THE PAINTER FROM SEVILLE

SONYA VAN DE GRAAFF

Imprint: Alaya Books

www.alayabooks.com

ISBN: 978-1-7636998-0-9

Alaya books

The world needs your story.

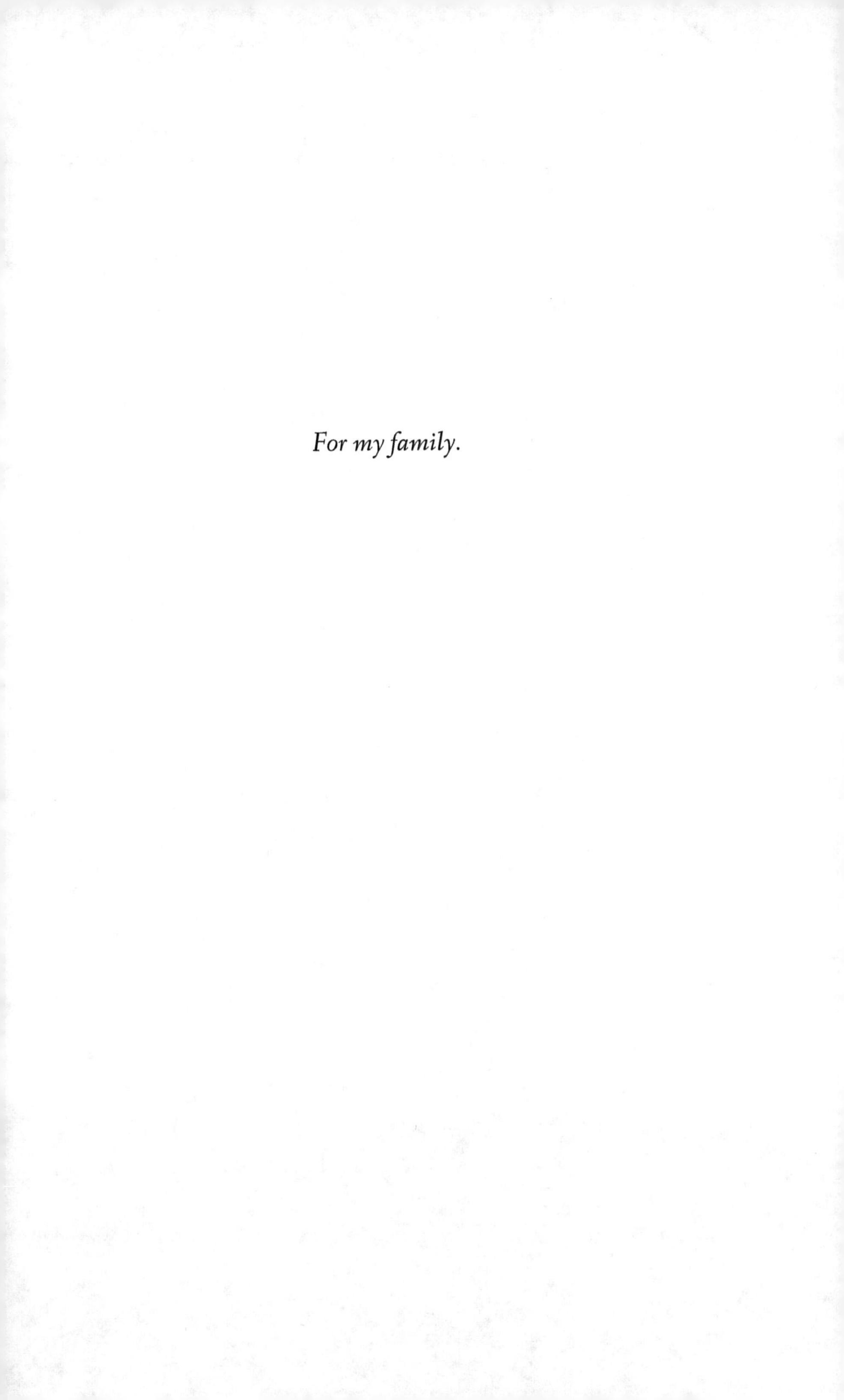

For my family.

That painter who has no doubts will achieve little.

— LEONARDO DA VINCI

PROLOGUE

The Rio Guadalquivir meanders languidly through the valley of Seville, as if pausing for breath on its long journey from the high mountains deep in the Sierra de Cazorla, before wending purposefully on, through the woodlands, olive groves and vineyards, to finally spill into the wild waters of the Atlantic Ocean. It evokes a world unto itself as if bestowed by a Divine scheme as a stimulus for philosophers, and a salve for those who have loved and lost.

In recent times, the river has seen the demise of the Moors and the rise of the Catholics. It has been witness to the consecration of the great Cathedral of Seville and seen the way in which the whole of the valley clusters elliptically around the great edifice like a defenseless body around its sun.

In the vestry of the Cathedral a priest resides. He leans against the soiled window ledge, his walking sticks within reach, and his thoughts centre on the young woman within his line of sight tending to her stallion in the forecourt of her home, the Palacio del Catedral. Only the Cathedral gardens separate them. She is of fine stature and singular beauty and yet, utterly unaffected by these attributes. Or perhaps – having no father to admire her, nor mother capable of advising her – she is simply unaware. He has set it as his own task to watch over her, for she is of a wilful nature and, in his darkest thoughts, a threat to herself and all he values.

At a tentative knock on his door, he reaches for his sticks and turns his focus to the interrogation he is about to conduct in readiness for the impending Inquisition.

CHAPTER ONE

AUGUST 1512

It was already approaching the time for lauds, and Francisca was still working at the fresco. She bent to dip the paint brush into the pigment and conceded defeat to some locks of her hair which persistently evaded their braided confinement. She held the handle towards the very end, and, with a fluid wrist, liberally applied the indigo to the wet plaster.

A breeze finally fluttered through the atrium, and the flares attached to the bannisters of the staircase flickered, breaking the even light. She took it as a sign, tossed the brush into a flask of solvent solution, and covered the plaster mixture and egg tempera with waxed paper so that they would not harden. She gathered the hems of her skirt and took care walking along the wooden planks and descending the rows of ladders, to the atrium floor.

Several months had passed since she had begun her work at the fresco and although she had made good progress, there was still much to do. She wanted it to be perfect, but she also wanted it to be complete in time for her Uncle Carlos's return. From several details in his last letter, she estimated that might be as soon as el Día de

Todos los Santos – All Saints' Day. That was not even three months away and so it was especially vexing she would not be at liberty to continue her work for some time.

As a consolation, as well as reward, she decided to grant herself the luxury of a viewing, for the very first time.

She had imagined some ceremony in the occasion, but the reality was that she went to the middle of the atrium with leaden legs and shallow breaths. By the fountain, she turned around, looked up, and braced herself for the truth.

She gasped.

It was beautiful and dramatic: more beautiful and dramatic than she had dared hope. Even through the clunky scaffolding, the vast wall seemed alive, vindicating her decision to apply wet plaster rather than to paint directly onto the etching.

She surveyed the wall along the horizontal line to check for narrative coherence, and was satisfied. The colour scheme imbued momentum, compelling the viewer to follow the storyline.

But the longer she looked, the more exasperated she became that she could not see the picture free from the scaffolding's obstruction. She had never had that privilege. Everything she knew of the picture was what she had discovered at close range on the planks of the scaffolding: dissolving the limewash, cleaning the wall, and applying the plaster and pigments, small section by small section.

The etching – her mother's last work – to which she had been applying the fresco had been concealed for a decade and a half under layers of limewash. She had only recently discovered the picture, hiding like a ghost in the wall, by a trick of the light. Her efforts at finding a sketch had proved fruitless. If her mother had drawn one, it had been lost – or destroyed. The only suggestion of a plan lay in the remnants of the perspective design. There was a hole in the wall where her mother had hammered a nail to signify the vanishing line, and lines were marked in the edges of the wall for the orthogonals, radiating outward from the hole.

Her eye kept returning to the uppermost corner, where the griffin soared in the big sky, and she imagined she caught its gaze. In the way of a certain magic that the early hours can conjure, particularly in one with scant sleep, Francisca opened a door in her mind and entered another realm. With all the power of a drug-enhanced state, she became the griffin with its body of a lion and wings of an eagle, and she burst out of the wall and wrested the entire picture – all twelve characters and the landscape – from it. Trusting in providence, she flapped with all her might, dragging the picture behind her. She rose up and up, navigating amongst the tangled fronds of the tall palms gracing each of the atrium's corners, until the picture broke free from the wall. The landscape and characters floated in the sky and shimmered with life.

She looked for what she had come for. Her mother. There, by the edge of a dry ravine, she found her. Tears streamed down her mother's face, and her arm – outstretched to Francisca's father – hung there, unreceived.

Her father's eyes were defiant and affixed to the sky.

There was no doubting it signified a rift between her parents, and it struck her with the force of a physical blow. Reconciliation was impossible: in a tragedy that had befallen the family when Francisca was a small child, her father had died.

Francisca heaved with unconsolable sobs – sobs that had never fully poured forth, but had needed to.

When she sufficiently restored, she looked again, to follow her mother's gaze. It directed her to the mountain peak, where stood a mysterious figure. Francisca soared towards it, and to her surprise, the character within reach of the mysterious figure was Marina, her mother's nurse – at the time of the picture, barely more than a child too, and her mother's chambermaid. Marina had angel wings, and Francisca sensed with growing fascination that Marina was a significant character in the picture.

When Francisca came to, she was slumped on the cool mosaic

floor, by the fountain's ledge, emotionally exhausted, but her mind was racing to catch up with her discoveries.

It was not unusual for a picture to contain symbolism, to suggest a metaphorical idea. Leonardo da Vinci regularly arranged aspects of his religious compositions in groups of three or subtle triangular formations, to signify the Holy Trinity. In the way he portrayed Jesus in *The Last Supper*, reaching for the bread and wine, he ingeniously signified the indivisibility of God the Father, Christ the Son and the Holy Spirit.

The symbolism in her mother's etching was of an entirely different order. The composition was complex. Its subject matter unique. The symbolism was certainly not obvious to Francisca. Whatever metaphorical message her mother intended to convey might only be evident once the fresco was complete.

Her musings were interrupted as the approaching dawn shifted the shadows cast by the flares, and the sound of the monks' low chanting from the nearby monastery drifted into the atrium. She could not afford to delay, so she picked herself up and steadily walked up the atrium stairs.

It took some time to adjust to the darkness of her bedchamber, but her eye was drawn to the silk stitching that shimmered on the spine of her favourite volume, Leonardo da Vinci's *Dreams and Visitations*, and soon her writing desk and the outlines of her journal, quill, and ink stand, neatly arranged, emerged.

She went to the windows to open the curtains and let in the light. At the nearby coat stand, she reverently felt the stiffened linen of the painting costume that had been her mother's and that had not been worn for a decade and a half. With a sense of destiny, she changed into it and, as she pulled the straps over her shoulders, she swallowed a lump in her throat. It was as if her mother was cloaking her in her genius and inspiriting her for the day ahead.

As she let out her long hair, she caught her reflection in the looking glass, and deftly wove her thick dark mane into a new braid. She watched her intense, almost black, eyes that she'd been told she had inherited from her father, and she imagined him inside the looking glass, proffering her courage. From early childhood, she had been denied the benefit of his guidance, and she'd had to find her own point of reference. That she had inherited his eyes – that most personal attribute of his likeness – she regarded as a secret power. Finally, she stole a glance at how her mother's painting costume looked on her. It fit perfectly and she realised that her mother once had been of fine figure and height too. But she was both relieved and disappointed to see nothing of what she had been told of her mother's former glamour. The painting costume looked like a commonplace sailor's uniform on her. Even so, she liked the way it drew a latent boyishness out of her.

Overwhelmed, she cut off the thought, and went to the windows, pushed the heavy mahogany frames wide open and inhaled deeply. The earthy smell of the stables from the forecourt below wafted up and she smiled to see the farrier already tending to Fiel, her loyal black stallion. The low thrum of the chanting monks vibrated on the air. She looked up and there were the last fading stars. Predawn pinks and purples streaked the inky sky and, in the deep golden hue of the sun pushing up towards the horizon, the cathedral pulsed, seemingly alive.

On the morning when her family had moved out of their small house in Santa Cruz, and into the Palacio del Catedral, Francisca's mother and father had accompanied her to her bedchamber on the first floor.

'The stars will cheer you if you awake in the night, Francisca,' her mother had said, showing her the gold-leafed constellations that she had painted on the dark mahogany ceiling. 'Our bedchamber is only across the hallway and Uncle Carlos's is next to yours.'

However, Francisca was too enthralled by what she had seen through the windows to acknowledge her mother's gesture. She could almost touch the cathedral and she levered herself up to the window ledge and perched there so her legs dangled down the outside wall as she held on to the lead drainpipe protruding conveniently by the window frame. She thought prophetically, if ever she might need to escape, the drainpipe would be sturdy enough to hold her weight, possibly even when fully grown.

'What is it that you see, Cisca?' her mother whispered, holding Francisca's waist tightly to keep her from falling.

'The dragon, Mama,' she had replied as she pointed to the cathedral.

In the cathedral's three-quarter profile from her vantage point, Francisca did not imagine God, but rather it seemed to her as a magnificent and menacing dragon crouching on its haunches. The mist rising from the ground seemed vapour emanating from the dragon's pores, the circular stained-glass window in the endless stone wall, its all-seeing eye, the flying buttresses fanning out, its folded wings, and the stone-layered side entrance doors, its gills. In the long days of her childhood, after the tragedy befell her parents and her grieving was at its peak, the dragon had been a loyal companion, and she had imagined tales of their heroic adventures.

Francisca drew the windows shut and picked up her hat and a satchel that she had carefully filled last night with the supplies she thought she might need. For luck, she touched the volume of *Dreams and Visitations*.

Catching her reflection in the looking glass again, she squared her shoulders and looked herself in the eye. 'I am Francisca Mendez. I am a painter,' she said to herself. 'Whatever might happen, nothing can ever take that from me.'

CHAPTER TWO

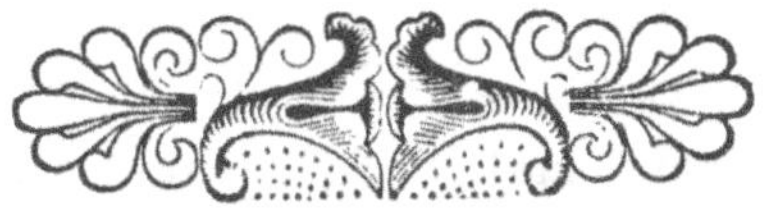

Quietly, Francisca entered her mother's bedchamber. The curtains at the terrace doors were still drawn, shutting out the burgeoning morning. Francisca went to her mother's bedside, and leaned in to kiss her on the forehead. She settled into a red velvet armchair beside the bed, and soon her mother stirred. She took one of her mother's hands gently, as though an injured bird, in her own, and allowed her mother time to adjust to her waking state.

'Good morning, Mama.' Francisca smiled and stroked her mother's cheek. Over the harsh years, her mother's face had sunken in on itself, her once delicately defined features now indistinguishable.

'I hope you slept well,' Francisca said.

Her mother opened her eyes, and her efforts to return Francisca's smile drew yet another fracture in Francisca's broken heart, but she had learned how to function with the pain, and barely noticed the new wound.

She had convinced herself that her mother's suffering was only transitory. Her mother had simply become cocooned and, when God ordained it, she would emerge, renewed. Their suffering would be over, and they would pick up where they had left off all those years ago, and life would be good again.

Francisca leaned in and, in a tone of conspiratorial excitement reserved for children and the aged, said, 'I am to become assistant to a master painter, Mama.'

Francisca sat back and, having uttered the words, began taking in the enormity of what she was about to embark upon.

'A letter from Uncle Carlos arrived from the Vatican, Mama,' she elaborated, concealing her growing anxiety from her mother. She needed to be strong and confident, not only for her own sake, but for her mother's too.

'Uncle Carlos wrote to say that he has finally chosen a master painter. He is from Rome – Señor Antonio Ceretti is his name.' Francisca waited to see if her mother showed any recognition in the name. Perhaps he had been known to her when she had been active as a painter. When her mother displayed no sign, Francisca continued, 'Uncle Carlos has commissioned him to paint canvases for the cathedral. He has already been working in the cathedral for some time. I am to offer my assistance.'

Nerves began to form a knot in Francisca's stomach as it occurred to her that the master might reject her. It would be unbearable. Painting had become her sanctuary. At the easel she could lose herself. It was where life took on possibility and excitement and she had come to see herself as a painter. She thought of the times in her life when fantasy had converged with reality, and how, painfully, she had learned to keep the two separate and distinct. What if she had been deluding herself?

And yet, she dared to wonder, what if Señor Ceretti affirmed her talent? Perhaps then, life could open up in ways she had never dreamed.

'It is strange that I have not noticed Señor Ceretti at work in the cathedral,' Francisca wondered aloud, but spoke on, in answer to her own question. 'I suppose the cathedral is vast.' She envisaged her dragon's lair. 'A painter and his canvas can go unobserved amongst the stonemasons and lead-light window craftsmen, not to mention the worshippers and priests.' The cathedral had only been consecrated a few years ago and was still bustling with specialist craftsmen applying finishing touches.

'Uncle Carlos said the master's brush has the grace and emotional restraint redolent of Bellini,' she continued, talking over her fears and hopes. She had never been in the presence of a painter of Bellini's technical mastery and fame. Bellini was ancient, and in the association, she imagined Señor Ceretti to be a severe, ascetic old man who could paint the smallest detail even with fading eyesight.

The light in the room lifted, and she looked into her mother's eyes and saw the daily battles that beset her, and she began to feel misgivings about her new venture on an entirely different level: how could she leave her mother for an entire day, days at a time? Her mother needed her.

At a sound from the threshold, she turned. It was Marina, and the feeling of the vision she had had in the atrium washed over her. Francisca had always seen Marina as middle-aged, but now, with the benefit of her vision, she calculated that Marina could be no more than seven or eight years older than she herself. Her mother's portrayal of Marina in the wall picture as barely more than a child – perhaps of twelve or thirteen – explained why Francisca had not recognised her image when she revealed her likeness in the etching. The vision had been revelatory, even though she did not yet know what it signified.

'Good morning, Marina.'

Marina nodded and smiled wanly in acknowledgement, and with her free hand sheltered the flame of a candle that she carried as she went to the other side of the bed. The light of the flame cast Marina's shadow like that of a timid deer. A deer was not the animal Francisca had associated with Marina and suddenly Francisca saw her as an untamed creature, rattling at the cage in muted rage at the life that had entrapped her. It came to her like one of life's truths – that servitude was not the life into which Marina had been born. Marina had the delicate beauty of aristocracy, Francisca saw as if for the first time.

'Good morning, Señora Mendez,' Marina said cheerfully to Francisca's mother.

She placed the candle in a lantern on the bedside table, and the soft light and shade soon settled and found their place in the bedchamber.

'I have been telling Mama that I am to become assistant to a master painter – all the way from Rome,' Francisca said, noticing strands of dull grey in her mother's hair, gaining another insight into the callousness of time's indifference. 'Uncle Carlos finally chose a painter to paint some panels for the cathedral, and he has instructed me to assist him.'

'I wish you well with it, señorita,' Marina said, as though it were an everyday matter.

A mischievous grin wriggled on Marina's face and she said, 'Perhaps, when he returns to Rome, you will join him.'

Marina's suggestion was fanciful, cruel even, for its impossibility, but the idea took Francisca entirely off course from her dilemma about leaving her mother. Venturing to Rome was not something she could ever realistically contemplate, even though she had dreamt it. Her place was with her mother. She had never travelled, and soon, she would be married. It had gone unsaid that Uncle Carlos had spared Francisca from marriage for the sake of her mother, but this time, he had signed off his letter saying:

> *Upon my return from this tour, your marriage may be delayed no longer. I have a betrothed in mind. It is an appropriate match.*

She experienced what she could only describe as a kind of seizure on reading the words. Once married, there would be no more fantasising about the life she had always imagined for herself.

She would be answerable to a man. She would be his possession. Her life would be over when it had barely even begun.

'Your mother always wanted to see Rome,' Marina elaborated brightly, implying both the possibility of Francisca taking her mother with her and Rome's restorative powers.

This took Francisca further yet off course, and an idea popped into her head. If she could win the master's good opinion, it might be possible to take her mother, under his protection, to Rome. Rome might be the place to revive her mother's spirit. She would convince Uncle Carlos of the merit in the plan, and indirectly, further delay marriage, perhaps indefinitely.

'Perhaps, Marina,' she said absently, trying to stem the fantasy from taking root.

'Will you be joined by other apprentices?' Marina asked.

Francisca was quick to correct Marina's use of the word *apprentice*. 'Uncle Carlos said I am to offer my assistance. An apprenticeship is not on offer, Marina,' Francisca replied stiffly. It would be unrealistic to think she could take on a formal training position. She was already nineteen years old, and apprenticeships lasted years and were almost always the reserve of boys. Elizabeth, Francisca's art tutor until recently returning to England, was the only woman Francisca was aware of who had had the benefit of an apprenticeship, and even then, it was as a favour to Elizabeth's father, the English ambassador to Milan. Elizabeth had been blessed: her master was the great Leonardo da Vinci.

'In answer to your question, I do not know if there will be others, Marina,' she added, realising she had not contemplated the idea of serving the master alongside others.

She determined to take control of the conversation.

'My immediate concern, Marina, is that I may not be home for Mama until the evening,' she finally said, stating the subject of her dilemma.

'You need not be concerned, señorita. I will be here,' Marina said, plumping up the pillows and encouraging Francisca's mother to sit more comfortably. As if reading Francisca's thoughts, she added, 'You must do as the archbishop said. Your mother and I will take a turn in the garden this morning after breakfast. I will not leave her side the entire day.'

Francisca looked across to her mother and saw all the reasons she could entrust her with Marina. There was affection for Marina in her mother's expression and her mother had, after all, included her as one of the characters in the wall picture, and even made her angelic. Then she remembered the way in which Marina had kept vigil with her day and night when her mother had returned so changed and they had buried her father in the palacio's grounds. Her mother and father had only meant to take a short holiday in the countryside, but something dreadful had intervened. Without Marina, Francisca's mother might not have survived the trauma – nor, perhaps, Francisca herself. During that time, Marina had become like family.

'Thank you, Marina.'

Marina smiled perfunctorily, signifying an end to the matter. 'I see you have found your mother's painting costume,' she said.

Francisca's interest was piqued, and she asked, 'Do you remember Mama wearing it? I found it when I was looking for the pieces of scaffolding in the basement. I had not thought to wear it until last night.'

The truth was that Francisca had believed it would be irreverent to put it on, until last night. As she was preparing for the coming day, she thought her mother would want her to wear it, for luck and fortitude.

'Do you remember Mama wearing it?' she asked again. 'She had made the costume so that she could climb up and down the scaffolding safely and with ease,' she explained, hoping to trigger Marina's memory.

'I remember like it was yesterday,' Marina replied, inhaling the nostalgia of those happier days.

'Do you remember Mama working at the wall picture?' she pressed.

'I do, señorita. It was a special time. She worked at it with urgency. It was like her life depended on it.'

Francisca sat up. Marina's description accorded precisely with her own observations when cleaning the wall, and the bold strokes had revealed themselves. Marina's words hung in the air, and the two women paused briefly, out of respect for the memory of how Francisca's mother had been before the trauma had taken hold of her and killed her spirit. Francisca wanted to ask Marina more questions, but it seemed inappropriate to do so in the presence of her mother.

'What will happen to the progress you have made with the fresco, señorita, now that you are required to assist this Roman master?'

'I will find time in the evenings, Marina. I still hope to have it completed for Uncle Carlos's return.'

Applying a fresco to the wall picture had become Francisca's anchor since discovering it on the day that Uncle Carlos had left for the Vatican, and it had kept her purposeful since he and the two others she loved most had left her: first Elizabeth – home forever to England to marry, and then Bernardo, her friend since childhood – voyaging to the Americas. When not by her mother's side, she had dedicated all her time to the fresco. The picture was her link to her childhood and a way of trying to understand it.

'Your uncle will be surprised to see it,' Marina said uncertainly.

Although she barely admitted it to herself, she had imagined too that, upon her mother seeing it complete, her spirit might thereby be restored.

It had not taken Francisca long to realise that someone must have applied limewash to the etching for the very purpose of concealing it. Had it been concealed because the picture was unfinished, and, since the tragedy, was destined always to be unfinished? Or because it was too upsetting to see? Or for another reason?

A trick of the light, caused by sun shining through a fine mist of rain, had revealed it to her as she had sat on the fountain's ledge and shed silent tears at her solitude. It was only the faintest outline, but it had been enough to trigger her memory. As she fell to her knees, she cried as lost memories, like a fractured looking glass, began to return.

She had searched the palacio for the scaffolding that her mother must have erected to etch the picture into the wall, and eventually found the pieces scattered in the basement. Alone, she assembled them and set to work to reveal the etching.

The composition was complex and intriguing, and like nothing else her mother had created. It covered the entire wall over the atrium staircase, all the way from the return at the top landing down to the floor. The picture was executed with a carefree virtuosity, like her mother had completed it in a matter of days and – as Marina had explicitly said – with a sense of urgency. It depicted an arid mountainous landscape, with twelve characters, three of whom were strangers to Francisca. Francisca imagined they served as witnesses to the story. The other characters comprised her family and their inner circle: her mother and father, Uncle Carlos, Father Alberto, Marina, Bernardo, Elizabeth, a mysterious figure at the mountain peak, as well as herself. What the story sought to tell – and whether it was sacred or profane – Francisca was not yet sure.

Although the picture was perfect as it was – the compositional structure beautifully balanced, and the light and shade exquisite – only a fresco would reveal the beauty of the landscape, the detail of the characters' expressions, and convey the story as she believed her mother had intended.

It was slow and painstaking work. Each morning, Francisca chose a small section of the wall to which to apply the plaster and paint the pigments. It would take her all day to execute. To set permanently, the pigments needed to be applied to wet plaster. There could be no room for error – it would be an ordeal to reapply the plaster and repaint a section.

Researching the proper fresco technique had taken days. She wanted the fresco to last forever. Elizabeth had told her the paint was tragically already flaking off Leonardo da Vinci's wall painting of *The Last Supper* because he had used the secco technique rather than applying wet plaster for the paint to set into.

She had set on a method. She knew to follow the lines of colour horizontally. On a picture this size, it was the horizontal lines that would provide visual coherence to the entirety. She had already applied a fresco to the landscape. She had painted the sky bright azure blue, reflecting the brilliance of a single star. The mountains were deep blue and purple tones receding into the distance, providing atmospheric perspective, a term Elizabeth had told her was coined by Leonardo da Vinci.

In the long hours alone at the wall, Francisca had considered various possibilities as to the picture's meaning, but none of them developed, and she supposed it would become apparent only once the fresco was finished and the scaffolding dismantled.

The bells of the cathedral's minaret struck seven times, and sunlight filtered into the room.

Francisca kissed her mother and, with a heavy heart, said farewell. She put on her hat, turned and again saw herself in the looking glass. She liked what she saw but, seeing the inappropriateness of wearing the painting costume outside the grounds of the palacio, she reached out and unhooked a long cloak hanging on the door hook, draped it over her shoulders, and tied the bow.

CHAPTER THREE

Approaching the gate of the kitchen herb garden, Francisca squinted into the harsh light at the cathedral sprawled out like a giant lizard lazing in the morning sun and she pulled her hat down. She had made the short walk through the cathedral grounds more than a thousand times, but her senses were so heightened today that she barely recognised the scene.

She pushed the gate open and steeled her courage to introduce herself to the great Señor Ceretti, whom her uncle had commissioned. She would impress him with her skill. Rome awaited, she dared to imagine.

Inside the cathedral, the scent of frankincense was overpowering, and she swallowed the choke constricting her throat. The *Kyrie Eleison* rang out. Father Alberto, who presided over the cathedral during her uncle's frequent absence, leaned over the pulpit, and sang out the call in his shrill tenor voice, and the choir replied, mesmerically, over and over, like an echo chamber.

She continued on through the great cavern, constantly returning her focus to the task of finding and introducing herself to the great Señor Ceretti. She wound her way amongst the endless forest of columns plunging down like stalactites. With each step, her tread fell more heavily as if she was wading through treacle, and her breath became tighter as her nerves began to get the better of her, but she had no choice but to continue. It was not until the very last section that she found him. She should have known: the Nave del Evangelio, that abutted the minaret and opened out to the old Moorish orange grove, was her uncle's favourite part of the cathedral. It would be here that he would want the first paintings to grace the walls of the cathedral.

Amidst the shadows there was a silhouette of an imposing figure. A boy approached, bowed and handed the figure a note.

'For you, Señor Ceretti,' the boy said.

The figure dismissed the boy, and as it leaned into the light of a flare to read the note, the man became visible. Francisca's mind turned on its axis. Señor Ceretti was nothing like she had anticipated. He was only about thirty years old and as beautiful as Saint Francis but with none of Saint Francis's humility. He exuded arrogance. He was tall and gaunt so that his high cheek bones protruded. He had thick dark brown curls and a beard. The lace of his linen shirt was loose, exposing the matted hair of his chest, damp with sweat and masculinity. Francisca looked away, and then, incongruously, saw a large knife tucked into the belt of his trousers, in a manner suggesting he was anticipating a fight.

His brow furrowed and pricked with sweat as he read the note. He destroyed the note in the flame and seemed deep in thought as he walked towards a nearby trestle table stacked with painting materials.

Sensing now was not the time to announce her presence, Francisca retreated into the shadows of a pew and watched on. He placed some chalk into a pestle and mortar, ground it into a mixture and spooned it onto his palette. He walked back to his canvas, donned his painting smock, and shifted the flare.

It revealed a painting, almost complete, but there was none of Bellini's emotional restraint or grace. The painting was emotionally fraught, with a deep restless agitation. It was like nothing she had seen.

The composition depicted Christ on the cross. It was a haunted Christ, whose gaze was not directed to God for mercy, but rather outside the canvas, to the viewer, condemning them personally for his fate. The paint was thick, like the consistency of blood. In the way the tendons of Christ's hands stretched and contorted with his own weight and his chest bulged with the effort to alleviate the pressure from his hands and shoulders, Christ struggled for his life. He had yet to accept the inevitability of his death and sacrifice.

The style was more like the realism of Grünewald of the Germanic countries than the Italian restraint she was accustomed to, and Francisca thought he must have studied there, or had exposure to German artists. The strokes of paint were unapologetically visible. Elizabeth had taught her to aspire to make the strokes imperceptible, so that the surface seemed as still as a pond, the technique perfected by Leonardo da Vinci.

At Christ's feet was a kneeling woman, her bereft countenance fixed on Christ's eyes. It was as though nothing else in the world existed apart from the two characters, and Francisca thought it was bold of him to depict only Mary Magdalene witnessing Christ's death. It was unorthodox and possibly blasphemous. The scriptures said that not less than three people had been present at any one time. The depiction of Christ's crucifixion in darkness, though unconventional, was possibly acceptable. Saint Mark had described a darkness passing over the land on the sixth and ninth hours on the day of Christ's sacrifice, and Señor Ceretti must have chosen to depict the moment of the eclipse. To single out that moment signified a darkness in the soul of the artist, Francisca thought.

It was the strong chiaroscuro technique – of deep shadow around the two figures – that created the startling effect, but she had never seen such dramatic execution. Would her uncle approve? Again, she thought he had been mistaken to think he had found, in Señor Ceretti, Bellini's disciple.

Señor Ceretti turned to look at a model posing in a half kneeling position and gazing to the heavens. Dazzling light shone through the stained-glass windows, illuminating the model's beauty.

All of Francisca's attention shifted to the woman. She was a painter's dream. She was simultaneously nobility and peasant. A singular pathos seemed to emanate from deep within her. Her face was proud and evoked the exotic with her fine ruby-studded nose and long auburn hair. Her mouth was full and yet soft and delicate. Her thin robes were dampened and clung to her slight yet curvaceous body. The woman brought Mary Magdalene to life. Francisca suddenly saw Mary Magdalene as a bold and sensuous woman, and a strange force drew her into this woman's world.

Señor Ceretti approached the woman and, as he towered over her, madness descended upon his face. Francisca sensed something dreadful was about to happen. The moment lengthened and she waited apprehensively. All fell silent. Another moment passed, and Señor Ceretti bent down and whispered something in the model's ear. As he returned to his full stature, the madness turned to wickedness, and a single tear fell from the model's eye. All of the boldness then shrank from the woman's face so she was left with only vulnerability.

Señor Ceretti strode back to the canvas, and the atmosphere altered; the particles in the air seemed to rearrange themselves, leaving everything misaligned. The tension was palpable, and in that moment, Francisca saw the impossibility of taking her mother to Rome under Señor Ceretti's care. Whether or not she might win his esteem, he would not be a man with whom she could entrust her mother's safety and care. There could therefore be no possibility of she herself going. He would not be her salvation.

The disappointment passed through her painfully, but quickly, like the superficial flesh wound of a darning needle. For all her hope, it had after all been but a brief fantasy and at least, she thought, there would be no imperative now to seek his approval.

She began to build a protective barrier in anticipation of the wounds he might inflict on her.

From her pew, Francisca looked over to the model. There was pain in her eyes, and she wondered what manner of man would have such power, and it struck her that a woman so beautiful could also be vulnerable. She wanted to go to the woman and comfort her. They caught each other's eye. The model shook her head discreetly, commanding Francisca to remain quietly in the shadows on the pew. Despite the brevity of the moment, the connection was intimate.

Back at the canvas, a self-satisfied smile spread across Señor Ceretti's face like a disease.

The model's eyes had hardened, and her jaw had set.

Whatever he had said, his goal had evidently been achieved, for the Mary Magdalene at Christ's feet had transformed into a vengeful one.

As Francisca observed the scene play out from the safety of the shadows, she did not feel like an outsider or an interloper. It was as if she had wandered into a drama unfolding before her, and although it was a drama not intended for her eyes, she was being woven within its spell. She was alive with curiosity and somehow aware of her mind leaping forward to a time where the drama would evolve into one in which she would become entangled, and her entire being expanded with a kind of fatalistic excitement.

As Señor Ceretti stood back from the canvas mid-brushstroke, Francisca's attention was inexorably drawn back towards the model and she watched her rise, take her belongings, and go behind the partition, presumably to change. She feared she might never see her again and decided to find a way to talk with her.

Simple decision though it was, there was a strong sense of consequences yet to unfold.

CHAPTER FOUR

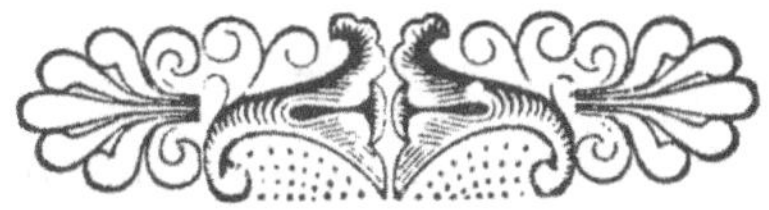

Hoping that Señor Ceretti would not notice her, Francisca quietly slid out of the pew and walked over to the doors leading to the Moorish patio. The patio was a tranquil place, conjuring a simpler time, long gone. An orange grove framed a small double-stoned fountain. Waters deep from the spring filled the fountain's central bowl and spilled over perpetually into a larger stone dish into which it was nestled. The waters, forever replenishing, seemed still yet alive, like the finest of paintings.

She stepped over the threshold and walked down to the fountain, dipped her hands in, splashed her face and neck, and was refreshed. As her eyes cleared, she spotted a bench in the shade of an orange tree, towards the tall wrought iron gates. She sat down, took a cigarillo from the case in her pocket and lit it by the flame of a nearby flare.

As she inhaled the dark nicotine, she looked over beyond the gates at the Cathedral square where the morning markets were already bristling with excitement. The scene evoked the Arabic bazaars she had seen pictures of. Bright red and orange tents cascaded over the entire space, and all manner of exotic goods and caged animals were on display. A cacophony rang out of traders bargaining and coins chinking in velvet purses. Somewhere, someone played a flute. A complex aroma of spices wafted on the air.

A fleet of ships must recently have returned from the Americas or the Canary Islands, and she brought to mind her childhood friend, Bernardo, somewhere out there on the open seas en route to the Americas. It would be months before she would see him again. Ships were known never to return and she tried not to fear for his safety.

By the gate was a beggar, his back to her. Even though he wore a loose robe, her painter's powers of observation discerned that, by his posture, he was a young man. A falcon with flaming rust-red plumage perched placidly on his shoulder. The man's hands were outstretched but the marketgoers were impervious to him. His face was shrouded in his hood, and she imagined him to be drawn with premature lines. She felt for him, so went over and pressed a coin into his hands and, as she did so, she had a strange sense that she knew him. She was about to say something kind, but he drew his cloak further over his face and did not turn to her but rather hurried away, and the falcon lifted off his shoulder.

Why would he conceal his identity and hurry away? Was he ashamed of his plight? Was he an escaped convict? Or perhaps he was unaccustomed to kindness. Her heart went out to him. Nevertheless, for all his suffering, at least he had freedom, and she envied that. No one would force marriage on him.

As she wandered back to her bench in the shade of the orange grove, she followed the course of the falcon's flight as it circled the minaret counterclockwise three times, and she recalled her vision, embodying the griffin and she felt the bird to be an omen.

The minaret's small, weathered bricks glistened like antique copper in the sun, exuding an aura of melancholy, and jarring against the limestone of the new cathedral to which it had become attached since the mosque had been destroyed. Temples to two different faiths were now combined, the Islamic relic now purposeless and subsumed into the Christian world. Could the destruction of a temple destroy the faith it had served? Or would the worshippers rise up in a simmering rage?

Her reflections were interrupted when, out of the corner of her eye, the model emerged from the cathedral and stepped down to the patio. She too exuded an aura of melancholy, rivalling the minaret's. As she approached with a lightness to her step, she also radiated grace and beauty, like poetry. Her presence completed the scene.

She wore a flowing blue dress with soft tan leather ankle boots, somehow expressive of herself and delightfully different to the stiff fashions inhibiting movement. In her left hand, she lightly held the straps of a linen bag slung over her shoulder and in her right hand, she carried a book bound in orange vellum.

As Francisca watched her approach, she felt that, in all her life, her decision to meet with this woman was the first thing she had actively chosen to do, and she was instilled with courage.

'Buenos días,' Francisca said, as she rose from the bench.

'Buenos días,' the woman replied agreeably.

She had clear grey-green eyes, evocative of a high mountain spring and that seemed to be a direct path to her soul. Her auburn hair shone in the sun. She could be almost thirty, Francisca thought. There was a worldliness about her, and Francisca wondered where she came from.

They stood face to face, Francisca slightly taller. Wanting something to do with her hands, Francisca took her cigarillo case from her pocket and held it out to the woman. The woman adjusted her linen bag and accepted her offering, and her soft breath fanned Francisca's face when she leaned in to light the cigarillo from her own. The gentle swell of the woman's cleavage rose and fell with her inhale and exhale of the smoke and Francisca did not avert her gaze. Her senses roused. It was a new and wonderful feeling.

'I could not help seeing that the master unsettled you,' Francisca said, feeling bold.

She herself might indirectly be responsible, since it was Uncle Carlos who commissioned Señor Ceretti. Perhaps Uncle Carlos had also engaged the woman to be his model. What did Uncle Carlos know of Señor Ceretti's character?

The woman seemed to consider Francisca's statement, but after a pause she said, 'The cathedral is filled with a strange unease.' She looked into the distance wistfully.

Her voice was like honey.

Was she trying to excuse Señor Ceretti's behaviour? The cathedral was the pride of Seville. It was bold of the woman to criticise it. Even so, it seemed that the woman had acute powers of observation. From childhood, Francisca had sensed a complex world of good and evil residing within the cathedral. It seemed to have nothing to do with God but sometimes it had disturbed Francisca that it was not during Father Alberto's sermons, but rather in her quiet times alone, that she truly felt God's simple benevolence.

'There is a priest – Father Alberto,' Francisca whispered, but paused before finishing what she might have said. 'Perhaps avoid him,' she finally settled on saying, but feeling she had been uncharitable. He had devoted his life to the service of God. She had scrutinised her objection until pinpointing it: it was his insistence that she stifle rational thought. He would have her mind shrivel to a seedling, when she wanted it to blossom like a rose in the morning sun. 'It is the work of the Devil,' he would hiss when she questioned something he had said.

The woman nodded, suggesting she understood. Francisca was glad to say no more on the matter.

Time was progressing too quickly. If only she could slow it down, and think of something meaningful to say, so that the woman would truly see her, and then she imagined the conversation to be like painting. That was something over whose direction she could hold some command.

Despite sensing the woman's reticence for the subject matter, Francisca pressed, 'As long as the master has not unsettled you.'

The woman seemed to recall herself to the present. She laughed mildly and replied dryly, 'Such a thing is simply one of Antonio's measures to connect with people: other people. There is almost nothing he would not do for his art.'

'What other measures does he apply?' Francisca muttered, surprising herself again with her boldness and feeling she should explain. 'I am to become the master's assistant. My Uncle Carlos, the archbishop, commissioned him.' She felt the colour rise in her cheeks again, this time at revealing her relationship to the archbishop as well as the favour implicit in the manner of attaining her position as assistant.

The woman looked intently at Francisca and finally seemed to be taking in her words. 'Do not concern yourself,' she said, the rich mellifluous quality returning to her voice. 'You will find him to be uncompromising, but he saves exorcising his demons for me.'

Francisca could see no band on the woman's matrimonial finger. What was her relationship with the master?

Noticing the woman's eyes on her clothing, Francisca looked down. Her cloak had come loose, and she took it as a chance to redirect the conversation.

'This painting costume belonged to my mother,' she said, touching the fabric, and feeling that she had revealed something deeply personal. 'She made it,' she added, as if that helped to explain.

The woman smiled and her face opened, and Francisca wanted to cleanse her of all her melancholy, so that the woman could be restored to her natural state of joy.

'My name is Isabel de Flores,' the woman said.

'A beautiful name,' Francisca heard herself reply as she accepted Isabel's outstretched hand. 'My name is Francisca Mendez.'

'And where are you from, Francisca Mendez?' Isabel asked whimsically, and in a manner suggesting she had a right to know.

'I'm a Sevillana by birth. I live in the Palacio del Catedral,' Francisca said, pointing in the general direction, 'on the other side of the cathedral, next to the alcazar. It is not a grand palacio,' she clarified quickly, 'but they refer to it as a palacio because it is where the archbishop lives.' She was suddenly embarrassed to have mentioned that her home was a palacio. 'If you ever need anything or would like somewhere quiet to be, you would be welcome to visit. It is usually only my mother and myself who are there. My uncle travels frequently.'

She waited for Isabel's response as she watched her exhale her cigarillo smoke.

'Thank you. That is very kind.' Isabel took the orange vellum-bound book, her hand obscuring the title. 'You had better go in,' Isabel continued. 'He will be ready for you soon.'

The encounter was over. Francisca's many questions about Señor Ceretti would have to wait for another time. So too would her curiosity regarding Isabel de Flores.

As she watched Isabel leave, a lone cloud drifted over the patch of sun where she had stood, as though Isabel took all the light with her, and Francisca found herself wondering if she had discovered something more prized than freedom.

CHAPTER FIVE

Back at her place in the shadows on the pew, Francisca watched Señor Ceretti apply the finishing touches to his haunted Christ, and she observed how he held the brush like an extension of his hand, and the mesmeric rhythm in the way he applied the paint.

He moved away from the canvas, looked to the rafters and crossed himself.

The click click click of Father Alberto's walking sticks warned of his approach. As he emerged from the shadows, he said, 'Ceretti, I see you have been hard at work.'

Señor Ceretti did not flinch. 'I trust you approve, Father.' Señor Ceretti's light baritone voice and accent suited him, but his tone of deference caught Francisca by surprise.

'My good man,' Father Alberto continued, flashing his blade of a smile and waving a walking stick perilously close to the canvas, 'I shall appraise your work once you have completed several canvases. That is when I will gain a sense as to your style and how it is that you tell the scriptures. In the meantime, I trust I am correct to assume the archbishop has explained what is required. You are aware of our ecclesiastical tastes here in Seville? They are somewhat more – let us say, *ascetic* – than the Roman style. We do not like too much perfection here.' He chuckled.

'Indeed Father, you can be assured that I am aware,' the master replied evenly.

'Excellent. It has been remiss of me to not introduce myself until now. While the archbishop is away, I take care of the cathedral's life and all of her parishioners.' Father Alberto turned to leave but he paused and said as if by way of afterthought, 'I am always here. You can come to me both for spiritual and practical matters. No subject is beyond my remit.' He looked meaningfully at Señor Ceretti as he said, 'For confession, be sure to come only to me.'

With that, Father Alberto left, the click click click of his walking sticks echoing throughout the columns of stone. Francisca thought of how confessing to Father Alberto made her feel so wretched, amplifying her sinfulness rather than redeeming it.

When Father Alberto was out of sight, Francisca rose from the pew and walked over to Señor Ceretti. She could delay introducing herself no longer. She calmed her fraying nerves by telling herself she could abandon her position at any time. She was under no obligation to work for him if it displeased her, she told herself.

'Good morning, master,' she said, hearing the nervousness in her voice. 'My uncle, Archbishop Carlos, told me to come. I am Francisca Mendez – I am to assist you.'

As though she was not there, he went over to the trestle table, wiped his hands thoroughly, hung the cloth on the railing and arranged it neatly.

At proximity, with his piercing emerald-green eyes against his tanned skin, he was so beautiful that she felt awkward returning his gaze, and she had to force herself not to look away. How strange that she could not look upon his beauty, she thought, or perhaps it was his impenetrable countenance, forbidding access beyond the surface, that repelled her.

He turned towards her, so all of his face caught the light.

Visible, even under his beard, was a deep raw scar across his left cheek, which did not spoil his beauty, but rather imbued his face with interest. Francisca visualised the slice of a sword and wondered what he did to provoke it. She recoiled as she saw he had caught her thought, and she cautioned herself to be more guarded in the presence of an artist whose powers of observation were possibly keener than her own.

'Your uncle made my commission conditional on accepting you as my assistant,' he finally said. 'He assured me of your gift, but the fact is – and shall remain so – I prefer to work alone. I will not have you touch my work. Over the years, apprentices have spoiled my intent, and I shall not abide it. I would have you clean my brushes,' he said dramatically, seizing on the idea. 'That at least, could be useful.' He laughed gleefully and walked away, leaving Francisca wishing she could sink beneath the flagstones and disappear. He was playing with her as a cat with a ground nesting bird.

He gestured in the direction of a mid-sized herringbone linen cloth primed with imprimatura stretched over a frame.

'See what you can do with that,' he said with resignation. 'Try drawing the martyrdom of Saint Sebastian, and at the end of the day, I will inspect what you have done and will instruct you accordingly.' He turned away and muttered, 'We will yet see about you cleaning my brushes,' and he laughed again.

Was he already set on rejecting her? Though she tried to convince herself that she did not need his approval, she could not abide the shame of him reporting to Uncle Carlos that she was not up to the task. For this reason alone, she determined to do her utmost to gain his approval.

She tried to recall if Señor Ceretti mentioned a style and she looked over to ask him, but he had gone.

Standing before the canvas, she felt – more than ever – both the risk and potential of the first stroke. Between herself, the charcoal and the canvas, anything could happen. It was as if a mysterious force was at work at that precise point, capable of setting the composition off onto an entirely different trajectory to that which she had intended.

She focused on her breath. Her hands stilled and she had a strong sense of her mother applying the first cut of the etching into the atrium wall, encouraging her. The blank canvas once again became her familiar friend and she immersed herself in the task.

The composition revealed itself in her mind and she applied the charcoal. In Saint Sebastian she imagined Bernardo. She knew his muscled body from the exercises Elizabeth had set her. He had been a patient and theatrical model, and Elizabeth had said he had the beauty of Michelangelo's *David*. Saint Sebastian and the lightning-struck tree to which he was bound took the foreground. On a rock by the tree was a scorpion, representing the evil of those who had orchestrated his fate. The background was a desert landscape, symbolising his desolation. Plunging and rising mountain peaks faded into the distance, in perfect perspective. She wanted to evoke an impression of a biblical place and time, whilst simultaneously conveying the feeling that, were it not for the arrow lodged in his abdomen, Saint Sebastian would have been dying from a broken heart.

She depicted Saint Sebastian's torso twisting in one direction and his head thrusting back in another, to suggest movement and his struggle in resisting his fate.

Elizabeth had told her that Leonardo da Vinci secretly cut open freshly dead bodies – a right permitted only to doctors – so as better to represent the human body in paint.

'Leonardo knows that flesh cannot be painted with the realism he demands of himself unless he understands the muscles and tendons that support it,' Elizabeth had told her, and she had shown Francisca a drawing that Leonardo had given her of the very same muscles and tendons.

When Elizabeth had first told Francisca this, she had shuddered, not only at the grisly images appearing in her mind, but at the idea that an artist of Leonardo's sensitivity could do such a thing, and she had asked Elizabeth, 'Is that not blasphemous?'

Elizabeth answered without fear in her voice as she explained, 'Some would say so, Francisca, but Leonardo believes that understanding the human body will not only help him be a better painter, but also bring him in closer communion with God. In fact, Leonardo believes it is his duty, as one of God's creations, to seek to understand all of nature. He sees it as a scientific endeavour, which is the basis for artistic endeavour. He is adamant that if the result of his learning contradicts previously accepted truths, then those same truths must be abandoned.' Elizabeth smiled. 'I agree with him. Don't you? We now know that Leonardo's beliefs are not new. The ancients from the Classical past – the great thinker and scientist, Aristotle, in particular – believed this too.'

The idea that humans could take it upon themselves to understand God's creations had unsettled Francisca at first. Everything she had ever known from Father Alberto's teachings shifted beneath her very feet, but she sensed the excitement of it, and she had spent much time thinking about it.

Father Alberto had preached subservience to God as well as the supremacy of tradition, and the word of God as expressed in the bible, but practising his sermons in the way he instructed had made Francisca's mind contract in a manner at odds with her inquisitive nature.

'After all,' Elizabeth continued, 'should we not seek progress of knowledge in all things? This is our natural state. Brunelleschi and Masaccio did this by applying their understanding of pure mathematics to develop perspective. Where would we painters be without perspective?' Elizabeth had smiled, as if to say the answer was self-evident.

When Elizabeth had first expressed these ideas, Francisca had wondered if anything might be possible, and, although she felt afraid, her mind took flight in its expansiveness, and she knew there could be no retreating from this way of being.

She applied some shading to Saint Sebastian. Even when applying a sketch, she thought in colour, and visualised the finished product. All the colours would be determined by reference to Saint Sebastian. For his pale skin, she would use lead white; for his strawberry-blond hair, lead tin oxide; for his clear, sky-blue eyes, azurite; and she imagined mixing lead tin oxide with a few drops of lapis lazuli blue, if Señor Ceretti would allow it, for his green loin cloth.

For the red desert background, she would use cinnabar, for the mountains, monochrome blue tones. She visualised making the mountains darken gradually and almost imperceptibly blurring into the edges as they receded into the distance. For the sky, she would apply ultramarine, fading into less colour saturation the more it approached the horizon, to account for the effect of the atmosphere on the appearance of objects in the distance. Elizabeth had taught her Leonardo's technique of atmospheric or aerial perspective, which perfected the lineal perspective technique that Brunelleschi and Masaccio had developed.

In the midst of deep thought, Francisca paused, sensing a presence behind her and she turned quickly. Señor Ceretti was standing behind her, watching. She tried not to flinch.

'Your uncle tells me I am to endeavour to fill this area by the time of el Día de Todos los Santos, when the Pope will be gracing us with His presence.'

He gestured expansively, suggesting the mad ambition of the task. Francisca agreed. A painting needed time to gestate and metamorphose naturally, and each layer of oil, no matter how thinly applied, needed to dry. It was a process, as Elizabeth had taught her, of allowing the image to reveal itself from the canvas. She knew Leonardo da Vinci worked on his favourite painting, *Lisa del Giocondo*, for over four years.

'I have a vision for how it must be,' Señor Ceretti said and, as though he had already shared his vision with her, he nodded in a manner expectant of a response, but she was at a loss as to what to say. 'If you really want to help me, you must do more than compose well,' he said. 'There can be nothing banal here.'

Her heart twisted at the verdict, and she rejected it. It was even worse than accusing her of poor draftsmanship.

She would not allow him to destroy her confidence. She would build a wall around herself.

'Tell me, why do you paint?' he asked.

The question caught her by surprise. She thought her work spoke for itself. She had found her own philosophy which, over the years, Elizabeth had patiently helped her to develop. Painting was her door into a world of dreams, transcending the here and now. It was the one thing over which she had some determination, but she was not ready to share these thoughts with him. They were too personal, too much a part of herself, and she could not entrust that part to him. She had her own fears too, about what painting meant to her, fears that went to her core. She had never shared them with anyone, not even Elizabeth.

The pressure built as she tried to formulate a response, and she was so determined to not reveal her true self to him that all she managed in reply was, 'I love to paint.'

'You love to paint?' he repeated, raising a mocking eyebrow. He took a deep breath and said, 'The only reason to paint, Francisca, is because life itself depends on it.' He looked her directly in the eye and whispered, 'Painting *is* life.'

In his passion, she found a chink in his impenetrability.

He took some chalk and absorbed himself in crushing it on a marble slab, and she hoped the interrogation was over.

Finally, he said, 'Since da Vinci, any man can draw with perfect perspective and apply paint so that it seems a real piece of fabric or an actual, seeing eye. He has taught us everything. Technique has been mastered. He has finished what Brunelleschi and Masaccio began.' He paused. 'So, all that is left, is to paint an idea. Painting must seek to represent an *understanding* – an expression of our plight on Earth. Christ is the perfect example. We should practise painting Christ every day.' His voice became distant as he continued, 'For this space, I want the human soul laid bare. Nothing must be withheld, there can be no compromises. We must show this brief moment between life and death; all the suffering we endure; all the suffering we inflict.'

In his words, Francisca sensed his solitude and the impossibility of bridging it, and – furthermore – that he knew this about himself.

As for herself, she had never thought about painting in terms of expressing something new. She had simply sought to do her best, but his philosophy sparked an idea. Maybe she could be a link in a chain. Maybe she could carry the torch from artists gone to artists yet to come, and she was awed at the thought.

'You must strip everything away that you use to console yourself. Every moment at the easel must be an agonising struggle. Can you do that?'

'Yes... yes I can do that, master,' she said quietly. There was no choice but to agree, though she was unsure how she could deliver what he demanded, even if she wanted to. He was not interested in what she had to offer. Was his goal to annihilate her?

'Every painting must sow a seed of discontent and doubt in the faith of every man. This will keep him returning here, to find certainty in his faith. He will not find it in my paintings. I will not stoop to give it to him.

'What we do here is the difference between life and death. There is a line. On one side lies emptiness. On the other, lies that which breathes for itself, which has its own energy and that lives on and rewards, long after I put down my brush. Every stroke of every painting must fall on this side of the line.'

There was something wild in his eyes as he looked about the forest of stone columns, seeking something there.

He seemed to look through her as he demanded again, 'Can you do that?'

'I... I will try,' she said quietly, keeping her thoughts to herself.

In his insistence that she emulate his style and adopt his

philosophy, and in making no effort to seek what she had to give, she shut herself down to him. She knew, even if she managed to do as he required, she would not share her artistic self with him. She felt new resolve to follow her own path, and in that moment, for all her riling against his speech, there was a level on which she understood, even now, that this new resolve might be a gift he had given to her.

He sighed and seemed to return to the present. 'Go home and think on what I have said. In the morning, when you have been well rested, begin applying paint to your Saint Sebastian.'

With that, Señor Ceretti dried his hands on the linen cloth, and left.

He had told her to return tomorrow. He had not dismissed her or reduced her to cleaning his brushes. In her relief, all her other feelings towards him seemed inconsequential and she wanted to rush home and share her success with her mother and write to Elizabeth. She would not be a disappointment to Uncle Carlos. His belief in her had not been misplaced.

As she watched him leave, she imagined him going home – to Isabel de Flores – and for a moment, her elation slipped away, and something began to take hold of her heart.

CHAPTER SIX

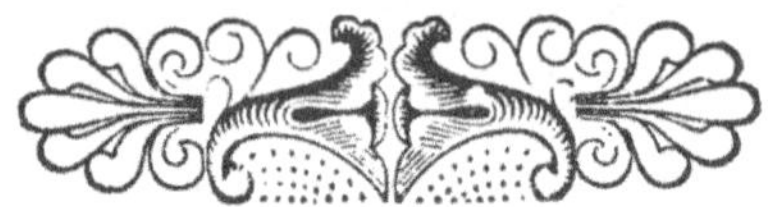

Francisca hurried home and ran up the stairs. She was bursting with her new experiences to share with her mother but, on entering her mother's bedchamber, she saw Marina standing formidably by the terrace doors, and Francisca faltered.

Refracted blood-orange light of the sunset blazed through the doors, casting Marina in a numinous silhouette, and Francisca again thought of last night's vision, and she regarded Marina with new eyes. She had a strong sense of Marina's connection with the mysterious figure on the mountain peak. What did the connection mean? Why did her mother depict Marina as an angel? She searched her mind for anything that the volume of *Dreams and Visitations* might shed light on.

'Your mother lacked interest in the garden this morning and has slept even more than yesterday,' Marina said, rolling her hand to suggest a pattern of decline, but Francisca did not want to hear it. She would not let go of the hope that her mother would recover, for if she lost hope, then so too would her mother.

'But you did take a turn in the garden together, Marina?'

'Yes, but the fresh air failed to buoy her.'

'And you were here throughout Father Alberto's visit?' Francisca asked anxiously.

'Yes, señorita. He bled her and she barely roused from her slumber throughout the entire procedure.'

Francisca looked at her mother's elbow to see the scratch marks from the venesection that Father Alberto had administered. The scars from Father Alberto's years of administering the procedure – which he had declared would alleviate her mother's suffering, but in fact only exacerbated it – made Francisca feel ill. She did not know whether she abhorred the bloodletting more than his administering of balms. She wanted to ask him to stop the treatment, but she did not dare, and she hated herself for her weakness and her fear of him taking precedence over her own convictions.

She sat on the edge of the red velvet chair and looked at her mother's sunken face. Ever since she was a child, she had feared losing her, and yet it was impossible truly to contemplate her passing. She could not imagine the permanent loss of her single unassailable connection to Mother Earth, to everything. She would be cut adrift and rudderless forever.

She kissed her mother's forehead, settled into the chair, and began to tell her about her first day as assistant to Señor Ceretti.

'I wonder why any master would leave Rome for the very edge of Christendom?' Marina asked, interjecting.

Francisca had not given any thought to the question, but it struck her as insightful. Uncle Carlos had had difficulty finding an artist of the style and quality he demanded. No Spanish artists seemed to satisfy him. He said he would rather the cathedral have no decorations than ones he did not love.

'Mama,' Francisca continued while she pondered the question, 'although his style is very different to mine, he seems to think I have potential. I am to return tomorrow, to continue with the task he has set for me – to paint the martyrdom of Saint Sebastian.'

'Were there other apprentices?' Marina asked.

Francisca tried to suppress her irritation as she explained again,

'I am Señor Ceretti's assistant, but, in answer to your question, no, there were no apprentices.'

'Forgive me my curiosity, señorita,' Marina said, bowing slightly and turning to the window.

Francisca's irritation dissolved and she regretted not having been kinder. Marina's life was even more stifling than her own, and her position with Señor Ceretti was the only event that had happened in the household in months. Since Bernardo and Elizabeth had left, there had been nothing to divert the long hours.

'Someone called for you this afternoon,' Marina said abruptly.

For a moment, Francisca thought it might have been Señor Ceretti's model, Isabel de Flores, and her heart leapt.

'He left no message, but said he might call again,' Marina added.

Francisca's mind quickly adjusted, and she felt Marina's eyes on her.

'What did he look like?'

'I do not know. He wore a hooded cloak that obscured his face. A tamed falcon was perched on his shoulder. His voice was familiar. Do you know who it might have been?'

'No. No, I don't,' Francisca replied uncertainly, but recognising in her description the beggar at the morning market and noting that Marina had found something familiar about him too. She could not guess how he could know her name, where she lived or why he might want to visit her, nor why he would hide his identity.

Marina took her leave and they bid one another good evening. Francisca turned to her mother and chose aspects of the day to share with her. She spoke about how Señor Ceretti held the brush and executed the paint strokes, about his style and philosophy. She wanted her mother to be proud, so she elaborated on the fact that he had told her to return to work tomorrow, to continue painting the martyrdom of Saint Sebastian.

When the sun finally set over the palacio's walls, casting the bedchamber in deep shadow, Francisca took her leave of her mother.

Back in her own bedchamber, she looked longingly at her bed but, out of the corner of her eye, noticed a blue envelope with Elizabeth's seal, perched on the stand of her writing desk. At once, she sat down, broke the seal, and read.

2 July 1512

My Dear Francisca,

I write with news of my husband's passing. Mercifully, his suffering was brief. The King granted an elaborate burial here, in the Greenwich Palace chapel. I take comfort that he is with God now.

There is nothing remaining for me here and I have found a place to go where I can live with purpose. I feel hopeful. I am to live in Wilmington, a hamlet on the south coast of England. Last week, the King commanded that it be reinvigorated with chosen settlers, for it occupies a small area of strategic importance within the Cuckmere valley and there is a port at the neighbouring village of Alfriston that smugglers have been frequenting but which the King wishes to take command of.

I, along with two other women from Court whose tastes and manners are congruent to mine, will depart in a month's time. With God's good grace, we should be celebrating the Feast of St Michael in our new home. Our other community members will arrive from different parts of the Realm. The King wishes for a diverse group, the good sense of which I intuit.

There will undoubtedly be much to accomplish before the winter sets in.

Finally on my news, you will be amused to know that I have formed something of a friendship with your compatriot and our Queen, Katharine. She wished for connections with her country which, understandably, she misses with heartfelt longing, although she confessed to being glad to have left behind the menace of the Inquisition. She mentioned rumours of the new Inquisitor Generale having his sights on Seville, convinced Sevillano conversos are continuing their Jewish traditions.

It seems Father Alberto may finally have his wish.

I mention it not to alarm you but rather to encourage vigilance, for there might be disturbances. Stay safe at the palacio. Do not venture out after dark, please. I promise to let you know if I hear more.

On a lighter note, Her Majesty presses me to converse about Seville in her desire to be transported back to Spain in her mind. I endeavour to conjure, in pleasing language, the colourful squares and orange blossom avenues that she prompts me to describe, but, alas, I see only the Palacio del Catedral.

All those years, did I venture so infrequently beyond its walls? It seems to me now that our daily routine comprised my entire world. Yet I felt boundless within its confines. At the time, I felt it was the same for you. Do you remember when I asked you of what you dreamed and you answered, This? At the time, your answer filled me with joy, though of course, I later learned how you longed to explore – and I loved you even more for answering me as you thought I wished to hear.

For Queen Katharine, I see the disappointment – and curiosity – in her eyes, as I struggle to fulfil her simple wish. Perhaps I will be able to explain it to her one day.

Now, I see I am rambling.

How excited I was to hear from your uncle of the work he has arranged for you with Antonio Ceretti. By the time you receive this you may already have started. Please tell me how you progress.

I saw some of Ceretti's work – which I remember vividly –

when my father and I visited Rome. Even then, it was clear that he was an artist of profound brilliance and unsettling depths of darkness. How did your uncle convince him to leave Rome?

I have no doubt you will learn whatever it is he has to teach you. I have said it before – only technique will give you the freedom to express all that your soul needs to say. But let him touch not your spirit, for it soars with clarity and joy in your work. It is not many whose work transcends their circumstances to achieve transfiguration – the very purpose of art, which I know you understand.

Have you had word from Bernardo? I have been thinking he should be home soon.

Please send my best to your mother, for whom I pray daily.

My best also to your uncle.

For you, Francisca, my love.

Elizabeth

Folding the letter back into its envelope, memories of the magical years with Elizabeth stirred. Elizabeth had provided the grounding required for her flights of fantasy at the canvas, and she had come to love Elizabeth like the aunt she never had. When Elizabeth's father retired from office earlier in the year and they returned to England, it was impossible for Uncle Carlos to not observe Francisca's grief. It was almost pure luck that the position with Antonio Ceretti arose.

Francisca penned a short reply, offering condolences for Elizabeth's husband's passing and wishing her well in her new home. She promised to write at length soon.

She did not respond to Elizabeth's enquiry about Bernardo. There had been no word since his letter in weak script that she'd had difficulty reading. She did not wish to worry Elizabeth.

Elizabeth's mention of the Inquisition coming to Seville alarmed Francisca. Francisca could not evoke the Jewish purge of her childhood as reality, although she had heard of that time when neighbours, even family members, informed on one another for fear of their own safety and security. Seville had moved on from that time. It had matured into a thriving and cosmopolitan city attracting a diverse range of people – scholars, traders and entrepreneurs – from all over the Mediterranean. The Maritime University taught aspiring captains of ships who came from all over Spain, to navigate the seas. The very fact of Señor Ceretti's recent arrival from Rome – the artistic capital of the world – was testament to its rising importance. Surely too, she thought, the Inquisition could not resume unless the archbishop ordained it, and she did not believe Uncle Carlos would do so. For all his ambition, he was a pragmatist, more interested in progress than purity of creed and thought. And yet, as she readied herself for sleep, a shard of anxiety fixed like a splinter at the edge of her mind.

Her sleep was restless. She dreamed of her father, and she was in the dream too. Hand in hand, they knelt by the ravine's edge, gazing into the abyss of the Inquisition.

CHAPTER SEVEN

The following weeks, Francisca and Señor Ceretti each worked at their canvases alone. It seemed to Francisca that he had erased her from his mind, and she tried to do the same as regards him. Even so, the idea that he had planted continued to germinate, and she found herself wanting her art to signify something. She wanted it to be a bridge from here to somewhere else, to be a point of reference on the continuum of tradition and renewal.

During these first weeks, she worked on three canvases at once, so she could attend to a dry canvas, while allowing the oils to dry on another. She worked long into the evenings, neglecting the fresco on the atrium wall. She would return to it, she told herself, as soon as she had made sufficient progress on these three paintings.

It was towards the end of a day during the fourth week, when deep in thought, she heard the mellifluous sounds of a woman's voice and turned from the easel. At the sight of Isabel approaching, the blood rose to Francisca's temple.

'I see you have been unleashed, Francisca.'

Francisca had barely spoken to Isabel since their first meeting, although she frequently had been aware of her presence, as one is aware of the sun.

Every day, Isabel brought lunch for Señor Ceretti, and Francisca caught glimpses of them eating in silence. She could not help observing that Isabel's efforts to cheer him were unsuccessful. He was irritable. From the way they were together, Francisca concluded they were a couple, whether they were married or not. She had heard of travellers living such lives. Once, when Isabel was unusually quiet and Señor Ceretti unusually attentive, Francisca saw a bruise on her cheek, and she knew it had been at the hand of Señor Ceretti, and she wanted to thrash him.

'You may observe Saint Sebastian. The other two are not ready,' Francisca said quietly, conscious of, and disturbed by, the degree to which she cared for Isabel's good opinion.

Disregarding Francisca's instructions, Isabel walked around the three canvases, viewing them from different angles, and while she did so, Francisca intently studied Isabel's profile. She thought of the muscles supporting her flesh, and the purity of soul that must lie within to express such natural beauty.

'I confess, I was sceptical when you said you were Archbishop Carlos's niece. My reservations were ill-conceived. You have a gift,' Isabel said in her worldly way. 'Your Saint Sebastian is original. It is quite different to the Italian versions and what I have seen of the Spanish.'

'Thank you.' Francisca's heart raced, and she blushed more deeply.

'There is a mystical quality, evocative of Fra Angelico, and, with your fluid movement and perfect perspective, Leonardo's teachings are evident too. It is like drifting in a forest valley in first morning mist.'

Francisca felt a tingling in her spine at the mention of Leonardo. Since Elizabeth's departure, she had been longing for the companionship of someone familiar with him and his work. Meanwhile, she suppressed the urge to laugh at the unnecessary misery of self-doubt she had endured these last weeks. It was contrary to her nature and learning to be indifferent to the opinion of her superiors, and, whether she liked it or not, she regarded Señor Ceretti as her superior. But having Isabel's good opinion felt of an entirely different order. It felt deeply personal, and all the more meaningful for it.

'It pleases me more than you can know that you appreciate it.'

After Señor Ceretti's criticism, Francisca had decided to alter the composition in two respects. First, to draw Saint Sebastian's expression darkly inwards, in line with the scorpion, suggesting accusation of those responsible for his fate. Second, to paint the shadow cast by Saint Sebastian's body in a direction different to that cast by the tree to which he had been bound, instilling a sense, not of him departing the world, but of being not quite *of* it. Since he had not commented on her work since their initial introduction, she had no way of knowing if he approved of her accommodations.

As Isabel turned to look at Saint Sebastian in more detail, Francisca contemplated the optimum light and shade to express Isabel's beauty. In the same way that flesh should not be painted without an understanding of the muscles and bone structure beneath, Francisca would never presume to paint Isabel's portrait without first understanding her thoughts and feelings.

Finding Isabel's eyes upon her again, Francisca was startled out of her thoughts, and she looked around to Señor Ceretti's work area. He was not there, and his materials were tidy, suggesting he had left for the day.

'Shall we get some air?' Francisca asked, aware – for the second time in her life – of not passively responding to the actions of another. Spending time with Isabel was something she wanted, and she felt something of the power of the griffin rise within her.

They stepped onto the threshold of the Door of Concepcion. The warm afternoon sun poured over the old patio walls. Citrus fragrance lingered on the air and the leaves from the orange trees rustled in the soft breeze. They sat on the fountain's low stone ledge. Spring waters bubbled quietly. Vapour riding a zephyr's crest anointed them.

The simple magic of the moment was undeniable, and they smiled at one another.

Isabel arched her back, sighed with pleasure, and whispered, 'There is something wonderful about the sun in the Seville sky. I could bathe in it all day.'

Francisca tried to slow her thoughts and she occupied herself with preparing two cigarillos. She held some paper to a nearby flare and cupped the flame to Isabel's cigarillo, feeling Isabel's soft breath on her hands.

'I am interested to understand how you came to paint?' Isabel asked after exhaling the smoke.

'It is what I know.'

'Yes, I can see that,' Isabel said gently. 'But I am interested to know how it started. There are not many women artists, at least, not many I have encountered.'

'My mother painted. When I was little, she showed me how to prepare the raw materials and mix the pigments. Earlier this year, I found my painting costume from that time.' Francisca shaped her hands to show the size, and she said, 'So small,' and she smiled wistfully. She'd discovered it wrapped inside her mother's painting costume amongst the scaffolding in the basement.

'What a wonderful way to learn. That explains your instinctive style.'

Francisca reached for a handful of stones amongst the gravel scattered about her feet and found a sharp one which she worked into her palm in an effort to dull her emotions.

'In the spring, I rediscovered my mother's last work. It is an enormous etching – a wall picture – over the central atrium staircase in our house.' As she spoke, she thought of all the characters it represented, and she wondered what it all meant. She felt guilty for having neglected it since taking on the role as assistant to Señor Ceretti. 'The picture was hidden under layers of limewash and almost a decade and a half of dust and soot.'

'How extraordinary. How did you discover it?'

Francisca was embarrassed to explain it, but Isabel's effect on her was disarming and she said simply, 'I was feeling sorry for myself on the morning that my uncle left for the Vatican. Elizabeth, my tutor, and Bernardo, my friend, had left earlier in the year, and I was bereft. It felt like I was being abandoned, and I started crying, right on the ledge of the fountain in our atrium. I didn't care if the servants saw me. Then it started to rain, but the sun was shining through it – it was a sun-shower. I looked up and there it was, hiding in the wall. It had been there all the time.'

'That is even more extraordinary.'

She did not wait for Isabel to ask her why the picture had been covered over in limewash, or who had done that. She was too excited to share the rest of the story. 'I don't know precisely what the picture represents but what I do know is that it is a desert landscape with a narrow ravine, and a griffin soars in a sky that is lit by a single star. There are twelve characters, including my mother kneeling by the ravine, my father, Uncle Carlos, and even Father Alberto.'

'From your description, it seems highly ritualistic: a star, a griffin, a woman kneeling by a ravine with a priest presiding...?'

Francisca looked at Isabel, stunned at the obviousness of her supposition and that she herself had not realised it. She replied excitedly, 'Yes, yes, it must depict a ritual.' She felt a step closer to unlocking its meaning.

'I should love to see it.'

The idea of showing it to Isabel was thrilling. 'Yes, I should like you to see it. It is obscured behind scaffolding but once it is finished and the scaffolding dismantled, I will show you.'

She wanted to share her knowledge of the technique with Isabel, thinking she would find it of interest, and she continued on enthusiastically, 'From the markings, my mother must have scoured it on the plaster wall with a stylus. I dissolved the limewash, cleaned it, and have been applying a fresco to it these last months, as my tribute to her. I know she would have intended a fresco –

with proper wet plaster – to have been applied. She loved vibrant colour.'

Her voice welled up. She recalled the feeling she'd had on that morning, of having rediscovered the essence of her mother.

'Your mother, she...?'

Francisca saved Isabel from having to finish her question. 'She is sick. More precisely, a tragedy befell her when I was a small child, and she has never been the same. So, you see, painting is what I turned to. It was the one thing of my mother that remained with me.' There was an openness of spirit in Isabel that, in turn, made her open up. It felt like being in a place without time or consequence.

'My father was killed.'

She had never uttered these words to another living soul, and she shook with emotion.

'Dios mío.' Isabel gasped. 'Who would do such a thing?'

With that question, a cloud lifted from Francisca's mind. *Someone* was responsible for her mother's interminable suffering. *Someone* killed her father.

She had always suppressed this darkest element of the truth. No one had ever talked to her about what had happened. Even Bernardo and Elizabeth had brushed over the subject. She presumed it had simply been to save her revisiting the pain. Uncle Carlos too had always told her not to dwell on the past, insisting nothing could change fate. On the two occasions when he had answered her questions, his replies had been inconsistent. Once, he had referred to it as an accident. Later, as an encounter with masked bandits. Rather than scrutinising what lay within Uncle Carlos's conscience, Francisca had been confused. She did not dare question him further.

Perhaps Elizabeth, Bernardo and Uncle Carlos had been motivated by love, but the fact was, Francisca's questions always lurked beneath the surface. Her questions were not going to disappear. She needed to talk about it. She needed to know what happened.

Her thoughts raced ahead of the conversation. She said, 'I am sorry – I do not know why I am burdening you with this.' She looked up and briefly searched Isabel's eyes as if the answer might be found there.

'Please do not apologise, Francisca. Some things are easier to say to someone you do not know well. It can help to see things differently.'

She withdrew into her thoughts, and she muttered, 'Maybe seeing my father being killed before her very eyes was what made my mother like she is.' She looked up, sensing she was on the cusp of discovering an important clue. 'It is as though her mind is locked in the trauma. She has not uttered a word in all this time. She is sleepwalking through her life.'

'Oh, Francisca. It is hard to see a loved one suffering.' Isabel placed her hand over Francisca's.

In response to Isabel's sympathy, Francisca's pent-up emotion boiled over. As the tears spilled down her face, she said, 'I do not know what really happened. I do not even know if anyone was ever found and punished. Uncle Carlos will not discuss it.'

If, as she believed, no one had been brought to justice, why would Uncle Carlos have mentioned bandits, she finally asked herself? It could have been a personal vendetta against her parents. It could have been anyone. She thought about all the characters depicted in the painting, and wondered if it might hold a clue to the identity of the perpetrator. That possibility seemed so obvious to her now. Her mother had completed the wall picture with urgent determination. Marina had commented on it too. Perhaps she had foreseen what was to befall them, and she wanted to record it as evidence, but the enormity of the idea was too much for Francisca, and she buried it.

'Perhaps you can speak to him about it?' Isabel suggested.

'Yes, perhaps.' But Francisca anticipated the difficulty of again broaching the subject with Uncle Carlos, and darkly wondered why he had always evaded answering her questions.

'Do you remember your father?'

How did Isabel know she needed to talk about him? It was like an antiquarian's spade had struck upon a fragile artefact buried in her soul.

'I had almost forgotten him, until I saw his likeness in the atrium wall etching.' On seeing the representation of him in the wall, she had cried with all her heart. It was like she was losing him all over again, and she understood she had repressed her memories of him as a way to protect herself.

'Lately, I have been dreaming of him.'

She recalled his image revealing itself as she had carefully brushed away the dust. His intense black eyes behind thin wire-rimmed glasses, were set within a strong but kind face, and he wore a simple black suit. She had been frightened to look at him, afraid of the emotions it might yield within her. She came to see that she had spent all those years willing herself to forget him, to spare herself the pain of losing him again and again. Having seen it, she worked hard to let it go, and she was now able to call him to mind and stay with his presence, quietly, as with a breath.

Revealing her mother's likeness in the young woman by the ravine's edge had brought with it its own pain – something yielded and something resisted within her. She had learned to lock memories of how her mother had been before the tragedy in the deepest recess of her mind. She knew to approach the place with reverence, like a pilgrimage to a sacred shrine. But, standing there before the young woman at the atrium wall, there she was, in plain view. Francisca had not been prepared for it.

Francisca's fear about the place of art in her life rose in her mind. Somehow it seemed connected. She dug the stone into the palm of her hand.

'Sometimes I think painting is merely something I cultivated to paper over the cracks of all the pain. I always feared that if I peeled it all back, there might be nothing at all. Maybe I am not a real painter after all. Señor Ceretti effectively said as much. He called my drawing of Saint Sebastian "banal".'

'Oh?' Isabel said, with a sharp inhale of air.

'I think he is barely tolerating my presence and use of his materials. But then, sometimes it is as though painting is the one thing that is real, that I can rely on and that is mine.' She looked up at Isabel, embarrassed at pouring out her innermost thoughts, and muttered apologetically, 'I suppose that makes no sense.'

'Not at all,' Isabel said firmly, dissolving Francisca's embarrassment. 'Your urge to paint is what you have known since your earliest years.' As if diagnosing Francisca, she said, 'I believe it is an intrinsic part of you. It is part of your nature.'

In what seemed like random threads suddenly beginning to connect, Francisca thought of her painting and the pain of her mother's suffering. The connection seemed tenuous but important, and she tried to concentrate. It was like grasping the details of a dream on waking.

She was daring to see things as they really were.

A seed of anger lodged within her. How could she have been so lacking in enquiry about how her parents came upon their fate? From the feeling taking hold inside her, she knew there could be no going back from this point. She must speak with Uncle Carlos when he returned, though she felt unsure whether she would believe what he would say, and she knew she had to find her own path to the truth. She had to find out how her father came upon his fate.

Isabel had given her the courage to see reality.

They bid one another good day, and Francisca went back into the cathedral. Before tidying her materials, she took a lantern to view Señor Ceretti's latest work. In the foreground lay a man in the shallow waters of a river. From the gaping wound to his neck and his blood flowing into the water, she recognised it as a depiction of the martyrdom of Saint Matthew. Saint Matthew's followers straggled up the mountainside, bereft at their loss. By the mountain's verge was a man, running away. He held a blood-stained knife. Francisca looked more closely and saw the villain was tall and gaunt, with piercing green eyes and a scar on his cheek. It seemed a dark caricature of Señor Ceretti.

What had Señor Ceretti's state of mind been, to depict himself as Matthew's murderer?

Regardless, the painting was compelling for revealing that hidden part of ourselves that despises beauty and love for fear of it abandoning us, or abandoning ourselves in it. Francisca could not help asking herself what it might mean to be in love? Would she lose herself or perhaps find herself? Even as she asked the question and saw, behind the veil in her mind her ideal of it, she knew the answer already.

CHAPTER EIGHT

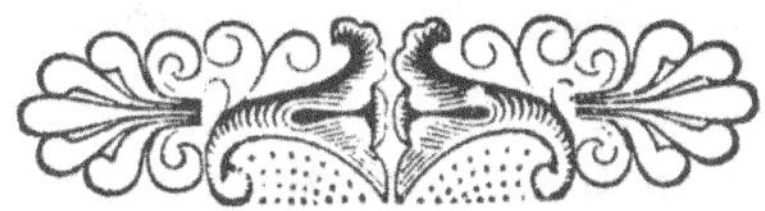

The flame of a single candle lit the small musty vestry study where Father Alberto worked at his desk. Volumes of reports, the pride of his life, lined the walls. Their meticulous details of Seville's heretics were to be evidence in the forthcoming Inquisition for which he had been agitating ever since the last cleansing which finished short of its purpose: producing a pure, Catholic Spain.

Conversos had been absolved and given leave to continue living in Seville on the proviso that they left behind their faith and observances. Only those Jews refusing to convert to Catholicism had been punished. With one or two exceptions, Father Alberto rejected the idea of the converso. His reservations had proven well-founded. Seville had become awash with observant Jews, and he had determined to conduct an interrogation of all conversos. There would be a test of the purity of their faith by none other than the Inquisitor Generale.

At a knock on the door, he returned the quill to the ink well and smoothed down his lank hair. He reached for his sticks and walked barefooted on the cold flagstone floor.

'Marina, come in.'

'Father,' she whispered hoarsely.

He ushered her in and they took their respective places by the round table.

'Well?' he asked, steepling his gnarled fingers.

'I have little to report this week,' Marina replied, feeling the walls close in around her. In Father Alberto's ice-blue eyes, she felt she had seen the soul of the devil.

'Marina, come.' Father Alberto encouraged. 'No detail is too small.'

'There may be something of interest,' she stammered.

'Yes?' he leaned forward.

'First tell me please, Father, are my mother's conditions improved?' she pleaded.

'Yes, yes, I continue to do all I can,' he replied impatiently.

'How do I even know if she is alive? Where is the proof?' She flicked the tears from her eyes. She was only twelve years old when they took her mother from her.

'Marina, you must have faith,' he extended his hands as though the proof lay in them. 'I told you last week that your mother will be moved to improved quarters. I myself will oversee it.'

'Might I see her?' She knew the answer but needed to ask it nevertheless.

'No. I would not advise it, Marina,' he clasped his hands, closing the issue. 'Now, what do you have that might be of interest?'

Ill with betrayal, she padded about her cloak and removed Francisca's journal. 'I must return with it,' she said.

Father Alberto eyed it as a snake to its prey. He squinted as he studied the words and turned the pages, committing to memory Francisca's private thoughts and correspondence.

'You have done well this week, Marina. If you find any more materials like this, be sure to bring them to me.' He rose to dismiss her.

Marina disliked Father Alberto's praise but she was glad that she was, for now, free to go.

CHAPTER NINE

Francisca watched helplessly as the man and woman begged for their lives. Their features were familiar, but she could not grasp their identity. She tried, but was unable, to run to their aid, and Fiel galloped to her side, carrying her to safety.

She jolted awake, and, as her mind settled into consciousness, she could no longer suppress the fear that had been growing within her and that had become clearer during yesterday's conversation with Isabel.

Her father's spirit was unrestful. He had died an unnatural death: he had been murdered, and the murder had been premeditated. She was convinced of it, and she knew it to be true, from her studies of *Dreams and Visitations*, which taught her about the meaning of these mysteries of the human mind.

Swiftly, she rose and changed into the painting costume. She knew what she had to do. There could be no more procrastination. She must complete the fresco to discover the secret that resided in her mother's last work.

Even as she went to the atrium staircase, she knew the sudden urgency was irrational: her father was dead, and her mother had been a shadow of herself for a decade and a half. Nothing that the wall picture could tell her would change these two facts. It would be sheer fantasy to hope that, in uncovering what had happened, it might somehow in turn restore her mother's health. And yet on another level, she told herself, if the wall picture held the answer to her parents' fate, then it was incumbent upon her to uncover it. For reasons she could not yet articulate to herself, it seemed imperative to complete it before her uncle's return from the Vatican. There was not a moment to lose.

The atrium landing was lit by the soft flames of the bannister flares, and Francisca peered through the gap between the wall and the scaffolding to try to see the picture in its entirety, but all she could see was a narrow wedge of colours all seemingly blended together. She walked down to the ground floor and stood in the middle of the courtyard to study it with fresh eyes.

Horizontally, the picture had three demarcations: the top two thirds comprised the sky and mountainous backdrop; the bottom third comprised the desert foreground; the meandering ravine in the middle divided the two and emphasised the perception of dimension to the whole. Overall, it was pleasingly balanced to the eye.

Laterally, there were also three sections. The first – between the top two landings of the atrium staircase – was the star and the griffin. The next section, between the second and third landings, was landscape. It was in the final section, between the third landing and the floor of the atrium staircase, that the main action took place.

All twelve characters occupied this space. The compression made it all the more dramatic. Francisca stood at the bottom of the staircase and looked up. For the first time, she saw the ingenious way in which her mother had connected them together. It was like a spiral. Small landings – liminal spaces – allowed the characters to appear that they belonged together in the narrative.

On the lowest level, three unknown characters huddled together on the desert sand. They were witnesses to the narrative, as in a biblical story. They were in mid-discussion, analysing what they had seen.

She imagined herself as one of the witnesses and she followed the spiral up to the next trio of characters: her mother, kneeling by the ravine; her father standing apart from her, with one foot on the fertile area between the ravine and the desert (and she noticed it was unclear whether his arms were outstretched or clasped behind him – it seemed the picture had been altered); and finally, Uncle Carlos, presiding over them in golden robes. To glean their expressions required some imagination, but she sensed from her close work at the wall that her mother seemed resigned, and her father sombre. Uncle Carlos's expression was more difficult to read.

She continued up to the next level, occupied by the solitary figure of Father Alberto. He sat on a fallen trunk in the shade of a withered tree. His face was obscured by his Franciscan friar's hood, but his signature walking sticks, placed obliquely in the shape of a crucifix, rested against the trunk of the tree. She continued up the spiral. The next cluster comprised the trio of Elizabeth, Bernardo, and herself. Elizabeth was in a posture of ushering Bernardo and Francisca up the mountainside. Elizabeth glanced back uncertainly to the ravine. Bernardo and Francisca were children, the age they would have been at the time her mother executed the drawing: no more than five years of age.

Where the spiral teetered, higher up the mountainside, was Marina, depicted as a girl with angel wings, of twelve or thirteen, as she must have been at the time of the drawing. Francisca looked up to the haloed figure that Marina was approaching, and her vision washed over her like a warm bath. She tried to grasp the insights she had felt within reach of, but they faded.

As she stood there anchored to the ground, observing, she understood that the picture represented a single moment in time. Something had happened immediately before it, something would happen immediately after it. Shortly after the etching was finished, her father had died and her mother's spirit was destroyed. Those insights seemed significant, and she thought how strange it was that she could be looking at the same picture but see it with different eyes, and in doing so, develop a deeper awareness. She promised herself that she would not stop studying it until she learnt its message.

The colours breathed with energy that only wet plaster could achieve. From the outset, she had reluctantly dismissed the idea of using oil, notwithstanding its superior subtlety of light and shade and glossy finish. Elizabeth had told her that oil would not bind in the plaster and would flake off, so she'd settled for the egg tempera.

The tones cascaded coherently across the horizontal line of the wall. She had started with the star, the sky, the mountains, and the ravine. The bright yellow star glowed against the lapis lazuli blue sky where the griffin soared. The thick plaster that she had applied to the griffin gave it the illusion of bursting out of the sky. The mountains receded in shades of blue. The ravine meandered across the wall in tones of brown and ochre.

She thought back to the day when she had made a start on the project. Focusing on her work had saved her from disappearing in the bitterness of her loved ones having left her. She bit her lip, swallowed the salt rising in the back of her throat, and forced the emotion down.

As much to check its stability as to vent her emotions, she kicked the scaffolding. It was steady and secure. Testing its limits, she clambered up to the penultimate level and walked across the planks to Marina and saw the child of twelve or thirteen, and affection stirred within her. Marina had joined the household as an orphan. She must have felt all alone in the world, but Francisca, being a small child at the time of Marina's arrival, had not given much thought to Marina's plight. Francisca climbed up the ladders, to the uppermost layer of scaffolding, to the figure ablaze atop the mountain. At the time she had uncovered it, she had thought it represented a kind of 'Sermon on the Mount', but her vision washed over her again, and she remembered the connection between Marina and the figure and wondered what it signified.

She felt the area by the haloed figure where she had last applied the plaster all those weeks ago. It was cool, the texture smooth and solid. The plaster had bound, and the paint set securely. Her pent-up emotions dissipated, and she decided to make a start there. She measured out a new pot of lime paste, stirred it well and scooped up a small quantity. Placing her feet hip width apart so that she had a solid base, she held the trowel securely. With her shoulders firm but also free, her hand made the swift, tight, semi-circular sweeping motions, and she took care to meet the cut edges neatly with the corner of the trowel and to tidy it with a smaller finishing trowel.

The rhythm restored her equilibrium. Her hands guided the trowel in quick, small motions. She smoothed down the plaster to prepare it for the spray of water and then the pigment.

Dipping the tip of a long paint brush into the pigment she applied the strokes liberally. She leaned back against the scaffolding and watched the pigment settle and set into the plaster.

Again, she dipped the brush into the pigment and, with small flicks, applied it to the halo. She held the brush loosely and kept her wrist relaxed, mindful of the cut in the plaster – and as she did so, she noticed that the area around the halo was different to the rest. It appeared to be cut into a panel. Sliding the brush behind her ear, she explored the area with her fingers. A pang of a memory began to stir, and she imagined she could see her mother's smile.

She was deep in concentration, but a chill rushed up her spine at the sound of a click click click. She turned abruptly, holding on to the scaffolding to sure her footing.

There, at the top of the atrium staircase landing, was Father Alberto. The idea of him entering and walking through her home freely filled her with unease. It was not his home.

And yet Uncle Carlos loved him and encouraged her to also. 'He was my mentor, Francisca,' Uncle Carlos had always said. 'He was more of a father to me than my own flesh and blood. People misunderstand him and I ask you not to judge him for his disability.'

She had tried to scrutinise her feelings. His disability had nothing to do with how she felt, and she had been upset that her uncle had so accused her. And yet, she was mindful that she had no rational basis for the way she felt about him. He had never done anything against her, nor, as far as she knew, Uncle Carlos. He doted on her mother, attending to her daily to administer his treatments.

'Do you ever sleep, Francisca?' Father Alberto asked, showing his small teeth as he leaned on his walking sticks at the precipice of the atrium staircase, and she imagined him tumbling down the great height to his death.

'I am keen to make progress for my uncle's return, Father,' Francisca said, trying to sound unperturbed.

'I saw the lantern still burning in your bedchamber,' he said. 'I came directly to ensure all was well.'

Francisca was concerned to not wake her mother, and so she climbed down the scaffolding and walked up the atrium stairs.

'I can look after myself, Father Alberto,' she said quietly.

It was the truest thing she had recently said to him. She had learned to live without the physical presence of those who had brought her joy.

He extended his lips in his blade of a smile, as if to say it was nonsense, and waved a stick at the scaffolding and said, 'I counsel you against continuing with this foolish little project. You do not know what you are doing.'

'Why would I abandon it, Father?' she asked, genuinely curious.

He spoke over her. 'You are not to question me, girl!' He stamped one of his sticks and shook with anger. Her mind resisted his command, but he was oblivious. 'Indeed, not only must you abandon it. You must cover it over with limewash, and this you must do before your uncle's return. Make it your priority.'

Francisca had no intention of doing as he commanded, and her mind soared with the freedom she had granted herself.

'There shall be no questions. Whilst your uncle is away, I have authority over you. Soon you will be married, and another man's charge.' He turned to leave, but then paused. 'Speaking of your uncle's return, you should know, I have it on good authority that Señor Ceretti's commission will not last it. Upon your uncle's return, the Inquisition will resume. You would best be advised to spend your time with the master for the remainder of his tenure and learn what you can from him.'

With that, he turned back down the hallway. She waited on the steps until the click click click was out of earshot. She was shaken, her mind awash with questions. There were too many to absorb. Why must she conceal the wall painting? Why would Señor Ceretti's commission come to an end with the resumption of the Inquisition and, more sinister yet, what relevance was that to Uncle Carlos's return home?

CHAPTER TEN

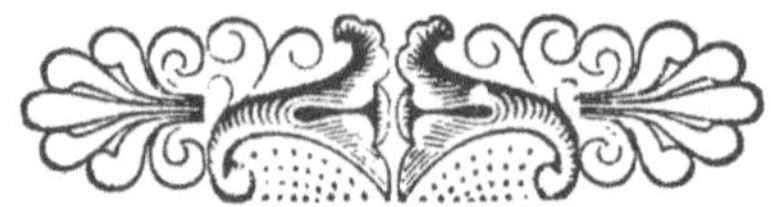

The following day, back at the cathedral, Francisca tried to put aside the previous night's encounter with Father Alberto. It had unsettled her, but she willed herself to focus on her work. She needed time to think and to decide on her course of action.

Fresh in her mind was the dynamic colour scheme she had achieved for the fresco, and she knew her strength lay in juxtaposing bold colours with clarity of perspective. Her aim was to see if she could translate this effect to the canvas. This is what she wanted to convey for Saint Francis's revelation in her depiction of him in the desert.

She became so absorbed in her work that she was entirely unaware of anything else until she heard a mellifluous voice utter her name.

'Francisca.'

She turned around and saw Isabel, seated on a pew.

'It is beautiful watching you at work.'

How could she not feel a rush of pleasure at Isabel's words?

Isabel rose from the shadows and came to her like a visitation.

'You do know, I hope, that your painting is true to your experience? Your use of colour is life-affirming. From all your losses, you have chosen life.' She placed her hand on Francisca's arm. 'How is it that you lure your viewer in by showing your intent with absolute precision, but then leave her to find the rest for herself?'

'You articulate perfectly my intent,' Francisca replied simply.

'With his gloomy darkness, Antonio would have us all fall into his canvases, never to return,' she said dramatically, bringing some levity to the exchange. Imitating Señor Ceretti, Isabel declared comically, *'Too much colour compromises drama.'* She laughed and concluded, 'Well, that is obviously not true.' She gestured towards Francisca's canvas for evidence.

Francisca laughed. 'Elizabeth helped me to explore colour and light, to express a feeling. She was apprenticed to Leonardo da Vinci, and so she was not afraid to experiment.'

'Your Elizabeth must have been a special woman,' Isabel exclaimed. 'The only woman, surely, to have worked in the great master's workshop.' She paused, and looked at the canvas, and said, 'Leonardo's approach is to seek the higher spirit that resides within us. You are fortunate to have that connection to the great man.'

'Do you subscribe to Leonardo's philosophy that we should strive to understand nature so as to commune more closely with God?' Somehow she knew Isabel's answer would, one way or another, seal their relationship.

'Of course,' Isabel replied easily, and Francisca resumed breathing. 'Leonardo is simply restoring Aristotle's philosophy which had been abandoned for too long. We must put the time of wilful ignorance behind us,' Isabel continued. 'Aristotle's approach is, self-evidently, humanity's only way forward.' She looked into Francisca's eyes. 'We must seek to be enlightened. God has, after all, granted us the gift of intellectual curiosity.'

That settled the matter, and Francisca's mind opened out like a flower in the midday sun. She would put all doubts of blasphemy behind her.

In an exaggerated Italian accent and dramatic gestures, Isabel recited Leonardo's teaching, *'You must observe the light, and see that which has the highest degree of brightness. Likewise for the shadows, you must see those that are darker, and study the way they join one another.'*

Together they finished Leonardo's lesson. '*And your light and shadows must blend, like smoke, without strokes or borders; sfumato.*'

They laughed together.

'It is good to laugh,' Francisca said, rubbing the tears from her eyes. 'I have been feeling embarrassed about the intense conversation yesterday. I said a lot of personal, possibly inappropriate, things. I think it is the solitude – I have forgotten how one ought to behave in civilised company.'

Isabel shook her head. 'I enjoyed our conversation, and I am glad we have moved beyond the polite stage. It is boring,' she said simply. 'I have been thinking all day about what you said regarding your parents. I hope you find the answers you are seeking.'

'I am determined to.'

'Shall we catch the last of the light?'

They passed through the Door of Concepcion, and sat on the fountain's low ledge in the warmth of the last light. Beyond the iron gates the merchants were closing their stalls and the taverns were beginning to fill.

Isabel placed her orange vellum-bound book on the ledge between them, revealing the gold-leafed title: *Occurrences with Light.*

'What is the subject matter of your book, may I ask?'

'It is a book of poems.'

'The poems must be significant,' Francisca observed. 'You carry the book like your life depends on it.'

'It belonged to my mother, and her mother before her.'

Isabel turned to a page in the middle and recited:

THREE QUATRAINS – by Rumi
A rider goes by, but his dust
of passing hangs in the air.
Look down this road through
the particles into infinity.
Who gave this soul to me?
The one who hooded my eyes
like a falcon's, who soon
will set me loose to hunt.
Flowers open every night
across the sky, a breathing peace
and sudden flame catching.

A fragile silence hung in the air.

As the words flowed through Francisca, she was filled with feelings for God and her mother and father, for Bernardo and Elizabeth. The sensations swirled through her body and soul.

'Those words...' Francisca began. 'It feels like something I thought lost or never imagined finding. It is difficult to explain.'

'Rumi lifts you up then sweeps you away,' Isabel replied.

'Who is he – Rumi?'

'He lived long ago. He was a Sufi who wrote poetry.'

'A Sufi?'

'A mystic. Sufis literally spin around the Arabian deserts, seeking God by annihilating their selves.'

'My head is spinning.'

Isabel laughed with her.

'Is that what you are – a Sufi?' Francisca asked. To define Isabel might unlock her mystery and help put the way she felt about her in its right place.

'Oh no,' Isabel laughed as though the suggestion was absurd. 'Though I like spinning around sometimes, and I like Rumi.'

'Tell me something about yourself,' Francisca asked. She

wanted to know the world Isabel occupied. She wanted to know everything about her.

'Like what?'

'Anything,' was all Francisca thought appropriate to suggest.

'All right then.' Isabel said. 'I am afraid of heights, but I want to go up the tower.' She gestured to the minaret that was glittering seductively in the soft dusk light. 'Will you take me up and mind that I do not fall?'

Francisca met Isabel's eyes. 'Yes, of course I will. The tower was the minaret that belonged to the mosque before it was replaced by the cathedral,' she said, blushing again, and wishing she did not.

All of a sudden Francisca recalled her father holding her by his side as they stood at the top, his wispy black beard flowing in the breeze. Love surged within her, and it was both a new and an old feeling. Isabel's eyes were exploring her. How much time had elapsed? She drew herself back to the moment. 'That was not telling me anything about you. Tell me something,' she pressed.

'I do not know,' Isabel said wistfully, looking up to the sky. 'I may soon be leaving here.'

The earth fell from beneath her and, before she could think, she exclaimed, 'But you have only just arrived. Why would you leave now?'

'I want to find my aunt. I have travelled the length of Spain following a trail of rumours. Now I hear she may not even be in Spain.' Isabel stood up and seemed intent on going. 'Come to my performance tonight,' she commanded abruptly.

'Your performance? Where?'

'A little place just outside the city walls – El Flamenco.'

'What will you be performing?'

'Some songs.'

'After all I've told you about myself, you only tell me now that you are a singer?' Francisca asked, at once in awe at Isabel, amused, upset, and embarrassed at herself.

Isabel's eyes sparkled. 'Getting to know one another is not something that needs to be the subject of a race.'

Francisca flushed with an awareness that she had not experienced before. She wondered at all that she might learn of Isabel in listening to her sing, but all she asked was, 'What should I wear?'

'El Flamenco is a place where you can be yourself,' Isabel replied. 'Perhaps wear your hair down.' She gently tugged the strands of Francisca's hair that had escaped from the confines of her ribbon, and Francisca was moved by her touch.

'You will find it in the alleyway after the arch of the last watchtower on the northwest city wall, on Camino Camarón.'

As Isabel set off towards the gates, Francisca gathered her courage and called after her, 'Where are you from?'

She imagined her to be from the mountains in the east, but she could not reconcile that idea with Isabel's perfect Spanish.

Isabel turned back. 'My mother told me we are from a land where the sun is always rising.'

CHAPTER ELEVEN

It was a still night when Francisca and Fiel set off from the palacio's forecourt. She had agonised over what to wear, and eventually settled on a flowing red skirt that she had forgotten she possessed, together with her favourite black lace shirt and black lace-up boots. Remembering Isabel's request, she let her hair down.

Light from a full moon shimmered through the palm trees lining the Calle de Garcia de Vinueza, and Francisca felt it exposing her inner turmoil. The thought of seeing Isabel perform at El Flamenco was exciting. She felt alive, and yet there was something about the intensity that frightened her. It was different to the intensity of her work. There, she felt in some degree of command. This was like entering unknown territory in which she might forever be lost. She was powerless under its force.

The bells of the minaret tolled. She counted ten and signalled Fiel a sprightlier pace. Flares by the convento cast freakish shadows of the gargoyles on the stone walls. Revellers, young and old, basked in the warm night air, their gaiety at odds with how she felt.

At the crossroads, a carriage thundered past, and Fiel only narrowly averted a collision, jolting Francisca from her thoughts. The driver cracked his whip, the whites of the poor animal's eyes betraying its fear. Inside the carriage was Father Alberto clutching his sticks, his lust for power written on his face, and Francisca recoiled. The carriage passed, and though she knew better than to look on, she did so, and what she saw so distressed her that it would haunt her for weeks to come. Shackled to the back of the carriage was a woman. She was an effigy of suffering, and yet, in her expression, Francisca glimpsed defiance and hope. It was like there was a protective aura about her.

The woman's prison uniform was the one worn by Royal Insurgents. She supposed the woman was destined for the Castle of San Jorge in Triana on the other side of the river, where political prisoners were incarcerated, most never to be seen again. During the purge of her childhood, Jews refusing to convert to Catholicism were incarcerated there. Her earliest childhood memories reverberated within her and she was transported back to Uncle Carlos discussing the problem of the conversos with Father Alberto. She could not recall the details, but she knew that conversos were absolved and permitted to continue living in Seville. Those refusing to convert presumably did so because they found the prospect of repenting of their faith and traditions worse than losing their freedom and worldly possessions.

Francisca felt sick for the woman and her indignity. She imagined a braver version of herself rescuing her, but the child within her wanted to retreat to the safety of home. In the end, there was nothing to be done but to carry on, crossing over to Seville's forgotten west side with its twisting lanes. She lost her sense of direction until, rounding a corner, she saw the familiar landmark of the recently constructed Iglesia de San Lorenzo, its childlike ochres and mustards lifting her spirits.

They arrived at a small path by the ancient tower of the Torre de Don Fadrique in the grounds of a deserted convent. Dangling off the branches of a dead tree was a colony of roosting bats. One cast off, dropped down and swooped up, as if on command of an invisible puppeteer. Fiel trotted on cheerfully, oblivious to the eeriness that Francisca sensed.

Finally, they passed under the thick stone arch of the last watchtower of the city wall, and emerged onto the desolate lane of Camino Camarón where Francisca dismounted and continued on foot. Halfway down the alley, by the lintel of a small door, she noticed a flamingo emblazoned in gold leaf.

Suddenly, the possibility that Señor Ceretti might be attending occurred to her and she considered turning back. His presence would be an intrusion on what she had imagined to be Isabel's invitation especially for her. On cue, a portly man in a purple smock greeted her and smiled in a way that made her smile back.

He whistled for the farrier and nodded towards Fiel.

'He will be well looked after, rest assured.' He took Fiel's reins and opened the door to El Flamenco.

The anteroom was like a magical cave. Pink and purple velvets and silks lined the walls. Lovers mingled amidst the shadows softly lit with dripping candles. A cocktail of burning wax, tobacco, and desire filled Francisca's senses, and she felt that she belonged and yet, at the same time, utterly alone. No one here was here for her.

She emerged into the noisy hall. Anticipation hung in the air. She went to the drinks counter and looked into the looking glass above, reflecting an enormous candelabra over a raised stage.

She jostled for a place, ordered a goblet of claret and drank it quickly. From her discreet vantage point, she saw that the hall was filled with small tables adorned with red and orange lanterns. Might Isabel and Señor Ceretti be amongst the crowd?

'Good evening,' a husky voice said.

Francisca turned to find that the greeting was intended for her and that the voice belonged to a magnificent creature with long black hair and sparkling dark eyes. She wore a full-length red velvet dress with a plunging neckline, revealing her elegance. The crowd made way for her as she approached.

'I am Gabriela Hernandez. Welcome to El Flamenco,' she said grandly, her smile filled with promises.

Francisca took the woman's hand and deduced that Gabriela Hernandez was the proprietor of El Flamenco.

'I am Francisca Mendez.'

Gabriela smiled mischievously. 'I know.'

'I am sorry, I am not sure we have met,' Francisca replied, flustered but beguiled.

'Isabel told me you might be coming and to look out for you,' she said, glancing at Francisca's empty goblet. 'Let me get you another drink.'

She wasn't sure what Isabel might have said to her but before having a chance to think further, the man behind the counter gave her a knowing smile and filled her goblet.

'Look, here she comes,' Gabriela said.

Isabel entered the stage. As the crowd whooped wildly, three musicians followed on behind. Her rich auburn hair was woven into a kind of crown on her head. Her robes were wrapped tightly around her, revealing nothing yet everything.

She raised her hands to the crowd in acknowledgement. The room became hushed and filled with expectation.

She scanned the crowd, and when she sighted Francisca, she smiled, sending a thrill straight through her.

Isabel stamped her foot, uttered a short, shrill howl, and the band started up in a collision of insistent pulsating rhythms. Francisca was at a loss to know how they combined the converging beats into one, but then realised it was Isabel who kept the beat together with a tambourine while she sang.

She harnessed all the energy of the hall and returned it, amplified.

The sounds were primal and Francisca felt she had always known them, and suddenly the lost songs of her father rose within her. She closed her eyes and listened to Isabel's voice wavering in a line between pain and ecstasy. The harmonies were like a question, followed by another question, and teasing out possible answers, but never quite settling. It was like being in a swirling ocean that scooped you up and kept you floating there, before releasing you, at last, on the final resolution.

Who gave this soul to me?
The one who hooded my eyes
like a falcon's, who soon
Will set me loose to hunt.

Francisca recognised the words of Rumi's poem. Through the music, her understanding of the words deepened.

The song told of a conquering of fear. If she were only to open her mind and believe, then she would be set free.

Her thoughts drifted to Rumi and Leonardo and their efforts to answer the deepest of questions. Rumi offered no answers, but his philosophy provided a path to accept the way of things. In Leonardo's study of nature, he knew that its secrets could never fully be understood, yet he was devoting his life in the endeavour. For Francisca, painting was like that – an effort to express life, even if only by an approximation.

Her mind stilled, like it had reached the centre of something, and she tried to stop thinking and to let Isabel's songs reveal their simple truth.

The crowd whooped and whistled. Isabel thanked them and promised to post notices of the band's next event. Francisca thought that, most likely, everyone felt as she did – that Isabel had been singing especially to each of them – and she tried to collect her emotions shifting beneath.

'Are you all right?' Gabriela asked, her eyes peering into Francisca's, and she smiled teasingly as she said, 'Do not fear, we are all a little bit in love with her.'

Francisca darted a look back at Gabriela, feeling her very thoughts and inner turmoil invaded.

Gabriela extended her hands out placatingly and laughed. 'I promise not to tell.'

A bartender gave Gabriela a bottle of liquor and three goblets. 'Come, let us go and see Isabel,' she said as she handed the bottle to Francisca. As they pressed slowly through the dispersing crowd, Francisca looked out for Señor Ceretti and wondered if he might already be behind stage. She felt sick at the thought.

At the end of a corridor, Gabriela rapped on the door and, without waiting for a response, entered. The room was barely a cupboard but cleverly designed with looking glasses and sumptuously decorated, befitting a star performer.

Isabel had already changed out of her costume and was taking off her make-up. Francisca noted Señor Ceretti's absence.

Isabel's eyes were ablaze as she asked, 'Did you like it?'

Gabriela folded Isabel into her arms, Francisca marvelling at the ease with which she did so.

'Darling. It was breathtaking,' Gabriela husked. '*You* were breathtaking.' She took hold of Isabel's shoulders and, as gently as if Isabel were a child, said, 'The band wants you to stay forever. And more to the point, so do I, and the whole of El Flamenco. You are what we have been waiting for all this time – ever since Valentina.'

At the name 'Valentina', the effervescence evaporated.

Who was Valentina? Did she mean something to Isabel? Francisca knew it was irrational, but jealousy's cold finger darted through her. Could Valentina be the source of Isabel's melancholy? She was in unfamiliar territory.

But the moment passed.

Oblivious, or perhaps inured to the power she wielded, Gabriela's face broadened with a smile, and she turned Isabel around like an item on display for Francisca. Isabel wore a comic look of being held captive, restoring the lightness.

'Francisca, do you agree? Is it not the case that Isabel is what Seville has been waiting for? Is she not needed here?'

Francisca tried to match the mood. 'She is indeed,' she replied, playing along.

'I am glad to be here with the two of you,' Isabel said, beaming. 'And I am glad you have made each other's acquaintance.'

The atmosphere lifted. The three women drew in, Gabriela poured the liquor, and they chinked goblets.

'Here is to Isabel,' Gabriela announced, and they laughed merrily. Gabriela tossed the liquor down. 'Now, I must return to my guests,' she said, leaving Francisca and Isabel alone together.

CHAPTER TWELVE

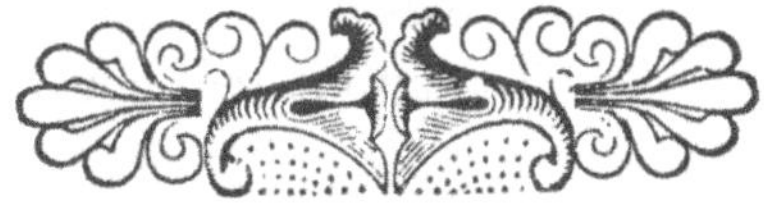

Gabriela's sudden absence made the dressing room feel twice the size, but there was no time for awkwardness, as Isabel took two shawls from the coat stand and suggested, 'Let's go outside.'

They stepped out onto the terrace and sat side by side on a small bench by the wall. A low, full moon shone through a thin wafer of clouds. Nearby, guards patrolled the city wall, and below, a small square lined with lemon trees thronged with evening revellers. The air was warm yet fresh, and they each draped a shawl around their shoulders. The intoxicating scent of Isabel's perspiration mingled with her musk perfume.

'I thought you modelled for a living,' Francisca teased, nudging her left shoulder against Isabel.

'The money is terrible, and the boss can be – let us say – difficult,' Isabel quipped.

They laughed and drank from their goblets.

'I thought Señor Ceretti would have come,' Francisca said, the liquor emboldening her to mention his name, and hoping that Isabel might reveal some fatal flaw in their relationship.

'It has been a long time since he has attended one of my performances.'

She would never miss one of Isabel's performances, but all she said was, 'Gabriela was right. Your performance was extraordinary.'

'I am glad you thought so,' Isabel replied without false modesty.

'You created a world. Tell me, how do you do it?'

Isabel looked at her meaningfully, her eyes lingering. Francisca wanted to reach out to her but applied all her focus to keeping her hands locked on her goblet.

'It might sound dramatic, but I imagine that all of this,' she said, gesturing expansively, 'might soon be gone.'

'Carpe diem?' Francisca asked.

'Exactly. I seize the moment and release the strings that tie me down. I fly. It must be similar for you, when you paint.'

'Yes, but perhaps in slow motion...' Francisca barely attempted a response. She wanted Isabel to do the talking tonight. 'May I ask you something else?' Francisca did not wait for Isabel's assent. 'I have been wondering how Uncle Carlos convinced Señor Ceretti to leave Rome for Seville.'

'He did not. We had already left Rome.' Isabel took another gulp of the liquor. 'By the time your uncle encountered us, Antonio was painting portraits for loose change in the main square of Barcelona. Carlos asked Antonio if he could paint Jesus like that, but what Carlos did not know is that Antonio was painting in his popular style, his take on Bellini – who he detests for his emotional restraint.' Isabel grinned. 'I hope your uncle will not be too surprised when he sees Antonio's work. Some would say it is blasphemous or unprofessional. In his mind though, it is a legitimate expression of the scriptures, and I think he feels more freedom in Seville to explore the boundaries.'

Isabel's explanation only produced more questions. Why would Señor Ceretti have left Rome without a commission secured?

'That at least explains why Uncle Carlos referred to him as being our new Bellini.'

'Actually, Antonio was reluctant to accept your uncle's commission. He had his heart set on a commercial rather than an ecclesiastical commission, but I convinced him an opportunity like this might not arise again. For me, Seville made sense too. I had not seen Gabriela for a long time, and I thought she might help make enquiries of my aunt's whereabouts.' Isabel laughed and tapped her fingers on the goblet. 'Gabriela knows everyone.'

'So, now that you are here, what do you think of it – of Seville?' Francisca asked, but really what she wanted to know was whether Isabel intended to stay for the duration of Señor Ceretti's commission.

'I love it. There is a sense that no one really minds what anyone else is doing, as long as it is *something*. It is how Rome was when I first moved there. I hope it lasts.' Isabel's voice turned distant. 'But I have heard that King Ferdinand wants to change it. He wants to restore the old ways.' She paused and, when she finally resumed, it was in the warm mellifluous voice that Francisca had become familiar with. 'Whatever my affection for Seville, I cannot live my life as a visitor in a city forever. There is no purpose to such a life. I want to be where I am needed.' She looked at Francisca expressively. 'Do you know the feeling of being in one place, when you are meant to be in another?'

'I do know that feeling,' Francisca said, imagining Rome, and clarified, 'but the fact is, my mother needs me.' She braced herself and asked, 'Where will you go next?'

Isabel's eyes became distant. 'I do not know. Gabriela is making enquiries about the whereabouts of my aunt – my mother's sister – and her family. I heard they were in England. It is difficult to give up the freedom of being on the road. That is how we all lived until my parents and I settled in Rome.' In a whisper, she said, 'But I need to find my aunt. I need to tell her my mother passed on to the other side. I want to tell her personally.'

Isabel's loss explained how she had been able to be sympathetic to Francisca's own loss, but Francisca wished she had shared it with her sooner. Did Isabel's melancholy stem from leaving behind her life on the road, or possibly her mother's passing? Yet she sensed it was something even deeper.

'I am so sorry, Isabel. Did your mother pass recently?'

'Last year already.' Isabel's collarbones contracted and expanded like wings of a bird as she contained her emotions. 'She had been ill for a short while. The end was quite sudden. I could not believe it.' She inhaled sharply. 'But belief or disbelief are quite irrelevant to the unassailable facts.' Isabel's eyes lifted to find Francisca in the luminescence and when she spoke, her voice was warmer than ever. 'I miss her, especially after I perform. She always encouraged me to make something of my voice so I could make my own choices in life.'

They sat in silence a moment.

'I am glad you are here – thank you for staying behind.' Playfully, Isabel added, 'Even though you missed the first half. I was left standing there, thinking you were not going to come, that you were not interested.'

'How could you have thought that? I needed to have time with my mother. It is difficult being away from her all day. She is so alone and dependent. I came as soon as I could.'

'Oh Francisca, I am sorry, and thank you. I should not have been so flippant. I did however think you might have brought a friend.' There was a hint of curiosity in Isabel's voice.

'The only person I would have brought is Bernardo, but he is probably somewhere between South America and the Mediterranean by now.'

Isabel tilted her head, her eyebrows raised quizzically.

'It is not like that. We have been friends since childhood. He and Elizabeth make me feel like I am not alone in the world, even though they are not physically here.'

'Such people are our true friends, to be cherished.' Isabel

cleared her throat quietly. 'I have been meaning to ask, how are you finding working with Antonio?'

'He does not say much to me.' Francisca did not elaborate that there was no respect in which it could accurately be said they were working together. 'I am learning by observation – the way he prepares the canvas with a dewy layer of darkness and captures glimmers of light amidst pools of shadows. But mostly, I am learning to trust my own voice. This has been the most helpful aspect of being his assistant.'

'I am glad you have come to appreciate your own worth and that you do not need to follow Antonio's philosophy. He is drawn to the shadows.' She gulped down the liquor and refilled her goblet. 'I wish he could just rest sometimes. But he cannot.' Isabel pointed to her head. 'He is devout and penitent.'

'Why? Why penitent?'

'His mother died in childbirth and his father never forgave him. It has afflicted his entire life.'

Francisca was suddenly filled with sadness for him. 'At least he has found an outlet to express his feelings.'

'I told you this so you can see that Antonio's philosophy is personal to his experience, and it is not the only path to making great art. You have your own experience, your own philosophy – you must believe in it and pursue it to where it might take you.' She looked into her eyes as she said, 'Believe in yourself. You must make a study of your own provenance. What you have is both a gift and a responsibility.'

Francisca felt the wisdom in Isabel's words, and she observed her face, so perfect in its arrangement of complex features, and she followed Isabel's line of sight up to the moon and again she felt in a dream.

There was a break in the clouds, revealing a cascade of stars.

'Here, it is said that each star is a gap in the universe, letting in the light of God.'

Isabel replied, 'Where I come from, it is said each star represents the soul of a loved one lost from the world.'

The silence folded in on them and, as their hands touched and they looked into each other's eyes, Francisca glimpsed the hope of what they might become to one another but did not dare express.

CHAPTER THIRTEEN

The Papal carriage traversed the sweeping coach road inland from Barcelona. Its black lacquered varnish shone in the morning sunlight, and the white cross of the Vatican emblazoned on the carriage doors sparkled. The sumptuous purple and gold velvet curtains, drawn for the occupants' privacy, did nothing to detract from the curiosity of passers-by, who stopped in awe at the splendid equipage. By the dust whipping up at the brow of the hill ahead, the livery knew the polish would not last the morning.

Cardinal De Praed and Archbishop Carlos felt rejuvenated, having stopped three nights in Barcelona. It had been an indulgence, though a much-needed one. It had been a long and arduous journey from Rome. The cardinal had suffered physically, and Carlos, spiritually. The final stretch to Seville via Valencia would have its own challenges. Due to the poorly made road, the Sierra Mariola was deceptively treacherous, particularly for the uninitiated driver. Carlos knew, having made the journey more than once. Before departing Valencia, he would take it upon himself to offer some advice to the coachman but he knew it would be a wasted effort; the Roman would be too proud to take any guidance, and

Carlos would be left with no choice other than to surrender to what might be.

The cardinal fell into a coughing fit and Carlos quickly located the spittoon from under his seat. Without any inhibition, the cardinal thrust his head between Carlos's knees, heaved forward and emptied the contents of his lungs into the spittoon.

Carlos smiled as he disposed of the contents out the carriage door and wiped his hand on his handkerchief. He retrieved from his day bag a small box he'd procured from his man in the Barrio Gotico, one of the small diversions Carlos had prepared for the monotonous journey. He presented it and lifted the lid, revealing a variety of chocolates within. The cardinal beamed a conspiratorial grin at Carlos and, quick as lighting, plucked one and popped it into his plump mouth. With his other hand, as deftly as a cat stealing a sleeping bird, he took the box. The atmosphere within the small cabin magically lifted.

'I am excited for you to see Seville, Cardinal.' Carlos had been bursting to tell him about it. He had been hoping the cardinal would have asked by now, but he had given up waiting. 'The river ports are quite a sight to behold too, when a fleet arrives in from the New World. Last year, I oversaw substantial extensions to the docks and Casa de Contratacion, simply to accommodate the sheer number of ships docking, and produce. Day after day: coffee beans, cocoa, fruit and vegetables, animals, the kind of which you have never seen.'

The cardinal's button eyes revealed themselves. 'Hmm, I should like to see that. We miss out in Rome.' His gravelly voice rose, and he waved a chocolate about. 'Coffee has not even reached us. And cocoa, only last year,' he said, his appal heartfelt. He reached across and touched Carlos's hand affectionately as he said, 'I enjoyed the samples you kindly brought to us in the Vatican.'

Encouraged, Carlos continued, 'We shall have plenty of time to look about and visit the markets. The palacio is comfortable. You will have an entire wing to yourself, and you will be able to rest and recover. When you are ready, you will find it is but a short walk to the ports and all the sights. And of course, our cathedral... Cardinal De Praed.' Carlos spread out his handsome hands as if to reveal the cathedral's beauty within them. 'It is a sight to behold. Of course, it has not the elegance of your Bramante and Michelangelo domes and cupolas, but it is magnificent in its own way.'

Carlos's voice trailed off in the absence of any sign of interest from the cardinal. These many weeks travelling from Rome, the two men had relied almost entirely on each other for company. Carlos understood the cardinal's well-being would go some way to ensuring his own, and so had endeavoured to be an amiable and thoughtful companion, taking care to discern the topics that most engaged his companion.

Despite Carlos's efforts, there had been long hours of silence. Carlos preferred such moments on his own. Indeed, it was in solitude that Carlos best kept his thoughts ordered, restrained, and disciplined. But, somehow, the cardinal's sheer size and overbearing character within the confines of the carriage had impaired his equanimity. At the lowest ebb, during the crossing of the Pyrenees, old troubles – that long ago he thought he had wrested – resurfaced. At times, Carlos longed to open the carriage door and throw himself down the mountainside. The old days, when the troubles started and tragedy befell the family, filled his mind.

But the haunting passed. Having battled through, Carlos felt stronger, his faculties sharper. It was Francisca who now occupied his thoughts. He rolled his rosary beads. Something must be done about her. Only he could bring it about. Marriage. It would not happen without his intervention; he saw that clearly.

It was painful to admit he had made an error of judgement as regards Bernardo. So much time had been wasted. Carlos had delayed escalating the issue, hoping Bernardo would take the initiative. Carlos had always envisaged a more ambitious and less free-spirited man for Francisca, but they had been inseparable. There was genuine affection between them, and he could see they made each other laugh. Sometimes Carlos would find himself smiling at the sheer joy of watching them.

But nothing ever seemed to *happen*. There was no tension, no stealing of glances or secret moments. Finally, Carlos reasoned he had no choice but to put Bernardo to the test and deal with the issue head-on, once and for all.

Carlos had offered to pay for Bernardo's further studies at the Maritime University, but Bernardo was too proud to accept.

Carlos had pressed the issue. 'Bernardo, I want you to be part of our family. The money – it is no matter. It can be yours to share.'

'I cannot explain. I am sorry.'

Carlos's temper rose, surprising them both. 'Then leave my house. Leave Seville. Until you do, Francisca will never be free.'

Carlos could not understand – what more could a man want from a marriage than friendship and trust? And if shared humour and money could be thrown in, then that was a bonus. Passion did not last.

So Bernardo arranged a placement as second officer on Vasco da Gama's next fleet and Carlos told him not to return until Francisca married.

Expecting to find Francisca inconsolable, Carlos was ready to do what he could to comfort her. She was tearful, but not in the way Carlos would have expected from a bereft lover. Carlos had postponed the issue by arranging Francisca's position with Ceretti, but it was nothing more than a device to keep her occupied until his return. His hand shook as he wrote the names of the families with eligible sons. What would he do without her?

At a bump in the road, Carlos clutched the carriage door handle. The cardinal winced in pain at his gout.

Realising he had drifted off into his own thoughts mid-discussion again, Carlos picked up the conversation. 'In any event, Cardinal, the cathedral is well-loved in Seville, indeed, in all of Andalusia,' Carlos enthused, thrumming his fingers on his robed knees. 'We have retained the minaret – repurposed it as a simple tower, so no offence can be caused. The cathedral has drawn the people together. Quite remarkable. We should be delighted if you could honour us with a sermon.'

'We will see about the sermon,' the cardinal spluttered. 'But I am looking forward to seeing your building. I've seen pictures – a curious rambling structure. I do not envy your task to fill it.'

Carlos smiled brightly. 'Ah. You well understand my challenge. But I had some luck en route to Rome. I commissioned someone quite special – one of Rome's own, in fact.' Carlos touched his nose.

'Well, who is your man?' the cardinal asked, his curiosity piqued.

Carlos smiled a little smugly, 'Ceretti; Antonio Ceretti.'

The cardinal's eyelids flicked open in a show of athleticism.

Carlos tried to swallow but the old lump in his throat surfaced.

'Ceretti?'

'Yes... from Rome.'

The cardinal blurted out, 'Ceretti – whose paintings are distinguished by their dark restlessness, almost heretical?'

'I am not sure about that, but is there more than one Antonio Ceretti? What is wrong?'

The cardinal waved a chocolate about. 'Only a handful of people know the thing. The Pope had ideas for him to paint some walls in the Vatican under close watch, but this... this *thing* put a swift end to that.' The cardinal's voice rose. 'If the Pope finds out he is working in a consecrated place on the commission of one of his own archbishops, matters could get awkward.'

'I... I had no idea. But what is this "thing" he has done?' Carlos stammered.

'Father Alberto knows it. He might see fit to tell you. Best always to speak with Father Alberto before decisions of significance.'

'So he keeps telling me,' Carlos muttered under his breath, feeling a fool.

The cardinal, evidently regretting his outburst, patted Carlos's leg. 'I'm sure we will navigate our way through. It is not the world's first diplomatic crisis, and it won't be the last.'

Carlos thought of Francisca, working under Ceretti, and felt panicked. He grappled for the right question. 'Is this – this thing you speak of – is it an isolated incident? Uncharacteristic of the man, I mean?'

'I could not say.'

Carlos pledged renewed resolve to find Francisca a husband.

CHAPTER FOURTEEN

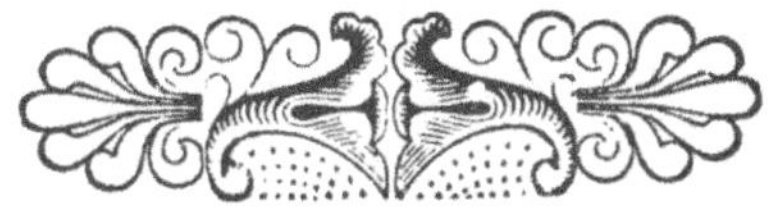

Several weeks passed, and Francisca developed a rhythm to her working day. During the daylight hours, she worked at the canvas in the cathedral, and during the hours after dark, at the atrium wall. Her work had a vigour and purpose, as never before. At times, it was like she was watching herself develop. Every day, she knew with greater certainty what it was that she wanted to achieve, and every day, she was a little bit closer to achieving it. Technically, she honed her vibrancy of colour by juxtaposing tones correctly. As words belong together in speech, so too do colours on a canvas. She polished her instinct for compositional harmony and perspective.

As regards the fresco, the characters required significantly more detailed brushwork than the landscape, and tangible progress was slow. She had worked her way down the characters and had completed the character of Father Alberto, and a justified sense of accomplishment filled her. Only once, while she was working at Father Alberto's character, did she contemplate his prohibition against her completing the fresco, and she silenced the voice of caution at the back of her mind.

She did not know when her uncle would be home, but she

estimated that, if she could continue at the rate she had been working, she would be finished within another two or three weeks, and she would allow herself a week to touch up any imperfections. Dismantling the scaffolding would take only a day or two. Uncle Carlos would need to be back for el Día de Todos los Santos, in time to welcome the Pope. She hoped that would be enough time. Frustratingly, she was no closer to uncovering the picture's secret, but she reassured herself that, once the scaffolding was dismantled, and she could see the picture without obstruction, all would become clear.

She stood at the easel in a patch of sunshine provided by a leadlight window, and applied the final layer of varnish to the Wisdom of Saint Jerome. Celestial light glowed through a grate in Saint Jerome's mountainside cave dwelling, illuminating his scroll and deflecting off the lion curled devotedly at his feet. The idea of light shining through the grate was Isabel's. Its impossibility would signify Saint Jerome's faith. The cave was set within a vast arid rocky outcrop, a harsh white-blue sky stretching out above. For all its biblical symbolism, it conveyed a tender domesticity between Saint Jerome and the lion. Francisca stepped away and resisted the temptation to look back. She would better judge success or failure tomorrow.

Each day, she observed Señor Ceretti at the canvas. Not once had he made a preparatory sketch. The entire composition flowed directly from his mind. His infinite patience as he sat back and allowed each layer of oil to dry seemed at odds with the restless agitation of his output.

Francisca tossed her brush into the flask of solvent solution and looked around. Señor Ceretti was nowhere to be seen but, out of the corner of her eye, she saw Isabel rushing towards her.

'Francisca,' Isabel uttered breathlessly. 'Is Antonio here?'

'I have not seen him all day. What is the matter?'

'There was a fight. Antonio fled the scene, and I cannot find him.'

On cue, a hollow thud echoed out and an elongated shadow appeared in the Door of Concepcion. A second later, Señor Ceretti himself emerged and stumbled towards them. His eyes were vacant, and he shouted incoherently.

Francisca sought out Isabel for an indication as to what to do, but she seemed transfixed, so she approached him cautiously, as she would a wild animal. There was a nasty gash by his right eye, and she recoiled at the stench of alcohol and manhood.

'Master, let us sit over there,' she said, bowing her head slightly, and she directed him by the arm to a nearby pew.

He yanked his arm away and overbalanced, nearly tipping the trestle table over. She reached forward and managed to catch his fall, but she could not hold him for long. Spotting a stonemason's wheelbarrow nearby, she called to Isabel, 'Look.'

Isabel recovered her senses and quickly wheeled it over and, together, they hauled Señor Ceretti in. He looked like a giant upturned crab with long gangly limbs protruding from its shell.

'We can't leave him here like this. Father Alberto will not abide intoxication in the cathedral,' Francisca said. 'Where is home?'

'Just a few streets away – off Calle Almansa.'

Outside, it was busy with the markets closing for the evening and the taverns beginning to fill. For other Sevillanos, it was just like any other evening.

A few people stopped, pointed and stared, some laughed, others frowned in judgement. They turned into the first side road. From there on, it was mostly a clear passage along the narrow lanes.

'I wonder how the other fellow is faring,' Francisca muttered as she maintained the wheelbarrow on a steady path.

'I have learned it is better to not think about it,' Isabel replied, running alongside.

At the corner of Calle Almansa, Isabel signalled to a building by the corner: one of the new elegant three-storey town houses made into apartments.

Francisca looked at Isabel. She hoped they lived on the ground floor.

'Wait here.' Isabel rushed inside, leaving Francisca on the street with Señor Ceretti in the wheelbarrow, trying to look nonchalant whenever people passed by.

Soon, Isabel called out her name and Francisca looked up to see her furiously waving from a platform extending out from the top floor. She then attached a large wicker basket to a pulley at the top of the building and eased the basket down to ground level.

Isabel's voice chimed out, 'The basket has doors at the front and back – they unlatch.'

Francisca's eyes widened.

'Put him in. It is the only way,' Isabel said, gesturing in a manner to demonstrate to Francisca how she might get him inside.

With grave misgivings, Francisca transferred Señor Ceretti from the wheelbarrow to the basket, thankful that he was all skin and bone. She tried to arrange him neatly, latched the door behind him, said a silent prayer, and hoped he would remember none of this in the morning.

She watched, aghast, as Isabel started pulling on the rope. Realising her post on the ground was futile, she ran inside the building, bounded up the stairs, let herself into the top floor apartment and rushed through to the front room. Isabel had made little progress. Francisca took a length of the rope, and together, they hauled and heaved.

When the basket finally rose level with the platform, Isabel signalled to Francisca to keep the rope steady. Isabel let go her length, took a nearby hooked stick, and pulled the basket over onto the platform, until it rested securely there. She opened the basket door and, together, they pulled Señor Ceretti out. He sprawled on the floor, blissfully unaware of his adventure.

'Antonio and I hauled the furniture that Carlos ordered for us in the same way,' Isabel explained, regaining her composure. 'Some was mahogany – heavier than Antonio.'

Francisca slumped against the wall, physically and emotionally exhausted, as Isabel poured a dark brown liquid into two goblets. They tossed it back.

Isabel poured two more and nodded encouragingly. 'It will calm you.'

They gulped down the second one, and, as they caught one another's eye, they fell to the floor and rolled about in helpless fits of laughter.

'You should have seen the look on your face when I suggested you put him in the basket! *Murderer*, you may as well have said!'

'I would have equally been a murderer.'

Señor Ceretti, green-tinged, emitted a pained moan and Isabel and Francisca caught sight of each other and burst out laughing all over again.

'Let's get him to bed,' Isabel suggested.

'When he sobers up, I hope he doesn't ask how he got up here.'

'I will say we helped him up but don't worry, he won't remember anything.'

They dragged him under the armpits down the hallway to the bedroom and lifted him onto the bed. Isabel shut the door behind them. 'Now, we can relax.'

CHAPTER FIFTEEN

Francisca followed Isabel down the hall to a small polygon-shaped corner room that led out to a large terrace. Isabel pushed open the doors, and they went outside to see the panorama of spires and domes and terracotta rooftops. Beyond, the river faded into dusk. Birds, flying in synchronicity, made their journey down-river for the night.

'It is breathtaking,' Francisca gasped. She had never seen Seville from this vantage point.

'Yes, it is a beautiful sight at this time of the evening, and every evening the light is subtly different.' They stayed side by side, watching the view. 'I will prepare some spiced brew. Please, make yourself at home.'

Francisca followed Isabel back inside. Adjacent to the corner room, there was a larger room with three big windows – an ideal workspace for Señor Ceretti, and she understood why he had chosen a top floor apartment. Paintings of Mary Magdalene modelled on Isabel and self-portraits of Señor Ceretti, modelled as Christ, were stacked against every wall.

Her eye was drawn to the sensual representations of Mary, and she saw the irony. The Christian story told of Mary Magdalene's transformation: in her love for Christ, she repented of her desires of the flesh, but these representations told of her as a woman, desired and in turn, desiring. There was a fatalism, suggesting that Mary and Christ's story was pre-ordained. Reflected in the paintings, Francisca saw Isabel and Señor Ceretti's own story and their life together and she felt out of her depth.

Isabel's dulcet singing voice emanated from the kitchen. The song followed an undulating harmony and a repeating, diminished fourth and sixth on the falling line. It was ancient, yet timeless in its elemental harmonies. It evoked something else for Francisca too, and she searched her soul. As the pressure built, she was transported back to her childhood.

She knew this song. Mingled with Isabel's voice was her father's light tenor, of all those years ago:

Durme, durme, sleep my little one, sleep without worry and pain.

She closed her eyes and returned to the mystical time of her childhood.

'Spice!' Isabel announced, smiling and unaware of interrupting Francisca's reverie.

'Thank you,' Francisca said absently, taking the goblet and trying to let go of the song and the memory of her father.

'By Señor Ceretti's productivity, I am guessing his current state of intoxication is not a regular occurrence,' Francisca said, gesturing to his work.

Isabel flipped through a cluster of canvases. 'Some people use their dreams to escape. Antonio uses Mary Magdalene.'

'Is it Mary or Isabel?'

'Sometimes I think the two have become one for him.' Isabel laughed wryly. 'Though he is yet to treat me like a saint.'

'But you are married?' Francisca had been wanting to know. 'For mere mortals, that is as saintly as love can be.'

Isabel smiled in a way that neither confirmed nor denied the question. She reached over to the window ledge and withdrew from a box two cigarillos. She took a wick and ignited it by the flame of an oil lantern and leaned in, to light Francisca's. Their eyes met briefly as her hands brushed Francisca's, but Francisca could not trust her feelings and she looked away.

As Francisca inhaled on her cigarillo, she emboldened herself and asked, 'How did you meet Señor Ceretti?'

Isabel looked distantly as she explained. 'Antonio attended my first ever performance in Rome. It was ten years ago. My father had recently died. It was a difficult time. Antonio came backstage and claimed me, there and then.'

Francisca could picture it and she said, 'His certainty made you certain.'

Isabel nodded. 'After two weeks, he told me I was his saviour. Through me he said he had found his true style.' Isabel shook her head as if shaking off the memory, and laughed. 'I will remind him.'

Francisca wanted to know more. 'What about you – before Rome?'

'Like I said, we were travellers.' A smile broadened on her face. 'My whole family travelled together. A day here, a day there, and we were on the road again.'

'It must have been invigorating, living like that. You must find me sheltered; I have never travelled.'

'Not at all, Francisca. You live your life up here.' Isabel touched her forehead. 'But yes, it was exciting, and there was also something about being on the road that satisfies the restless soul.'

'So why did you stop and why did you choose Rome?'

'So many questions, Francisca.' Isabel smiled, but quickly looked away and drew on her cigarillo. 'It all ended one terrible day. There was a fire at our camp,' she said, breathing heavily. 'It was devastating.' Her voice trailed off into nothingness. She closed her eyes.

'Dios mío, Isabel. How dreadful.'

'It is all right,' Isabel said, flicking her tears away and pulling herself up. 'But honestly, I cannot talk about it.'

'I think I now understand your melancholy.'

'Am I melancholic?'

'I feel it,' Francisca said. 'Beneath the surface of your cheerfulness and good humour.'

'Come, let us drink the spice and relax. We deserve it.'

Isabel led the way back to the corner room and they nestled amongst the cushions scattered around a table.

'So, here we are.' Isabel's eyes gleamed brightly, and she leaned forward, folding the fabric of her dress amongst her arms. 'I did manage to see your Saint Jerome, by the way, despite Antonio's theatrics. Congratulations.'

'You liked it?'

'I did. You captured Saint Jerome's kindness in the way the lion is curled up devotedly at his feet. Compositionally too, it is understated and yet dramatic. All the action is crammed into that small cave.'

'You have seen it precisely as I intended.' Francisca beamed. 'Señor Ceretti will probably find it banal.' She parodied his manner. '*You must capture all of man's suffering.*'

They laughed and, though conscious of being discourteous towards Señor Ceretti, it felt good to laugh.

'I suspect he will tear it all to shreds when we are finished,' Francisca concluded.

'It would not be the first time.' Isabel laughed again. 'When he told me you were tackling Saint Jerome, I assumed you would show his wisdom, like all the others. Bo-ring! All that wisdom!' Isabel exhaled the cigarillo smoke dramatically. In an entirely different voice, she said, 'Your version is beautiful. You take your viewer to another place and time, one that is better than the here and now.' She chuckled. 'Antonio will have us all immersed in his hell with him.' She tapped some ash into a small bowl and said, 'I think your two contrasting styles juxtaposed in the cathedral will be fabulous. It will be the reason people come to the cathedral.'

'I hope you are right, Isabel. I have said it before, but I hope you know how much it means to me that you like my work.'

'How could I not? Why do you think I have been loitering about the cathedral every day, even though the place is eerie?'

'Isabel. You should not say such a thing.'

She chuckled breezily. 'Why not? It *is* eerie. You find me irreverent, but I know you do not mind.'

'What makes you think I do not mind? The archbishop is my uncle,' Francisca said, but with humour in her voice.

'Intuition!'

Francisca inhaled the cigarillo, gathered her courage, and asked, 'Tell me – that song you were singing in the kitchen. It was a lullaby, was it not?'

'Yes, my father would sing it to me when I was a small child.'

With tears in her eyes, Francisca said, almost to herself, 'My father would sing it to me too. I had forgotten until I heard you sing it.'

Isabel leaned in and urged, 'Francisca, talk to me.'

Francisca was too agitated to remain seated. She rose and looked out through the terrace doors to the sky.

'After Papa was buried in the garden, I would look in his wardrobe every day, remembering how he wore his clothes. He had always looked so fine. Then, it became every other day, and then only sometimes, until, over the years, he slipped away from me. It is only since I started working on the fresco that memories of him have been returning to me.'

'Your father was buried in the garden of the palacio? Not in the cathedral grounds?'

'Yes.'

Isabel said nothing but Francisca could see she was taking in that information.

Francisca needed some air and went out to the terrace. Isabel followed.

'I thought applying the fresco to my mother's wall picture

might yield up the answer, or at least an insight, to what happened, but I feel no closer to discovering it.'

Isabel took another gulp of the liquor, and they gazed out to the infinite sky, scattered with brightly shining stars.

'Do you suspect she foresaw what was to happen, and represented it like a prophecy in the picture?'

Francisca breathed more freely to confess it and she said, 'Yes, that is what I have come to think, but of course it is possible it was simply a picture that she etched to express what was on her mind at the time. Either way, it was the last work she completed before fate intervened, and life has never been the same.'

'Let me come and see your fresco. Perhaps it requires a third person's perspective.'

'Yes, I am stuck.'

'Let us go now.'

'As in, *now*?'

'Yes. Why not? It is a clear sky.'

CHAPTER SIXTEEN

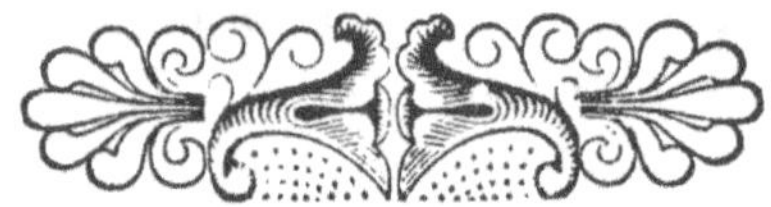

Francisca and Isabel hurried through the lanes to the palacio, Francisca acutely aware of Isabel's presence beside her. It felt like they were embarking on something new together. What information would Isabel glean from the fresco? Would she share her insights, freely and unguarded? As they entered the palacio's forecourt, Fiel muttered in his stable while he slept.

'That is Fiel, my stallion, snoring.' Francisca grinned. 'Here, this way,' she said, her nerves steadying as she led Isabel through the circular forecourt.

They passed under the arches and entered the atrium. The night air was still and cool here. There was an Elysian calmness which was like entering a sanctuary, far from the chaos of the city.

Isabel whispered, 'What a beautiful home you have.' She looked up at the palms, their fronds gently rustling, as if in conversation together. 'It is a whole world, in and of itself.'

'Yes, I am fortunate in that respect.'

The conditions were excellent to view the fresco. Light from the constellations flooded the wall, and the flares on the staircase bannisters lit strategic areas. It was magical, and Isabel gasped.

Francisca was impressed too. The wall had never seemed so vibrant.

For once, Isabel was speechless.

'I know the scaffolding makes it difficult...' Isabel squeezed her hand to silence her, and she strode about, viewing the wall from different aspects, whispering inaudibly to herself.

Francisca could wait no longer for Isabel's assessment. 'Do you have any theory as to what it might mean?'

Isabel tore her gaze from the painting.

'Even your lively descriptions had not prepared me for this,' Isabel breathed quickly. She searched Francisca's eyes and whispered, 'In answer to your question, yes, I do believe I understand the meaning behind the picture.' She looked around suspiciously, took Francisca's hand and said, 'But let us not discuss it here. Let's return to the apartment.'

And so, the two women set off purposefully once more through the star-lit streets, back to the apartment Isabel shared with Señor Ceretti. Francisca's nerves were in shreds with curiosity by the time Isabel ushered her onto the terrace and poured the remains of the spiced brew.

'Francisca, there is no easy way to say this, but they say the truth is like sunlight cleansing a festering wound, so I shall share with you what I believe the painting reveals.' She paused and inhaled the air as she said, 'Francisca, you were on the right track. The wall picture depicts your mother's baptism, and I believe it was your uncle who baptised her.'

All the blood drained from Francisca's body with the verdict, and she sat down heavily.

'The symbolism confirms it, Francisca. The star is six-pointed, which signifies the Star of David, a Jewish symbol of utmost importance, as you no doubt know. The griffin is another Jewish symbol, representing power and wisdom.'

Every word Isabel uttered was like a knife cutting Francisca's flesh.

'There are twelve characters – the same number as Jesus's disciples. The ravine – the place of your mother's baptism is also significant. There is barely a drop of water.'

Francisca listened in silence, with a strange sense of having known these things but suppressing their significance. She brought to mind the vision in which she embodied the griffin, and the griffin had known that the ravine had once flowed with clear mountain water.

'I believe your mother intended to convey that her baptism was flawed. In other words, her conversion was not of her free will. Your father stands aside from her, signifying that he refused to be baptised. He is the only figure in the entire picture who is linked both to earth and to sky! Have you noticed that the mountains plunge down so that, in the perspective in which your mother represented him, his face and upper body are in the sky? In terms of the perspective plan, your father is also the point from which every other aspect vanishes. In other words, he is the vanishing point.'

Francisca marvelled at Isabel's insights, as well as her technical knowledge. She was right – her mother had inserted the nail hole in her father's right temple. All the orthogonals ran from it.

Francisca's voice quavered as she said, 'It signifies that he is the one true figure – the one who stayed true to his nature.' It was as though she was losing her father all over again. 'It is difficult to accept.'

Isabel continued, 'You must believe it. Your safety depends on understanding it.'

'What else did you see? Did you detect any rift between my parents?' she asked, not knowing if she could bear the answer.

'That I cannot yet tell you. I need time to think on the remainder.'

Neither dared say the obvious, the idea of which had stealthily been growing in Francisca's mind despite her internal protestations: someone in the wall painting murdered her father; someone in the wall picture caused her mother's misery and pain, and so dreadfully changed the course of her family's life.

They leaned against the balustrades and looked out to the diminishing sky.

Isabel's musk perfume wafted in the space between them.

'Francisca, listen to me,' Isabel whispered, a sheen of sweat forming on her forehead. 'One thing is clear. From what we now know, you need to forget about getting to the truth. It will bring nothing but danger to you. I think Father Alberto was right: you should apply a limewash to it.'

This is not what Francisca wanted to hear. She looked ahead to where the river merged into the sky's inky canvas.

'If someone is responsible for my parents' fate, it needs to be avenged. *I* need to avenge it,' Francisca replied.

'Francisca, listen,' Isabel repeated, taking Francisca's hands in hers. 'Dark times are returning. I have just travelled the length of Spain, across Aragon and deep into Castile.' Her voice felt distant, like an echo. 'King Ferdinand wants his legacy to be a pure Catholic Spain. He wants Jews out, along with everyone else who does not conform to his idea of what it is to be Spanish. He is even turning families and friends against one another in fear.'

'Your words are frightening me!'

'Francisca, I have no wish to frighten you, but what I say is true. We are entering troubling times, and it is better that you know so you can make informed decisions. Ferdinand is determined to finish what he started at about the time your father died. You do know, don't you, that your father died at the height of the Inquisition?'

Francisca's mind felt like it would explode with the information. All she managed in reply was, 'Uncle Carlos has never spoken of the Inquisition. At least, not as anything relevant.'

Isabel continued relentlessly, 'People are blind to what is happening. I have seen Jewish people openly observing the Sabbath.' A hard edge surfaced in Isabel's voice as she said, 'You

Sevillanos think your liberties are indestructible, but you are wrong. Liberty and progress are the most valuable of gifts, and they are fragile. They can be shattered if not fought for and protected.' She snapped her fingers dramatically. 'Your liberties are built on the shifting sands of good fortune.' She shook her head. 'Be careful, Francisca.'

Francisca followed the line of Isabel's sight, out towards the river, resplendent under the constellations.

As though thinking out loud, Isabel said, 'Maybe that is why your Uncle Carlos is a fervent Catholic. Maybe, back then during the purge, he was too scared not to be. And he excelled at it, they believed him – and made him archbishop.'

She looked at Francisca, clear-eyed, taken by her own theory. 'It is possible, is it not? In fact, how else do you explain the wall painting?' Decisively, Isabel said, 'Forget about the past, Francisca.'

Isabel's theory was too much for Francisca to take in. What did Uncle Carlos forsake? Was it only his religion, or his family too? She began to tremble, and she said, 'I could do with something stronger to drink.'

'I will get us something.'

She tried to think. Isabel's advice was incompatible with her need to know the truth, and she did not see how unearthing what had happened all those years ago could possibly be dangerous now.

Isabel returned with a tall bottle and two small copas and placed them on a mosaic table. She smiled briefly and poured the syrupy liquor.

'I cannot believe I have lived my whole life without muscatel.'

'It is essential,' Francisca agreed, attempting a smile.

They drank quickly and Isabel poured two more copas and they leaned out over the railings again.

'What are you thinking?' Isabel whispered, nudging her hip against Francisca's.

'I do not know. It is difficult to make sense of it all.' Francisca frowned. 'Do you not think it is wrong to deny what you are? If my parents were Jewish – if *I* was born Jewish – and if I was forced to convert, do you not think I have an obligation to resist this?' She thought back to the woman shackled to the carriage, destined for the Castle of San Jorge. It could have been her if circumstances had been different.

A kernel of an idea developed in her mind, and her eyes lit up. 'Maybe I could help. I could ask Uncle Carlos to talk to the King to persuade him to reconsider his plans, and to allow life to go on as it is.'

'No.' Isabel shook her head decisively. 'That is not an option, Francisca. Some things cannot be won, no matter how much you want them. Some people cannot be saved, no matter how hard you try. Sometimes, the tide of history is simply against you.'

'You speak like you know.'

Isabel's look went straight through Francisca and her voice cracked as she affirmed, 'That is because I do know.' She said gently, 'When this madness passes, you can live the life of your dreams and honour your parents.' In the way Francisca found so thrilling, Isabel tilted her head back slightly, showing her noble profile in three-quarter view. Her auburn hair glowed against the starry sky. 'Let us assume you find out what happened – what then? Will you paint better? Will your mother recover?'

Although Isabel had asked her questions rhetorically, she had expressed the idea that had been taking hold in Francisca's mind these past weeks. She had the answer: *Yes, I believe my mother will recover if the truth is revealed.* But she said nothing.

'What will you do?' Isabel finally asked.

Francisca did not need to think before replying, 'I am going to finish the fresco.'

'You have courage, Francisca, and, for someone so young, you have suffered many losses.'

'As have you.'

Isabel's voice hovered on the air as she said, 'Your pain runs deep and is part of who you are.' As though she was reading

Francisca, she added, 'While it resides here' – Isabel touched the area of Francisca's heart – 'where the light enters you, your art will be safe forever.'

Francisca wanted to believe her art was safe within her heart and not a contrivance to paper over the cracks of her pain. She scanned Isabel's beautiful face, and her artist's eyes became a lover's gaze. Restraint disintegrated. In the soft starlight, the mystery of an ocean resided in Isabel's eyes, and it seemed to Francisca that she was truly being seen for the first time. She felt no embarrassment or self-consciousness. She opened herself for Isabel to see, and Isabel's lips parted. An arcane force drew Francisca's right hand to Isabel's left hand. Their fingers touched and lightly explored. Time extended. Nothing else existed.

Isabel took hold of Francisca's shirt and drew her closer. 'Like a dream,' she whispered, and leaned in.

Their breaths intertwined. Their lips touched and they explored cautiously and tentatively, recklessly and with certainty. An entire world resided in their kiss and they could not let go.

Señor Ceretti's voice cut the air. 'Isabel!' The spell was broken.

'I had better go,' Francisca said.

Isabel followed Francisca to the door. Something had changed, but Francisca was afraid the moment would forever be lost.

'I will see you at the cathedral in the morning,' Isabel said.

'Yes,' Francisca replied but there was no time to take in Isabel's expression. She did not want to leave like this, when they had barely even embarked on this new journey. Francisca began, 'Isabel, I...' But she was too lost to continue. Feeling the torture of the long hours that must pass until she could see Isabel again, she left.

CHAPTER SEVENTEEN

When Francisca emerged into the street, the air seemed impossibly light, too light to hold Francisca down, and she ran and ran, feeling unbound. Exhilaration surged through her. She cried and laughed and called out to the stars, 'Tell me!' *Have I finally been let in on a secret, that others have always known? Has the joy of life been denied me until now? Have I merely been existing?*

By the time she returned home and to her bedchamber, she had run herself to exhaustion. The exertion was what she had needed: it was the only way she could endure the feelings surging within her.

She drew the curtains closed, changed into her nightgown, and was about to settle into her bed when she spotted, waiting patiently for her on her writing desk, a blue envelope. As she opened the seal she slid into the bed sheets.

My Dear Francisca,

The joy your last letter brought me is difficult to express. It arrived on the second day of my own arrival here at the priory in Wilmington. To see the palacio's parchment and your familiar handwriting on my writing desk, on return from my day's toils, made the priory seem home.

Regarding your apology for not writing at length – please do not feel under pressure to write until time for quiet contemplation permits it. I can well imagine how all-consuming your work with Ceretti must be. But I confess, I do long to hear about it.

On the topic of Ceretti, I feel I should tell you something.

In the week prior to my departure from Greenwich Palace, I was fortunate to cross paths with Torrigiano, who arrived from Rome for a period of residency. He has been searching for a new home since finding himself unpopular in Italy after having broken Michelangelo's nose in a temper of artistic jealousy. King Henry commissioned him to design some statues for the garden – and indeed, why should he not? The artist's creation may be quite separate to his temperament, as we know. Every artist is, after all, subject to all human weaknesses.

Naturally enough, while greeting Torrigiano over tea, I mentioned your work with Antonio Ceretti in Seville Cathedral. I tell you, although I had not met Torrigiano before, I discerned shock in his eyes. That, together with his apparent desire to redirect the conversation, betrayed something hidden in his mind. I did not press him on it immediately, for there were others about. However, later that day, I sought out an opportunity to speak with him alone.

I found him in the forecourt to the hunting grounds, idly observing the roses, still glorious in their late summer bloom. For his gratification, I spoke in Italian. We exchanged pleasantries, primarily about his country (in respect of which I took care to speak most highly and with some detailed and current knowledge). Having so flattered and impressed him, I fancied I had won his favourable opinion. Immediately, I took the opportunity to turn the conversation back to Antonio Ceretti and, in a straightforward manner, asked him to reveal the reason for his evident shock, which I told him had not been lost on me.

He led me to the edge of the rose garden, by the border to the hunting ground forest and confided in me that, almost a year ago, Ceretti disappeared from Rome, suddenly, and without a word. No one knew to where, or why he went. It was not long before the rumours spread, and it is this that I must tell you:

Ceretti was obliged to leave Rome.

Word has it that he was under compromised circumstances – whether he left covertly or under Papal instructions, Torrigiano did not know. He could tell me no more.

I do believe he knew no more.

I asked him to share any new information with me, whatever its nature and however reliable. I explained the altruistic reason for my interest: that you were my charge for many years, that I take special interest in you and your continued development and that you are still young and unmarried and therefore vulnerable.

He gave me his solemn promise to do so. As I left Torrigiano, a furrow lingered on his brow.

I had hesitated to tell you but, ultimately, I decided that you should benefit from the information, such as it is. Despite Torrigiano's fraught temper, I believe him to be honest. Insofar as his information extends – which admittedly is limited – I believe it sincerely to be told.

You, Francisca, must form your own view of Antonio Ceretti's character, based on your good judgement and experience of him. In the meantime, you must take care.

Now, to other matters.

The setting of Wilmington Priory is even more idyllic than in my dreams. The morning air is sweeter, the bird song more lyrical, the land more serenely pastoral than ever I have known. Not only that, but the villagers are delightful, civilised and welcoming. Our closest neighbour, who lives in a charming, thatched house called the Chantry, is also a widow and someone with whom I feel a rapport. We have agreed to walk over to Alfriston and dine together at one of the finest inns in the area – the Star – on the eve of the feast of Michaelmas.

In short, my new home is more than I had hoped, and I am optimistic for the future. How I would love you to come and see it.

Indulge me while I tell you a little more about it. The priory, and indeed the view from my bedchamber on the second and top-most floor, is marked by a 'Long Man'. It is the form of a man etched in chalk, deep in the large hill formation that overlooks our little establishment. His vast stature occupies the entire length of the hill. Although his form is a mere outline – with no facial features or other characteristics distinguishing him as warrior, priest, leader or otherwise – he resonates a resounding calm goodness. The locals say the ancients created him as a call to the sun for good harvest. I do believe this to be true, for I have never seen such an abundance.

Our days are filled with physical labour that the produce demands. We work hard to forge out the new life that God has fated us. The priory itself, as well as its herb and vineyard terraces, must be brought into a habitable and useable condition. My companions are amiable and hard-working, and I feel we are of similar mind.

We are prioritising those works that must be done before the onset of winter – which, difficult to believe, will fast be upon us. I know not how the monks lived in the priory in the state we found it.

Even so, I have rarely been so full of hope. Our labour is not only for ourselves, but also for those who will come after us. I am only fully alive when there is something greater at stake than myself. Nurturing you has taught me that. You brought me the greatest of joys.

Now, I must sign off.

Please keep well.

With this I send my best love to you, Francisca,

Yours,

Elizabeth

Francisca slumped into her pillow, her mind reeling with the revelations about Señor Ceretti. She looked at the constellations painted on the ceiling and tried to think. Suddenly, all her questions began to fall into place. Whatever Señor Ceretti's compromised circumstances were, they explained three things: why he had left Rome without a commission; how it was that Uncle Carlos had so readily secured him; and how it was that Uncle Carlos was able to attach the condition of her being his assistant. Señor Ceretti had no choice and no bargaining power.

Gradually, the question arose in her mind: did Uncle Carlos know of his banishment? Isabel had said that Uncle Carlos had intercepted Señor Ceretti in Barcelona, at which time, Uncle Carlos would have been en route to the Vatican. Francisca reasoned it was very possible he was ignorant of Antonio's circumstances. She could not imagine Uncle Carlos commissioning him – quite apart from arranging her position with him – had he known Ceretti had committed an act justifying exile from Italy, possibly on the Pope's edict.

Francisca thought back to what Isabel had said – that Señor Ceretti had been reluctant to accept Uncle Carlos's commission – that he had wanted a commercial commission, rather than an ecclesiastical one. If it had been the Pope who banished him, then presumably accepting a commission within the Church would be an insult to, and in defiance of, the Pope?

Her next question caused her to sit up. Should she tell Isabel? But what, precisely, was there to tell? The information, while cogent in Elizabeth's hand, might seem insubstantial in conversation – baseless, slanderous even. She reread Elizabeth's words: ... *rumours spreading, that Ceretti was obliged to leave Rome...*

For now, Francisca decided there was insufficient detail to justify it. It was, after all, only a rumour, in Torrigiano's words. It may be nothing. The idea that Isabel might already know did not even occur to Francisca. Francisca resigned herself to the fact that she would not find answers to her questions immediately. She sank back into the pillows, and with her body still swirling from Isabel's kiss, fell to sleep: a still, deep sleep.

CHAPTER EIGHTEEN

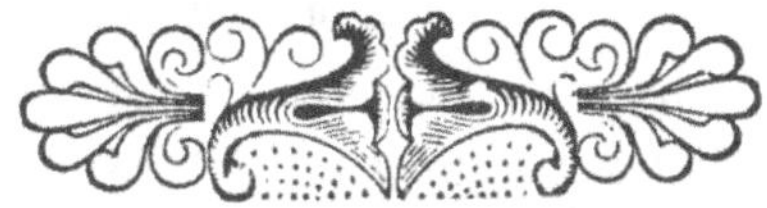

Francisca awoke before dawn, sprang from her bed and headed for the cathedral. A composition, vivid in detail, had appeared in her dream, and she needed to apply it to the canvas. She would make a seamless connection between what was in her mind's eye and what the viewer would see and feel.

The stars guided her through the cathedral gardens. In the predawn light, the limestone glimmered like the dragon's scales. Once inside the great cavern, it was as though she could hear the dragon's breath, but she was unafraid and she hurried, as if late for an appointment, to the Nave del Evangelio.

On a small canvas, she applied an outline in black chalk. She worked rapidly, the charcoal barely keeping up with her mind's instructions. Mary was in three-quarter profile, her chin slightly elevated, her lips parted in hesitant longing. Viewers would not know of what it was she yearned. Francisca knew every contour, ridge and hollow, the texture of the flesh, and she imagined she knew the emotions stirring within her soul.

By carefully layering the pigments and oils, Mary's grace would come to life. It would seem as if the image already existed in the universe, and that all she had done was apply it to the canvas, in a similar way as Michelangelo and his sculptures – they were already complete within the marble block; he had said, all that was required of him was to chisel away the superfluous stone.

Within a mystical cave setting, Mary, Mother of Christ, held her infant son in her arms. Her expression elicited her contradictions: her courage and fear, strength and vulnerability, certainty and doubts, loves and losses. In the depth of her expression, she searched for something – or someone. The viewer would be left to guess what or who, beyond the frame, it might be. A perceptive viewer would see that her countenance was sensual, her smile, a lover's smile.

Ironically, this might be the one painting in which a viewer might question their faith. *This* was what would keep them returning to the cathedral, she thought.

The morning came and went. In her focus on her work, she had not noticed the passage of time nor, more significantly, that Isabel had not come as promised. Nor did she notice Señor Ceretti's absence. Finally, she stretched and looked about. Already, it was dark. Night was setting in.

The last words Isabel had uttered the evening before returned to her – that she would meet Francisca at the cathedral in the morning. Francisca quickly cleaned her materials, and set off, with the sole purpose of finding Isabel.

CHAPTER NINETEEN

After Isabel had bid Francisca goodnight, she needed time to compose herself, but Antonio called out again.

'Isabel!'

Hesitantly, she went to the bedroom. An unsettling mixture of joy and guilt rushed through her. When was it that life had begun to unravel? When was it that she had become someone to whom things happened? It seemed long ago that she felt in command of her life. Longer still, perhaps, that she had been able to reach Antonio.

'Come here, woman.' Antonio slurred, 'Was that Francisca I heard?'

'I am here,' Isabel replied, not daring to approach him. 'Sleep for a while, Antonio. You will feel better in the morning.' As she began to close the door, she muttered to herself, 'I hope we will both feel better in the morning.'

'Don't go, Isabel. Join me.'

'I am not tired.'

He untangled the bed sheets, hobbled to her and seized her by the arm. 'Isn't it enough that I endure Francisca all day, without you bringing her home?'

'Endure her?' she exclaimed. 'You barely talk to her.'

'I never wanted an assistant, let alone for that assistant to be a woman and my commissioner's niece.'

'How is it that we see the same thing so differently?' She tried to release her arm. 'I see that Francisca is helping you meet Carlos's impossible deadline. I see that your different styles will transform that dreadful space into something alive and exciting.'

He let her go and shook his head, rejecting her analysis.

'I wonder sometimes if you appreciate the pressure that I'm under and the compromises I'm forced to make. Do you think I want to share my work with an amateur, a nobody, and a woman?'

'I know you do not mean that,' she said as gently as she could, sensing she must try to appease him. 'Francisca has a singular talent – brilliance even – and I know you see it in her work. You will curate it so that your contrasting styles strike awe into worshippers. When it is complete, it will be clear that what you have achieved here will be just as important as anything you achieved in Rome. You are leaving a mark here, in this part of the world.'

'This place is insignificant.'

When had she stopped sympathising with him? When had she recognised as petulance that which she had previously viewed as his struggle?

'That is not true, Antonio. And once people see what you have done, other great artists will come. In any event, Rome will still be there if you want to return.'

He looked up at her, a glimmer of hope in his eye.

'If the Pope likes what I'm doing here, certainly, I would return. But will you come?'

She could not go down this path. 'You know I need to find my aunt. Until then, I cannot know what the future holds.'

He took her in his arms, but she did not yield to him and when he bent to kiss her, she turned her face.

'What is it?'

'I am tired.' She avoided his eyes.

'Not three minutes ago, you said you were not!' he shouted, looking at her as though he could see a truth within her that he had not seen before, and making her feel exposed.

He pushed past her, went to the kitchen, and returned with two bottles of liquor. He unhooked his coat and slipped a bottle into each of the pockets.

'I do not think you need any more alcohol, Antonio. Please.'

'I need some air.'

'Antonio. Please, don't leave like this,' she pleaded even though she wanted nothing more than to be on her own.

He slammed the door.

Isabel's hands shook with tension and she needed to sit down. She was sorry for the way in which Antonio had departed, but also relieved to have the apartment – and her thoughts – to herself. She could not settle, and so went to the terrace doors, seeking clarity, but thick clouds had smothered out the light of the stars.

How was she to find a way through her emotions tonight? She knelt down and forced herself to block out her current problems. Her thoughts drifted to her mother. When her mind felt still and calm, she guided her thoughts to the place she ventured only rarely. It was too painful: Lucena – her and Antonio's beloved child.

After Lucena's death, she and Antonio had almost separated. They coped with her loss in different ways, and Isabel had felt abandoned by Antonio. Now, she queried whether Lucena's death was the unspoken tragedy that had kept them together. As she prayed, she felt a tugging at her heart – the only evidence she required to believe in life's higher force. It was how she knew life continued on, transmuted to another form, beyond her comprehension.

Tonight, the old pain met with new pain: that her life with Antonio may finally have come to an end. She felt it come towards her, and soon it began to occupy her. She recalled their young love, when she had been proud to inspire in Antonio the discovery of his true style. It had seemed to her that she was the only woman in the world who could have inspired that in him. They were meant for one another. It had taken her some time to realise that the price of Antonio's adoration was possession. He had occupied every piece of her body and soul, to the extent that she felt annihilated. He was controlling and demanded she share her every thought and feeling and disclose every movement. It was only with the elapsing of time and the gradual recovery of herself that she understood such love was not the kind of love that she sought. It was too intense. It was not sustainable. She understood that his behaviour derived from his insecurity. He had lost his mother even as he was entering this world, and so, naturally, feared losing Isabel. But the fear that drove his behaviour was self-fulfilling and served to push her away. She needed room in her life to be herself. She needed space between them, and she had tried to reframe their relationship, but he did not understand, or if he did, he would not accept it.

If she was not to drown in her feelings, she needed help, so she returned to the bedroom, dragged the trunk out from under the bed and opened the tiny, concealed drawer that contained a fragile, gold-threaded scarf that had belonged to her mother.

She gathered her hair and wound the scarf around and around until it sat like a shrine on her head. She attached a chain to an urn, and held a lighted wick to it until the coals lit. She sprinkled crushed spices on top, and as it began to smoke, she swung the urn in interlocking circles around the room. The vapours extended to every corner and its magic began to take effect.

With her hands extended, she began to turn, and she uttered quiet murmurs until her meditation became deep and profound. Time, as a dimension, ceased, and she entered a space without judgement, where the pain of broken promises healed, where life and death became the same and renewal possible. She let out a cry into the night.

When she awoke, the sun was far into the west. She had slept through the night and most of the next day. The apartment was quiet. Antonio had not returned.

Her mind was filled with questions, but she was not afraid. What might it be like to lose everything? Would it mean finding herself? Would it be like casting off from the shore, no land in sight? Her skin tingled. She looked at the vast sky. The sun had almost completed its wide arc and she realised that she was late for her appointment with Gabriela.

CHAPTER TWENTY

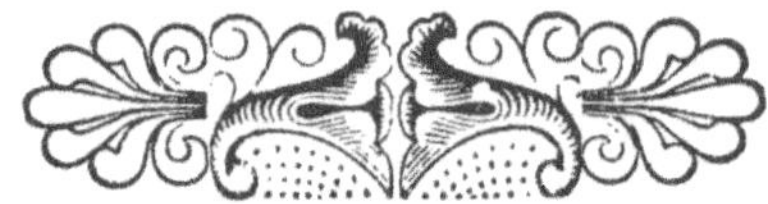

Gabriela ushered Isabel into her apartment, uncorked a bottle of claret and poured it liberally into two goblets. Gabriela drank and paced the parlour floor. Isabel sat quietly, waiting for Gabriela to reveal what was troubling her.

Mid-step, Gabriela stopped and in a gravelly voice said, 'It seems word has found its way to the wrong quarters about our gathering.' She gripped her goblet with both hands. 'If the fact of the gathering itself is known, it will not take a leap of logic to discover what it is that we are planning.'

'Gabriela, slow down,' Isabel pleaded as she settled into the cushions. 'Please, start from the beginning?'

'Isabel, what I am saying is that there may be an informer.' Gabriela's voice rose.

'Que horrible, Gabriela. Do you mean an informer amongst us, the Insurgeants Royale?'

'That is precisely what I mean.' Gabriela's strides quickened as she continued. 'I had taken great care to try and prevent this, but, as we feared, a new delegate was appointed by the Inquisitor Generale. He has his methods of persuasion, as we know too well.' Her frown merged into a half smile as she added, her husky voice restored to itself, 'Fortunately, we also have our own informers.'

Isabel tried to think. 'We must outsmart them.'

'Of course, but the question is, how?'

They searched one another for inspiration.

Suddenly, all became clear to Isabel, and she slapped her hand on the table. 'Gabriela, we must push ahead with the gathering. We settled on the date for the very good reason that it is when the guards at the Castle of San Jorge will be distracted with the arrival of the new prisoners for the Auto-da-fé. King Ferdinand would not imagine we could be so bold.' She paused and when she spoke next, her voice was steely. 'We cannot buckle at the first sign of pressure, Gabriela. That is precisely what they want.' Hesitantly, she added, 'Unless to do so would make Valentina's situation worse?'

Gabriela finally lost her composure and reached for a chair. 'Her situation could not be any worse,' she cried, her voice choking. 'My sources tell me that, not only is she incarcerated in San Jorge, but she is also in solitary confinement – her feet chained, her wrists shackled to a wall. She can hardly keep food down. I have not slept for days.' Tears poured forth.

Isabel crouched down and put her arms around Gabriela as she said, 'Then it is clear. We must press ahead as planned. We must keep our resolve. In any case, to reschedule now would be dispiriting for all of the Insurgeants – which we cannot afford. And there may be no better opportunity. Time is not a luxury we have. I know the delegates from Las Alpujarras are already en route. We have discussed strategy countless times...'

'You are right,' Gabriela said excitedly, pressing Isabel's hands as she returned to her feet. 'I have been too emotionally involved. We can hold the meeting right here.' Her voice strengthened. 'We will get word out that El Flamenco will host some entertainment. There is nothing suspicious about that.'

Her enthusiasm was infectious, and Isabel added, 'The band and I can be the entertainment. They would never think we would hold the meeting right here after a performance, before charging San Jorge.'

At the mention of San Jorge, Gabriela broke down again. 'What did Valentina ever do to deserve this living hell? Was loving me so vile? Is being Jewish hurting anyone?'

'You are right. These things are private matters,' Isabel agreed. 'The world will not always be this way. But nothing will change without a fight. We must be strong, Gabriela.'

Gabriela squeezed Isabel's hand and said with renewed conviction, 'Yes, you are right.'

'Come, let us sit on the terrace and watch the stars.'

Arm in arm, they went outside and looked, open-mouthed, at the drama unfolding before their very eyes. A sirocco was whipping up. They had been so absorbed in their conversation that they had been unaware of the Saharan sand appropriating Seville.

'It is as if a band of orangutans has been let loose,' Gabriela said above the noise, and they laughed a much-needed laugh.

Huddling together, they returned to the safety of the parlour and settled back into the cushions.

'Where would I be without you?' Gabriela muttered, 'Do not leave Spain again. I could not bear it.'

'Gabriela, you know I must find my aunt. Antonio is already anxious about it.'

'How is Antonio?' Gabriela looked over at her. 'Does he still have his temper?'

'It is the artist's prerogative, it seems.' Isabel thrummed her fingers on the table nervously. 'He is finding this commission particularly difficult. Yesterday, he picked a fight with an innocent man and got so drunk that Francisca and I had to take him home in a wheelbarrow.'

Gabriela chortled. 'If only the genius of the artist were reflected in the character of the man.'

Isabel looked away. 'Afterwards, he complained about the compromises he is forced to make by sharing the cathedral with

Francisca. And, of course, he made me feel like I was to blame for his circumstances. He left.' She showed her hands resignedly. 'And now I have no idea where he is.'

'I am sure he is safe. Antonio knows how to look after himself.' Gabriela chewed the inside of her cheek and ventured to ask, 'Might Antonio sense the alchemy between you and a certain someone else?'

Isabel looked up in shock at Gabriela's perception.

Unperturbed, Gabriela added gently, 'Even a blind man could see the chemistry between you.'

Isabel's cheeks burned and her hands shook. Although Gabriela was her dearest friend and she trusted her with her life, she was not ready to discuss Francisca. She needed time.

'I cannot talk about it,' she said, and drained her goblet.

'All right.' Gabriela smiled. 'It's all right, Isabel.'

There was one thing, however, that Isabel did want to discuss. It was the one thing she could not share with anyone else. 'Gabriela, I am sorry. Forgive me. I will talk when I am ready. But there is one thing I have been wanting to speak about for some time. It is difficult to put into words.'

'Try,' urged Gabriela.

Isabel tried to arrange her thoughts into something she could articulate. 'I had come to think it was our daughter's death that drove us apart, but lately, I have come to think it is her death that is keeping us together.'

Gabriela immediately understood. 'You are joined in your grief?'

'Yes. Not only that, but my guilt. How could I leave him to suffer on his own, after all we have lost together?' Tears streamed down her face as she looked to Gabriela for answers.

'Isabel, grief and guilt can become like a tumour if you let them. Honour the life your mother granted you and live it with all your heart. Even amidst grief, there is life and light to be found. Find a place for Lucena in your heart and nourish that place. Grief and life *can* coexist.'

As Isabel sobbed, she began to understand that she needed to find a place for her grief to reside within her. Until then, she would never be free.

Gabriela held her in her arms and let her cry until she had no tears left to fall.

CHAPTER TWENTY-ONE

Francisca hurried home and changed into a skirt and blouse. She sat down and penned Isabel a note which she thrust in her pocket. As she closed the gates of the palacio behind her, it was only vaguely that she noticed a strange chill hovering in the air. She was too preoccupied. Why did Isabel not keep her promise to come to the cathedral? She replayed last night's scene over and over, like a spinning orb and tortured herself with the possible interpretations, none of which provided any comfort. Perhaps she had overestimated the significance of the kiss. Perhaps it had meant little to Isabel or perhaps, in the cold light of day, Isabel regretted it and confessed to Señor Ceretti. Of all the interpretations, this last one was by far the most torturing, but it also explained why Señor Ceretti also had not come to the cathedral. She reddened at the idea.

By the time she reached the cathedral square, the chill had become a raging wind, silencing even Francisca's very thoughts. The streets had become a swirl of sand which pelted her face and spun in little twists like whirling dervishes. The wind rattled the gargoyles angrily inside their stone casings.

She had heard of the sirocco and seen fear and awe in the eyes of those who had survived it. Each grain of Saharan sand, it had been said, carried the secrets of a thousand years. The sirocco had been said to sweep all in its wake, even small cities. There was no doubt this was what the storm was.

Recklessly, she ventured on, determined to find Isabel or at least leave her the note. She clutched her shawl which she arranged to cover her mouth and nose. In the relative calm of the narrow lane off the cathedral square, she felt in her pocket for the note.

Dear Isabel,
I had expected to see you at the cathedral this morning. I hope our conversation did not upset you. I apologise if I behaved inappropriately...

To fill in some white space on the page, she had mentioned too that, having reflected on her good counsel, she had resolved to think further before pursuing the truth surrounding her parents' fate. Her hand had shaken, and she had struggled to hold the quill as she wrote the words. She had been too nervous to read the note over and she told herself that any feebleness or lack of precision in her expression would serve to mask the anxiety that had compelled her to put quill to paper.

What was this feeling that had been consuming her since she had set eyes on Isabel? It was both exhilarating and frightening in its authority, and, like a drug, she was powerless over it.

Finally she reached Calle Almansa. There was no shelter from the storm here. She clung on to her shawl and shaded her eyes as she sought out Isabel's apartment, but it was barely visible through the sand. Yet, she saw enough to be sure that no light shone from within. She tried the door to the building, but it was locked. She took the note from the pocket of her skirt and began to slide it through the gap, when, suddenly, she visualised Señor Ceretti intercepting it and she snatched the note back.

With one hand shielding her eyes, the other clinging to her

shawl, she leaned into the storm and, to give herself time to think, struggled on in the direction of the port.

The river was alive. Twirls of water spun in tall columns, slapped back, sucked in, and rose up. It repeated, over and over. The galleons tied at port, usually formidable, were like children's toys as the wind tugged at the ropes that tied them down. How could they possibly survive a storm out at sea, she thought? Bernardo had told her of the great raging swells as high as mountains and low gaping troughs as deep as the very ocean floor. Nothing was safe in a storm at sea, he had said.

As she struggled on, her thoughts darkened, and another, more likely, explanation for Isabel and Señor Ceretti's absence occurred to her. She stopped mid-step. What might Señor Ceretti be capable of doing when fuelled with alcohol after a fight and stung with jealousy? She thought back to the bruise that had appeared on Isabel's cheek all those weeks ago.

She cursed the self-referential thoughts she had been indulging in and began to retrace her steps. The wind was behind her now and propelled her on with a power such that she struggled to not become airborne. In no time she was back outside the apartment building, and she tried the front door again. It would not open. She rattled the handle and pushed her weight against it. It did not yield. She took a few steps back and called up to the apartment. 'Isabel!'

A man approached. She called out, 'Señor – have you seen Señorita de Flores or Señor Ceretti? They live here.' She pointed up to the building, but her words were lost to the roaring wind.

'Have you not heard – it's the sirocco.' She read his lips as he hurried away into a nearby lane: 'She must be mad.'

There was only one thing to be done. For this, she needed Fiel.

The sirocco had sequestered Seville. No landmark, square nor street was recognisable in the swirling red dust. Francisca tucked her head in behind Fiel's neck and trusted him to find the way. Her thoughts whirled with dark and disconnected images – of Isabel and Señor Ceretti arguing, of Bernardo lost at sea, Elizabeth unhappy amongst strangers in Wilmington Priory, and of her impending marriage.

She looked up at a stone arch. They had already arrived at Camino Camarón. El Flamenco was only seconds away. Her heart pounded as she tried to think what to say to Gabriela. How could she make light about venturing out, on a night like tonight, in search of Isabel? She rehearsed her opening sentence as she looked up to the terrace of El Flamenco.

What she saw played out like a scene from a bad dream. Hand in hand, Gabriela and Isabel stepped out onto the terrace. They shaded their eyes and looked up into the storm. Gabriela leaned in and whispered something, to which Isabel laughed, and, arm in arm, they returned inside. There was an unmistakable intimacy in their demeanour, and she imagined Isabel and Gabriela as lovers. Instantly, Francisca's world collapsed. The wind knocked all the breath out of her lungs, and she gasped for air. Could it be that what had happened between them last night was simply a matter of the moment for Isabel? Did it mean so little to her?

Fiel needed no command, and it was as though he flew through the alleyways behind the high city walls and onward and onward. When they reached the river crossing at the Puente del Herra they did not even slow down at the mid-point to allow the guards to interrogate them. Francisca would deal with any consequences of defying their authority later. They not so much crossed the bridge as leapt over it.

On the coach road by the river, Francisca cried into the storm, 'Mas rapido!'

Blood tears rained down from the heavens.

Beware, those who cross me tonight, Francisca thought. She was in the mood for an altercation.

They entered the woods of pine, elms and chestnuts, and the

thick canopy sheltered them from the storm. A tawny owl hooted. They ventured on. A nightjar warbled. A heron crooned. Two wolves scuttled across the path.

At a small clearing, light shone silvery on the soft grass. Francisca dismounted. The sky was clear, the stars visible. The only sound was a gentle rustle of leaves. The sirocco, it seemed, had finally passed. The woods had been spared the havoc it had wreaked beyond.

She spread her shawl over a large flat stone, curled up and hugged her knees to her chest. Her mind emptied and she fell asleep, and, at last, dreamed the dream that had been eluding her.

Scene by scene, in intricate detail, it played out before her. Right here, in this clearing, her parents' carriage came to a screeching halt. The horses kicked out and bucked as two masked assailants reached into the carriage and grasped her mother and father by the neck, threw them to the ground and, with a swift wield of an axe, severed her father's head from his body. Her mother, cowering on the ground, shrieked to God for mercy. They kicked her head, leaving her for dead.

Francisca's heart thumped wildly, and she awoke abruptly to a sound – distinct and rhythmic. It could only be human footsteps. She shuddered with fear and looked over to Fiel, and she saw that he too was alert to it. The steps approached, and a foreboding, that this truly was the place where her father was murdered, descended. Had the murderer come back to find and deal with her?

As she rose, she slipped on the pine needles. Fiel neighed, exigency in his tone. Somehow Francisca regained her balance and she sprung onto Fiel's back. As fast as they dared, they retraced their path back through the woods. Thunder rumbled distantly. At last, they emerged from the trees and started back on the coach road. Fiel broke into a gallop, full speed. Francisca clutched his mane. Biblical lightning illuminated the electric red sky over Seville. The minaret seemed on fire. She dared not look back.

By the time they reached the Puente del Herra, Francisca had regained her composure, and she slowed down for the guards. Although she would not have known what to tell them if they interrogated her, she need not have worried, for they waved her on.

Finally, they entered the safety of the palacio's gates. She secured Fiel in his stable and walked through the arches and into the atrium, too exhausted even to glance at the fresco. At the top of the atrium staircase, she paused and held on to the bannisters to catch her breath and collect her thoughts. It was then that she sensed an unnatural silence and she clung on to the railings at the precise moment the silence broke.

Glass shattered.

She leapt down the stairs and ran to the reception room. Amid the splinters of glass splayed out on the tiles was a large stone. A piece of parchment was wrapped around it, bound with a soft wax seal. Francisca tried to control her shaking hands as she broke the seal and peeled the parchment from the stone. Crudely rendered in black ink was a representation of an owl. The blood drained from Francisca's body with the threat implicit in the message and its form of delivery: the owl was a derogatory symbol of the Jews.

Someone, other than Isabel, knew her secret. But how? It was only last night that she herself discovered it.

She rushed back through the atrium courtyard and unfastened the heavy iron-framed gates, mindful of the precious seconds that had been lost in locating the stone and reading the parchment's message. The air was still. Not a soul was to be seen in either direction. A falcon darted out of the shadows and fluttered about, and, with no other sign to guide her, she ran towards it. Fear and rage drove her on faster.

In the distance, through the curling mist, she discerned a tall, hooded figure.

'Coward!' she shrieked.

For a split second the figure paused but then ran on, beyond the cathedral. It was impossible to catch him.

She must rush home and check on her mother. What if the

intruder had harmed her? She did not know how long he had been inside the palacio's grounds, nor precisely where he had been.

She turned suddenly but was winded and knocked to the ground. A bird screeched. Frightened and stifling a scream, she peered up. The hands extending down to her were somehow familiar. She looked up to the face that belonged to the hands. There was a hood shrouding the features, and she knew it was the young man she had seen begging at the morning markets on the day she'd first met Señor Ceretti, and she breathed a sigh of relief, knowing that he would not harm her. She looked into his eyes and looked again.

Can this be real? Her eyes widened. 'Bernardo?'

'Francisca, yes, it is me, your Bernardo.' His chin trembled. He looked her in the eye and in a lighter tone said, 'And this is Ángel, who has been my friend these last months.' The falcon flapped down to perch on his shoulder.

'But are you not in the Americas?' Francisca asked, unable to believe her eyes and ears.

'I returned,' he said, his eyes wet with tears. 'There was a man on my ship who made me fear for my life. I dived off and stowed away on a passing galleon.'

'Oh Bernardo! I wish you had come to me.'

She reached out and took his hands, and they fell into each other's arms.

CHAPTER TWENTY-TWO

'How is your mother?' Bernardo whispered from across the hallway. His blond hair glistened, fresh from a bath.

Their reunion at this specific moment in time seemed nothing less than a miracle. 'Thankfully, it seems she was not disturbed,' she replied as she closed the door to her mother's bedchamber behind her. 'Try to get some rest now, Bernardo. There will be time yet to talk.'

'Francisca, I will never forget you permitting me to stay here in your home,' he said, and, as Francisca pressed his hand, tears again welled in his eyes.

It was going to take some time to grow accustomed to his changed appearance. The muscles that once had seemed an integral part of him had vanished and, in the way his eyes seemed too big for his face, he was more like Perugino's ascetic Christ than Michelangelo's David that she had always seen in him.

'Bernardo, you are the brother I never had.'

She could not tell him the hurt she felt on account of the fact that he had not sought her out when he had been most in need. What shame, when he had finally returned to Seville, had driven him to live on the streets, and not seek out his family or Francisca?

Her questions would need to wait until he had rested and regained his strength.

Inside her own bedchamber, her bed seemed a dream of luxury. She sank into the feathered mattress and sighed with the simple pleasure of being horizontal. She traced the intricate pattern of gold stars carved into the dark mahogany ceiling and, in the way of the mind's mystical tendency when drifting into sleep, her thoughts floated.

She had so many questions. Were tonight's two incidents – the footsteps in the woods and the intruder in the palacio – linked? Were they designed to threaten her, or, perhaps, to warn her? Was the message of the owl on the stone directed at her or possibly another? Could it have been a message for Uncle Carlos, the messenger ignorant of the fact that he had not yet returned home? As for the identity of the intruder, there were few clues. From a distance, the hooded man appeared physically formidable, but nothing about him seemed familiar. There was also the drawing of the owl wrapped around the stone. The drawing had been crudely rendered and unlikely to be from an artist's hand.

At least one thing was clear – someone, apart from Isabel, knew the secret of her Jewish background. She suspected, too, that someone knew she was in pursuit of the truth about the tragedy that had befallen her parents.

Her final thought, and a dark one, was of Isabel and Gabriela, together on the terrace of El Flamenco. Tormenting though the image was, sleep saved her from dwelling on it any further.

CHAPTER TWENTY-THREE

Antonio awoke in darkness, disorientated and aching all over, but no longer feeling sorry for himself. There was a steady heat, like a thick blanket covering his back, and he turned to feel a vast stone wall exhaling the heat of the day, and that is how he remembered retreating to the safety of a monastery amidst a mighty storm. There was nothing to keep him here, and carefully – in case he had suffered a forgotten injury – he levered himself up from the ground and shuffled in the direction of a faint light.

He stumbled out into a simple square bordered only by the monastery and a small church. A thick carpet of red sand covered every surface. He'd left Isabel in a temper and must have slept through the next day and all of that night – and, of all things, a sirocco had intervened.

It somehow stunned him into feeling alert, and all he wanted was to make peace with Isabel and return to work.

He hurried in the direction he hoped was home. How long ago it had been since he and Isabel had been in the effortless flow of love and life together. It was destroying him but he did not know how to fix it. When she had told him she was leaving Rome to go in search of her aunt, he knew it was also her excuse to finally leave him, but like a drowning man clinging to a vessel, there was no loss of dignity in joining her. There simply had seemed no alternative, and the timing was striking. An acquaintance had tipped him off that a Papal order would imminently be issued against him and he would be forced into exile. He needed to be seen to be leaving on his own terms, not in humiliation, but he could not reveal his plight to Isabel. He had made Rome his home. His own. And it had made him the artist he had become. Rome was part of his very identity.

Isabel had not shown any resistance, and they had embarked on the journey in what he believed was a shared unspoken hope that the change would revive their relationship.

He chose one of the side streets and strode on, turning left then right and straight on, and the unloved lanes soon gave way to broader streets with the familiar town houses. Comforting smells of last night's suppers lingered in the still air, and it was then he felt ravenous. He had not eaten for more than a day, and he stepped up his pace.

The design of the city began to unfold, and, in the distance, the top layer of the minaret came into view. Even it was dusted in the red-tinged haze of the Saharan sand. Rounding another corner, a water pump appeared, and he drank liberally, bathed his face and chest, washed his shirt. A glimmer of optimism lit his soul as he began to see a way forward. Seville would be the place to start again. He would make it happen. He potted out a plan for their second chance. He would bury deep within him all the darkness. Even as he thought it, he knew it would mean he would not be able to paint, or at least, not in the same way, but the loss would be worth it if he could live his life with Isabel. He could become a carpenter, he thought. Making furniture would not require him to plumb the depths of his soul, and he was good with his hands. He would marry Isabel, and father another child with her, and he would be a devoted husband and a kind father. He would listen to Isabel and put his trust in her. He would re-learn how to love her, and he imagined himself as a blank canvas, and giving her the brush to paint it in at her discretion. He would not bleed her of her light, but rather reflect it back to her.

As he approached the convento in the Plaza de San Francisco, the heavens opened, washing all the sand away, and it seemed a good omen. He sought no refuge and hurried on. Soaked to his very skin, he ran up the stairs, fumbled for his keys and as he struggled with the lock, he put his weight behind the door, and almost fell into the apartment.

Isabel stood before him.

'I was about to apologise for making such a racket,' he said, smiling uncertainly. 'I hope I did not disturb you.'

'I'm glad you are safe, Antonio,' she said without emotion.

'These last days have been difficult, Isabel,' he said, attempting to justify his behaviour and absolve himself, but he could not meet her gaze. 'I am going to get some food and head back to the cathedral, while I am feeling well. Carlos will be mad if he comes back to find...'

'What, Antonio. To find what?'

'To find that I have not made as much progress as he hoped – as much as he has a right to expect.'

'I will prepare your food. Change into some dry clothes.'

She was wearing the silk nightgown he had bought for her in the early days of their love, and hope rose in his heart. He took hold of her waist and drew her close, forcing her to meet his eyes.

'Have you missed me?' He could not help the question. He was burning with a need to know whether she still wanted him.

'You're soaking wet, Antonio,' she said stiffly.

'Answer me,' he insisted.

Her eyes were tired and he said gently, 'I have missed you. You are all the light there is in me. You give me fortitude to paint the darkness.' He attempted to laugh, sensing he had said too much too soon.

'Let us talk later when you have done some work and we both feel rested.'

He should have let her go but he held her to him and implored, 'Isabel, let us try for another child.' His very life lay in the palm of her hands, but it was as if she did not even hear him. She freed herself and repeated, 'Let us talk later,' and she went to the kitchen to prepare his food.

CHAPTER TWENTY-FOUR

Early the next morning – now two days since Francisca and Isabel had last been together – Francisca opened the gate to the cathedral grounds and, eyes cast downwards, made her way through the meandering paths behind the main avenues. She did not want to see anyone or be seen.

Amidst the turmoil of her emotions, she had resolved to continue with her work. There was much to be done, and she would achieve nothing staying at home and agonising. Bernardo needed to rest, and she needed to allow him that.

As she sloped on, she pondered on the technique required to apply cochineal glaze to Mary's hands once the layers of oils had been applied when, as she rounded a corner, there, seated on a bench by a birdbath, was Isabel.

Francisca's cheeks burned. She had not wanted to encounter Isabel in this way.

'Hola.' Isabel greeted Francisca with a raised hand and open smile.

It seemed she had been expecting her. In the bright light, Isabel's eyes were luminous.

Francisca's voice dried up, and she was unable even to return Isabel's greeting.

'Antonio is at the cathedral already,' Isabel said as her gaze drifted to the mid-distance. 'His Christ Resurrected is like a demonic king. What your uncle will make of it, I can hardly imagine.'

Francisca's entire body tightened and she said, 'Isabel, I have been worried. Did you not think I might be concerned when you didn't come to the cathedral yesterday, as you said you would?'

'I have been worried about you too, Francisca. But, after our discussion, Antonio left in a rage and did not return until early this morning. I have been anxious.'

Isabel looked into Francisca's eyes, and Francisca saw her exhaustion, and all her defences crumbled.

'I was alone, trying to think. It nearly drove me crazy.' Isabel pulled at her auburn hair theatrically and laughed. 'So, I went to see Gabriela. She has matters of her own to deal with.'

'I thought Gabriela might know where you were, so I went to El Flamenco last night – I saw you both on the terrace from the street.'

'You were out in the sirocco? Francisca! You could have been killed. Why did you not come inside and be with us?'

'I did not want to intrude. You and Gabriela seemed...' Francisca struggled to find the right words and settled on, 'In an intimate moment.'

'Francisca, Gabriela is my oldest, dearest friend. She is like a sister to me.'

The tension in Francisca's mind disintegrated. The air between them settled and harmony restored.

'You seem different, Isabel. Lighter, somehow,' Francisca said, observing that Isabel's melancholy seemed to have lifted.

Isabel smiled and nodded vaguely in answer, and then, in a change of direction said, 'I saw your Virgin Mary with Christ Child.' She took Francisca's hand. 'It is beautiful. You see Mary as a philosopher, then?' Isabel suggested playfully.

Francisca would not allow herself to be drawn in and replied, 'It is for the viewer to decide.'

'Of course.' Isabel nodded and added, 'Your ability to paint from memory is remarkable.'

Francisca looked into the sky at a point of the arc above the sun, seeking time. She sought a matter-of-fact tone as she said, 'It is not so remarkable – observation is an artist's primary skill of trade.'

'Do you observe me, then?' Isabel smiled, teasingly.

'If looking with attention to detail is observing, then, yes, I observe you.'

'You observe me differently to the way Antonio observes me.'

'That is, I suspect, because I see you differently. Every artist captures a different essence of someone. It is, after all, the essence the artist sees.'

'What is the essence you see?'

'Isabel, if I was a writer, my task would be to find the words, but I am a painter. The answer lies in the strokes and contours of the paint and the colour tones. I have failed in my task if I need to provide a commentary.'

Isabel smiled wryly and nodded. 'By its state of progress, I am guessing you have had little sleep?'

Francisca reached down and scooped up a handful of gravel from the path and sorted them through. Until now, she had not thought to tell Isabel about last night's drama, but, before considering the wisdom of doing so, she disclosed everything – the interception in the woods, the stone thrown through the window, the chase.

Isabel's voice rose as she cried, 'Francisca! All this happened last night?'

'This was wrapped around the stone.' She took the owl drawing from her pocket.

Isabel studied it and whispered to herself, 'The derogatory sign for the Jews.' She took Francisca's wrists and searched her eyes as she barraged her with questions. 'But you are unharmed? That is all that matters. Were you going to go straight to work without telling anyone – you were not going to come to me? Who else knows about this?'

Francisca struggled to keep track, but she simply replied, 'I believe only Bernardo knows. But he does not know about the owl sketched on the parchment.'

'Bernardo? But I thought Bernardo was bound for South America?'

'He has returned.'

Francisca saw the whirling of Isabel's thoughts behind her eyes. 'Francisca, listen to me,' she said, looking around to ensure that they were entirely alone. 'We may not have much time. For now, you must tell no one what has happened.' She spoke with such conviction that Francisca trusted her judgement.

'Tonight, meet me at El Flamenco. Be sure to bring the parchment with you.'

CHAPTER TWENTY-FIVE

Father Alberto regarded Antonio's depiction of Christ's expression at the moment of his resurrection. There was nothing apologetic in Christ's victory over death and those who had betrayed him.

'I like this Resurrection of yours,' he said, shuffling towards Antonio, and pointing a stick at the easel. 'The boldest version I've yet seen. You have captured Saint Paul's scripture.' He patted him on the arm. 'I respect your pluck.'

'I am gratified, Father,' Antonio replied.

Father Alberto gestured to the space. 'Show me around.'

'Certainly.' Antonio himself had not even looked over the sum of his work, and he felt pleased to do so now, with someone who seemed appreciative.

At the Martyrdom of St Matthew, Father Alberto craned his neck to see Antonio and said with a hint of amusement, 'I'm not sure what the archbishop will make of this one. Bolder yet! What's this fellow been doing, then? Applied the knife to Matthew's neck?' He gestured mischievously with one of his sticks to Antonio's neck.

Antonio smiled calmly. 'It is for the viewer to decide.'

They worked their way around to Mary Magdalene and Christ Crucified. 'Yes,' Father Alberto nodded excitedly. 'She *is vengeful*. Mary Magdalene was no waif.' He nodded with unrestrained approval.

Antonio passed over Francisca's latest unfinished work depicting Isabel as Mary, and continued, to his Judas with Christ. He was proudest of this in the way it seemed to settle a truce between the two men. There was a hint of a suggestion of the two being as one – like opposite sides of a coin.

But Father Alberto paused before Francisca's painting of Mary and said, 'Hmm, but this one – Mary with Christ Child – is different. Dreamy.' He stood back, making room for Antonio to observe too. Father Alberto knew full well this was Francisca's work.

He persevered. 'That look – it's a look of romantic love – the Infant Christ is a ruse. She is not even looking at him – she's looking beyond him, to someone beyond the frame. We are left wondering who it is that captures her attention.' Father Alberto regarded Antonio keenly.

'You have an eye for detail, Father,' Antonio responded. Curious, he walked back to see the painting.

Antonio stood before the canvas and recognised Father Alberto's observations. There was a sensuality and tenderness in the portrait. It was more beautiful than any he himself had made of Isabel. It dared explore her pathos, and, in what felt like a revelation, Antonio understood that there was something more to Isabel and Francisca than he had thought. He felt confused and foolish.

Father Alberto was gleeful. 'This is not right. You've overstepped the mark here, Ceretti. I will need to think whether I can recommend the archbishop display this one to the public.' He was enjoying taunting Antonio.

Antonio controlled the rage seething within him and managed a tight-lipped reply. 'I defer to your good judgement, Father, of course.'

Finally, the tour ended.

'You've made good progress, Ceretti. I expect the archbishop will be pleased with that at least.' He said, 'Walk by me. I want to talk with you.'

Antonio slowed his pace and shortened his stride to keep in step with Father Alberto. He hunched his shoulders in an effort to match the other man's stature.

Father Alberto said, 'Cardinal De Praed will soon be arriving with the archbishop. They have come directly from the Vatican – a long journey.' He paused, leaned on his sticks, and peered up at Antonio and said meaningfully, 'I'm sure I don't need to explain. The cardinal cannot see you here. Do you understand?'

Antonio was speechless. He stopped mid-stride. His resolve to lock all the darkness inside was forgotten, and it exploded out of him like a burst boil. He reached for a pillar to cushion his fall.

In an instant, he was transported back to the nightmare of that fateful night in Rome. Desperately, a young man – barely more than a boy – had lashed out with his knife, cutting Antonio's face. Antonio had lunged with his sword. The boy's eyes betrayed his surprise. As Antonio withdrew his sword, his opponent slumped forward and fell into his arms. He held him for the brief, yet eternal, moment, as the blood flowed from the young boy's body, and he breathed his final breath.

Something in the shadows caught Antonio's eye and he saw, lurking there, a familiar figure. In panic, he ran all the way to the Tiber and there he washed the blood from his clothes and body. Only then did he feel his face on fire, and he knew the wound would never heal. It would be a constant reminder of what he had done. The next day, he considered going to the authorities. How could he explain that the man had provoked him, or perhaps that it was an accident, or possibly self-defence? Could he explain that, if only his patron had not looked at him that afternoon in the way that reminded him of his father and had made him feel like nothing. But, in the end, he decided against it. He felt his entire life had been leading to this point, the proof of the indictment on his character confirming what he had always known: he was not worthy of love, just as his father had always said. The die had been cast at his birth.

Father Alberto looked down at Antonio with hatred. He hissed, 'Ceretti. Ceretti – get a handle on yourself, man. Get up. I'm telling you – there is a comfortable house where you can stay. All your materials can be sent on. You will lose no time. You can continue your work discreetly from there.'

Antonio finally collected himself and shakily rose to his feet. He gasped, 'The light. The light will not be the same. I cannot reproduce the light of the cathedral elsewhere.' Antonio extended his hands helplessly.

'You will have to manage.'

'How long will the cardinal be in Seville?'

Father Alberto shrugged. 'Some weeks. I cannot be sure.'

'May I bring my wife?'

Father Alberto resumed walking. 'That is entirely up to you. Think of it as an opportunity to have some time away.'

'May I ask – is Archbishop Carlos aware?'

'You may not,' he said disdainfully, and as he disappeared from view, he added, 'If you have not yet confessed and wish to do so, you know where to find me.'

CHAPTER TWENTY-SIX

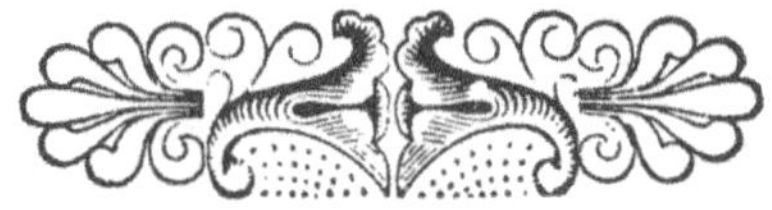

'Welcome.' Gabriela smiled and ushered Francisca into the parlour.

The shapeless linen shift that Gabriela wore could look sensational only on her, Francisca thought.

Subdued candlelight warmed the parlour. Terrace doors opened out to a large patio where Isabel, standing in profile, gazed up to the stars. The sirocco had scrubbed the sky clean and Francisca felt, if she held out her hand, she might grasp the stars.

But something in the sombre mood, and Isabel's countenance, told Francisca that last night's dramas had been the topic of conversation between the two women.

'Francisca, what would you like to drink?' Gabriela asked, pulling handles attached to a large globe, and revealing a variety of bottles arranged within.

'There is so much to choose from. Surprise me.'

Gabriela took one of the more exotic-shaped bottles, poured its syrupy liquid into two goblets and handed one to her. It was delicious, reminiscent of medjool dates. Francisca looked back out to the terrace and caught Isabel's eye, smiling softly back at her.

Gabriela ushered her out to a seating area arranged around a mosaic table on the terrace.

'Salud, ladies,' Gabriela said with a twinkle in her eye, raising her goblet.

'I was concerned you might not be able to leave Bernardo,' Isabel said.

'He needs to rest and eat. I have made sure the cook will look after him.'

Gabriela took charge and said, 'Francisca, I will come straight to the point. Isabel has told me what happened last night, which brings me swiftly on to some matters Isabel and I want to share with you. These matters are grave – so grave that people's lives depend on our absolute secrecy. And this in turn brings me to a matter that gives us cause for concern – there may be some things that conflict with your uncle's interests.'

Francisca sucked in the air, but before she could respond, Gabriela held up her hand and continued, 'Be that as it may, I do not know what is in your uncle's heart.'

Gabriela sipped from her goblet and looked directly at Francisca as she continued, 'Regardless of any conflict of interest you may feel, you will be unable to share *any* of our discussion with him – or anyone else. Isabel's high regard for you is why I am prepared to share this with you.' She looked Francisca in the eye and asked, 'Tell me if I should proceed?'

Without hesitation, Francisca replied, 'I understand and accept your terms. Please, go on.'

'First, Isabel will seal our circle of trust,' Gabriela said.

Isabel crossed her arms, held out her hands for Gabriela and Francisca to do likewise, and they linked hands. Isabel uttered an incantation in a haunting voice and language unknown to Francisca. A ripple of energy flowed through the three women, and Francisca felt she had been inducted.

A cold breeze rushed through the terrace. Gabriela tugged at her earlobe, suggesting the night may be listening, and they returned inside where they settled into low cane-woven chairs.

'Francisca, did you bring the parchment?' Isabel touched her hand lightly.

She took it from her pocket, unfolded it and gave it to Gabriela.

Gabriela frowned as she studied the crudely sketched owl, and said, 'Francisca, please, tell us, from the beginning, what happened. Try to tell us everything, omitting no detail, even if it seems inconsequential.'

Francisca relayed the entire story, even mentioning her supposition that her mother's nurse had witnessed key moments of the evening. By the time she finished, Gabriela had refilled their goblets twice over.

'Francisca, what Isabel told you about the Inquisition is true. The Inquisition will soon resume, right here in Seville. Unlike last time, however, it will test purity of faith. There will be no option to convert. The Inquisition will have the full force of the Pope's authority – King Ferdinand will have broad discretion, and, of course, he will want to impress the Pope with his ruthlessness. The Inquisitor Generale has travelled all the way from Toledo to set up office here' – she pointed beyond the terrace – 'at the Castle of San Jorge in Triana.'

Although Francisca felt the seriousness in Gabriela's tone, she could not absorb the meaning, nor understand how it was relevant to her.

'Francisca, your uncle is, at this very moment, accompanying Cardinal De Praed to Seville. The cardinal will oversee matters. According to our reports, they are scheduled to arrive imminently.' Gabriela asked, 'Do you understand?'

Francisca felt like she was sinking into the pit of the Earth. 'Are you suggesting that Uncle Carlos would support an Inquisition? He is only interested in what is good for Seville – trade, art, and the higher things.'

Gabriela explained, 'Francisca, life is changing. The King is unhappy about our liberal ways. Pressure is being applied on all major centres to follow his edict. Religion is at the heart of the change. The opportunity to convert came and went with the last Inquisition. This time, the faith of all first and second generation conversos will be put to the test and the burden of proof will be on them to establish the sincerity of their faith.'

Gabriela went to the globe for another bottle of liquor and took three fresh goblets.

As she poured Francisca's glass, she said, 'Isabel has told me of the wall picture your mother made. You, your mother and Uncle Carlos, as first-generation conversos, may need to testify. You need to be prepared if you are called upon to defend your faith.'

Francisca looked across at Isabel for help, but her complexion was blanched. Isabel nodded, confirming that she could take Gabriela's word as true.

With more of a practical tone in her voice, Gabriela said, 'Francisca, the important thing is that the work of the Inquisition is already well under way. Royalist sources are gathering evidence for the Auto-da-fé – which will be soon. Their methods are nefarious – and highly effective. They coerce families, friends, and servants to inform on one another. They do this, not only for expedience, but to instil distrust and drive a wedge amongst us, so that we each stand alone. Do you see? Instead of uniting against the authorities – for it is they who are the common enemy – they throw us off course, making us mistrust one another.'

Francisca felt ill to think she had been living in ignorance. The veil lifted from her mind. Nothing would ever be the same. Nevertheless, she clung on to what she thought she had always known and said, 'But my uncle is the archbishop. Surely no one would question his faith.'

'Perhaps, but there is also another point of view. He might especially be at risk because of his position. The King does not approve of Carlos's liberalism. He may be using this cleansing as an opportunity to denounce him.'

The idea chilled her to her very bones.

Gabriela leaned in, and touched her arm, and finally said, 'But, Francisca, I believe that someone is trying to protect you – to warn you.'

'Protect me?' Francisca asked, feeling confused.

She held the owl parchment up as evidence. 'In my opinion, this was delivered to warn you – to tell you to forget about the past, about your heritage, and to accept the way things are. The person who authorised its delivery knows you are on a trail for answers to find your father's murderer. I believe this person also fears your enquiries will reveal inconvenient facts that will compromise not only Carlos, but other important people too. Perhaps the Church establishment itself.'

'But how can I forget about the past? My childhood was stolen.' Francisca held her head in her hands and whispered to herself, 'Someone killed my father. Someone ruined my mother's life.'

'Yes, but there is nothing you can do to change these facts, Francisca.'

Everything was slipping away. 'That may be true, but there must be justice.' And though she dared not say it, she still believed the truth could set her mother free of her trauma.

Isabel and Gabriela exchanged looks.

'Francisca, if you really are resolute on the matter then we can help you,' Gabriela whispered.

'Help me. How?'

Gabriela nodded, giving Isabel her cue to continue. 'Gabriela leads the Andalusian Insurgeants Royale.'

'The Insurgeants Royale?' Francisca repeated, incredulous.

Gabriela's silence confirmed Isabel's assertion.

Isabel offered cigarillos from a box on the table. Francisca's hands shook when she took the lantern to light the tobacco.

'Francisca, there are many people who believe the Inquisition and King Ferdinand – and even the Pope – are contrary to the interests of Spain and the Spanish people. I am one of them.'

'As am I,' Isabel chimed in.

'How many members are there in the Insurgeants?'

'Many, many thousands.'

'They could bring about an uprising. There could be a revolution.'

'We do not want any violence but we will do what is required.'

'This is a lot to take in.' Francisca looked from Gabriela to Isabel and, in sudden realisation, she said, 'You must risk your lives, being involved in something like that – the Insurgeants – it would be treason. Why... why would you risk your life for it?'

Gabriela's voice was resolute as she answered, 'The idea of a society where everyone should be the same – think the same thoughts, feel the same feelings, worship the same God in the same way – is contrary to our varied natures and experiences.' Quietly, she added, 'And for me personally, I have no option but to fight this. Someone very dear to me – Valentina – has been incarcerated interminably. We have reason to believe she is now in the Castle of San Jorge. A rabid dog would not be treated as badly.' Tears welled up in Gabriela's eyes.

'What happened?' Francisca asked, and she remembered the name Valentina from Isabel's dressing room all those weeks ago. Things were starting to fall into place.

'She is Jewish and refused to convert. When they took her away, I became like a mother to her child, but they stole her from me too. I do not know where she is or even if she is still alive.'

Francisca's eyes were being opened to new things – both terrible and wonderful.

She looked towards Isabel.

'Isabel has her own reasons,' said Gabriela.

Francisca hung on Isabel's explanation, wondering if this would be the key to unlocking her mystery.

Isabel kept her eyes lowered as she said quietly, 'I have seen too much suffering to sit by and watch. I have to do *something*.' Francisca heard the emotional constriction in Isabel's voice as she continued, 'Members of my own family died at the hands of people incited by King Ferdinand's hate. It was they who set fire to our campsite. I saw it all happen.'

Francisca declared, 'My God, what you have both been through.'

A poignant and respectful silence ensued.

Francisca could remain seated no longer. She rose and paced the length of the parlour.

Looking into the eyes of her companions, she said with conviction, 'I do not know what some of my family members might be guilty of, and I do not know precisely what I might, by association, be guilty of. But I do know that I belong here, with you and the Insurgeants. Let me join you. Let me try to help. Maybe somehow, I can even help Carlos – maybe he has been drawn into something he cannot escape from.'

Gabriela rose too and held Francisca by the shoulders as she said, 'Think about it. Once you join, your loyalty must be to the cause – there can be no mixed allegiances. Whatever you decide, Isabel and I will do what we can to help you.'

CHAPTER TWENTY-SEVEN

By the time they bid good night, El Flamenco was closing for the evening. There had been no performance tonight. Those who had come had done so in search of companionship, to share the toils of the day in a convivial ambience with like-minded souls.

Isabel and Francisca emerged into the warm night air. The farrier approached with Fiel in tow. 'He is a beautiful specimen of a horse,' he said, handing Francisca the reins before disappearing into the side entrance to El Flamenco.

'He is so gentle,' Isabel said as she stroked his muzzle.

'He likes you,' Francisca replied as Fiel nuzzled into Isabel.

'If I ever own a horse, it will be a white mare, as a companion for Fiel.'

'He would like that, I'm sure,' Francisca smiled as she adjusted the stirrups for Isabel and said, 'Let's ride home.' She cradled her hands to help Isabel up and insisted that she take the saddle for comfort and safety, and she handed her the reins. Francisca hoisted herself up behind, lightly holding the ridge of the saddle, and they quietly set off. Fiel knew the way and they each drifted into their own thoughts.

Francisca's mind was filled with the evening's conversation.

Nothing would ever be the same. That her life had been lived in ignorance of fundamental truths was confronting.

She needed time to consider her uncle's position and she reasoned that, if he was a converso, forsaking his faith, then he might also have forsaken his family. She needed to know what his true motivation was to convert. Was it worldly ambition? Or fear for his own life? The bitterness of these thoughts pervaded her soul; if not her uncle, who could she trust? The very foundations of her life would crumble if he had been involved in her parents' fate.

Without warning, Fiel slipped on a cobblestone, momentarily losing his balance. Francisca clutched the back of the saddle to steady herself.

'You can hold on to me,' Isabel said. Her voice – tender and somehow feeling out of time – ricocheted off the buildings lining the narrow lane.

How many times these last many days had Francisca fantasised about something very much like this – to be close to Isabel, and alone, together? A physical yearning had taken hold of her. She had tried to convince herself that, if she could let it run its course, she would survive it and the madness would pass. But there was another part of her that knew it was much more than simply desire.

She released her hands from the back of the saddle and held on to Isabel's slender waist, feeling the softness of her hips and belly.

She stirred inside.

'So quiet, Francisca. What are you thinking?'

'Many things,' she said, collecting her thoughts. 'Uncle Carlos has been good to me, but I can't help having thoughts I don't want to have. It is as though I don't know him. Why has he never spoken of these things with me – to help me understand?' She shook her head. 'I don't want to feel this way – not towards him.'

Her words found and occupied a space in the ether.

'Yet who can we truly know?' Isabel asked. 'Even ourselves.'

'If Carlos was in some way responsible for my parents' fate, I cannot be philosophical about it.' Now that she had said it, there could be no going back.

'You do not yet know if he was involved.'

'But I am going to find out.'

The quiet majesty of Iglesia San Lorenzo marked their return to the edge of the familiar city centre. Fiel continued southeast, towards the palacio, rather than directly south, towards Calle Almansa. Neither Isabel nor Francisca corrected him, and they yielded to his choice.

The top layer of the minaret, magical in the night's light, became visible above the rooftops. It seemed symbolic: the world the minaret had been built to serve had long since vanished from Spain. The country had changed and, if Gabriela and Isabel were correct, it was about to change again.

'Francisca let's climb the minaret,' Isabel suggested.

'Now?'

'You said you would take me, and I do not want to go home just now, not after what we have been talking about.'

At the Puerte del Perdon, they dismounted and walked together through the Patio de los Naranjos. Francisca found a sheltered corner and tied Fiel's reins around some hooks. From the compartment inside his panniers, she removed a large set of keys linked together on a long, thick metal chain and looped it over her head.

'Francisca the gaoler,' Isabel chuckled.

'And you will be my prisoner,' Francisca joked, and then explained that the door to the minaret may be locked.

With all her weight, she pushed against the mighty Door of Concepcion. It was stiff. She tried one final effort. It gave way.

She crossed the threshold, Isabel close behind. The door closed behind them, and it let out a long sigh, as if defeated.

Inside, all was silent. The silhouettes of the canvases were scattered about the vast space like an archipelago. Francisca stepped forward, clearing some large stones and stonemasons' tools. Isabel gasped as she tripped. Francisca reached for her, and they carried on, hand in hand. Francisca continued assuredly, hoping, in turn, to instil confidence in Isabel.

The great cavern amplified their footsteps, the scent of frankincense from evensong lingered, and a draught whistled through the columns. A flare in the altar illuminated the cross like a beating heart. It was the light of the stars, shining through the lead-light windows, that guided their way.

'It is so dark,' Isabel whispered.

'I will borrow the flare from the altar.'

Isabel kept tight hold of Francisca's hand as she said, 'Are you allowed to do that? Is not the crucifix required to be illuminated, for always?'

'Perhaps,' Francisca conceded and so they continued on in the dim light.

At the opening to the base of the minaret, Francisca tried the metal door, but it was locked. She took the key chain from her neck, and, after the third attempt, the key matched the lock. She opened the door, making sure to lock it behind them.

They entered a small antechamber, which was neither part of the cathedral nor the minaret. It was built as a structural connecting feature when the mosque, to which the minaret had belonged, was destroyed.

The light was lost here, and they could barely see. Isabel held tightly to Francisca's hand.

'In a few turns, there will be a break in the walls,' Francisca reassured her, 'and then we will have some light.'

They kept to the inside of the shaft, Francisca feeling her way as they progressed slowly up the ramp.

Francisca said lightly, 'They say Queen Isabella refused to walk up. They had to find her a donkey.'

'I expected stairs, not a ramp. It is a pleasant ascent,' Isabel said.

'The Al-Andalus designed it that way so that a person could

ride a horse up to the top. They would go up at least five times a day for prayer.'

'How do you know all this?'

'Papa told me. He would pretend to be my horse as he carried me up on his back.'

'Are you starting to remember more about him now?'

'Here and there. The other night, after I saw you and Gabriela outside El Flamenco, I went to the forest and felt sure I came upon the location of the attack. I saw it all take place, in a dream. It was detailed and seemed real.'

'Your papa's spirit is unrested. It sought comfort – possibly help – from you.'

'Do you think so?'

'That is what I believe.'

'I am determined to find his murderer. Poor Papa. I have been wasting so much time.'

As Francisca had promised, when they rounded another turn, light poured in through a viewing point. They looked out, enjoying their well-earned aspect to the outside world – an elevated view of the Patio de los Naranjos, and Fiel, patiently waiting.

They no longer felt afraid. It seemed that they belonged to a world all of their own here in the minaret.

Soon, they came to a private chamber.

'This one is for the mayor.'

Through the metal grilled doors, it looked like a shrine, filled with family memorabilia and a place of Christian worship, with an enormous crucifix and elaborate representations of Christ and Mary, Mother of God. An abundance of vases, filled with fresh flowers, decorated the area.

Francisca explained, 'There are two other chambers. The top one belongs to the archbishop.' She smiled, 'It is quite different to this one. I painted a fresco on the walls and furnished it with a divan and cushions – I wanted it to be a place for reflection, away from worldly concerns.'

A wooden door slammed below, the sound reverberated, startling them both.

'You will not be afraid of heights by the end of this, I suspect,' Francisca said, trying to make light of it.

'No, I shall have died of fright instead.'

They laughed nervously. 'It is probably just the draught,' Francisca suggested.

'Might it not be Father Alberto? Does he not live in the vestry attached to the cathedral?'

'He will be at Matins with the priors in the monastery now.' To break the tension, Francisca challenged, 'I shall race you to the top.'

Before Isabel could reply, Francisca gathered her skirt and ran off, up the ramp, leaving Isabel no choice but to accept the challenge. Around the next two turns, Francisca slowed her pace to allow Isabel to catch up.

'Wait!' Isabel cried as she approached.

Francisca complied, but Isabel, running at full pace, overtook her and chuckled.

'That's cheating,' Francisca cried, and chased after her.

The atmosphere lifted. Finally, at the last few paces to the top of the ascent, Francisca drew level, but Isabel took hold of her waist. They wrestled one another for first position, giggling and gasping for breath. Isabel's back was against the wall when their eyes met, and Francisca inhaled her musk perfume, mingled with the salty sweat from their exertion. Desire coursed through her.

'That is one way of curing a fear of heights.' Isabel laughed uncertainly.

Francisca recovered herself, took Isabel's hand in hers, and led her over to the outer perimeter of the tower. Beneath the glittering stars, they could imagine that they were alone in the whole world. In the middle of the night sky, Ángel soared and imprinted her silhouette against the moon. The river sparkled, reflecting the constellations. The olive groves extended beyond the forests in neat, dotted lines.

'It is so beautiful,' Isabel whispered. In a fold of Isabel's shawl, her collar bones pulsed with her breath.

Francisca leaned over the low brick barrier. 'Look, there's the palacio, the alcazar, and the Puente del Herra.'

'I am not leaning over,' Isabel protested but tentatively, she approached the balustrades.

Just beyond, downriver and on the other side, Triana and the bleak Castle of San Jorge consumed all the light.

They walked to the next side. Beyond the city walls, Francisca could see El Flamenco. 'Look!'

They called out together, waved and laughed. 'Hola, Gabriela!'

Directly above, Francisca found the constellation of Lyra, which had always been her point of reference for England. She pointed to it and said, 'A thousand miles over there, is England and my Elizabeth.'

'They say the land there is delightful. I am beginning to believe my aunt may be in England. I am expecting to hear soon.'

'Elizabeth says it is a special place, although the weather is not always favourable. She has moved away from London to a village by the south coast that she feels is her destiny.'

'Maybe you could visit her.'

'I will not leave Mama for so long.'

Isabel squeezed her hand. They went over to the other side and Isabel pointed. 'Rome.'

'I want to see Rome one day – Leonardo, Michelangelo and Raphael – that would be a dream come true.'

'You must go. You can do anything you set your mind to – you do realise that, Francisca? You are extraordinary. Once people see your work here, you will be in demand from all over Europe. You will see.' Isabel's eyes sparkled with the magic of what she had said.

'Well, that would make me the only woman artist to be in demand anywhere. Do you think you will ever go back – to Rome?'

'Honestly, I do not know what the future holds.'

'Well, wherever you are, you can imagine me, here, looking out for you.' She pointed at the sky. 'We will be gazing at the same constellation – of Lyra. See that star there, at the edge of the beak of the bird? That is where we can meet.'

'Francisca, don't. I don't want to think about leaving you.'

'But you *will* leave. I can foresee Señor Ceretti and myself, toiling away in the cathedral, forever striving to fill it with your perfect image.' Francisca flashed her a self-deprecating smile, only to find Isabel's gaze already upon her, and all Francisca's insides melted.

Francisca gently tugged a lock of Isabel's auburn hair, without a thought as to what she was about to utter. 'Only some weeks ago, I did not know of your existence and now... now I do not know how I am to be without you. I tell myself it is ridiculous, but it does not change how I feel. What are you that you do this to me?' Francisca whispered, 'What is this, between us?'

Isabel's eyes blazed through Francisca. She took hold of her blouse and drew her closer. Desire could be contained no longer, and they surrendered to a mysterious command. Their lips touched. They kissed, tentatively, slowly, exploring one another's mouths. Their breaths merged and they kissed deeply and hungrily.

They wanted more, and a place where they could take one another in their arms. Francisca whispered, 'Come with me.'

She led her down one round of the ramp to a carved wooden door. She selected a key from the chain and unlocked it. Light filtered in through the narrow window. On the walls was a fresco of an Arcadian fantasy, Francisca's signature style evident. This was not a place for Christian worship or a shrine to a family; it was a place for dreams.

Isabel loosened the laces on her blouse, revealing more of her cleavage, and she guided Francisca's hand there so she could feel the fullness of her breasts, and her nipples, pert with wanting. In turn, Isabel hastily unbuttoned Francisca's shirt and lingeringly kissed there. They fell onto the bed, and feverishly explored each other's bodies through their remaining clothes and they caught sight of one another's eyes, revealing all their certainty, uncertainty, fearlessness, and fear. All the light and all the dark, all the yes and all the no of their souls, was written there.

'Are you sure you want this?' Isabel whispered.

'I have never been so sure of anything,' Francisca replied, and she guided Isabel's hand to her desire.

Urgently, they undressed, hands and feet intertwining, and they kissed like their lives depended on it, tasting one another, inhaling one another and their sweet perspiration, wanting to know every corner.

Isabel eased herself onto Francisca, and her hair flowed down. Their feet, hands, thighs, and limbs, and all of them, entwined as their bodies pulsed in synchronicity, and they lost themselves in one another. It was as if they were speaking a language that they had always known but never before uttered. Without any inhibition, Francisca took Isabel's throbbing source of desire to her mouth, and Isabel opened herself to Francisca, writhing with pleasure, and they moaned rapturously, until neither could hold back any longer. All the energy of the cosmos flowed through their bodies and souls, and created something new, like an alchemical reaction, out of the stars.

Afterwards, they held one another close.

'How beautiful you are,' Isabel whispered and lightly kissed Francisca. 'You were true to your word; you made sure I didn't fall.'

'I am the one who has fallen.'

'We have fallen together, but we are safe, in each other's arms,' Isabel murmured. 'Imagine, if you could capture this feeling in paint, we could have it forever.'

Francisca toyed with a lock of Isabel's hair and kissed the nape of her neck.

'I captured something of it in your portrait, don't you think? The way you make me feel – the way I sense your courage and fear, your strength and vulnerability, your loves and losses. Your beauty. All of you. I wanted to show all of you in your portrait.'

'That's what I felt when I saw it. I wanted you to tell me yesterday.'

'I was not ready to tell you. The very first time I saw you, I felt something, tugging here.' Francisca touched her own heart.

'I felt your eyes on me.'

'And then I talked too much.'

Isabel sighed a laugh. 'No. Not enough. I wanted to know everything.'

'They would call this witchery, wouldn't they – King Ferdinand and his Inquisitor Generale,' Francisca said.

'We must be careful. Think of poor Valentina.'

She allowed that thought to seep into her mind. The idea of taking this love carefully could not have been more at odds with how Francisca felt. She wanted to shout it out at the top of the world.

'That night, out on your terrace, you told me to forget about my Jewish heritage, that some things cannot be won just by wanting – and yet, you are a fearless Insurgeant Royale. How does that work – tell me?'

'I only wanted to protect you, Francisca. Once you cross over, the world is a very different place.'

She felt Isabel's words to be true. The bells chimed three strikes. There never seemed enough time to be together.

'I suppose we should go back down and rescue Fiel,' Francisca finally suggested.

They gathered their clothes that were strewn across the floor, dressed, and started back down the ramp.

As they ventured out into the night, Francisca said, 'Come to the palacio with me. Let us be together for the night.'

'I should go back.'

Francisca felt a tear at her heart. How could Isabel return to Antonio? She swallowed her feeling and simply asked, 'Will you be all right?'

But Isabel seemed lost in her thoughts and did not answer.

Francisca accepted that there had been no articulation of any understanding between them. No expectations had been declared, nor hopes shared, and yet, Isabel returning to Antonio could not have felt more wrong.

Should she tell Isabel what she knew about Antonio being forced to flee Rome? If she did not tell her now, then the opportunity would pass.

She settled on asking, 'Isabel, why did Antonio leave Rome?'

Isabel's brow furrowed and she answered absently, 'I told you – he needed a change. And he did not want me to leave without him.'

Francisca helped Isabel dismount Fiel and her ecstasy turned to wretchedness, as she watched Isabel disappear into the shadows.

CHAPTER TWENTY-EIGHT

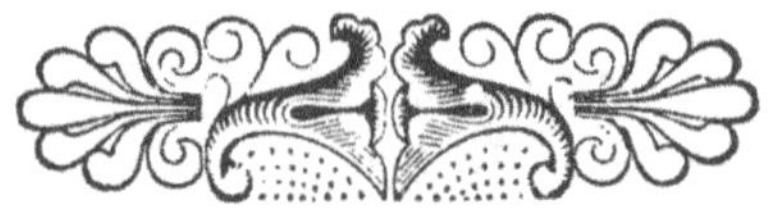

Francisca felt in no state to return home. She rode Fiel beyond the city walls and followed the river upstream to a place where her mother had taken her when she was a child. By a sandy stretch of the river's edge, Fiel grazed on tufts of grass. Francisca stripped off her clothes, neatly folded them on a rock and glided into the cool water. She swam in long, strong strokes and, when she reached the middle, floated and lost herself in the ocean of stars above.

Afterwards, she dried herself down with a linen cloth from one of Fiel's panniers. They trotted back leisurely through the ancient olive groves, and it was so perfectly peaceful that Francisca wondered why they had not done this before. It was not until break of dawn that they returned home.

At the gates to the stable yard, Francisca sensed change was afoot. The house and grounds were alive with purposeful activity. It was not long before she discovered the reason. By the archway to the atrium courtyard stood Uncle Carlos. Despite her recent doubts, instinct prevailed, and she leapt down from Fiel and into her uncle's arms, overjoyed.

'Uncle! I was not expecting you so soon.'

Carlos laughed joyfully and held her to him. 'My girl,' he said.

His eyes looked tired, and his hair, once charcoal black, was tinged with silver. How he had aged. With all that had happened, and all that she now knew, she thought how she too had changed.

'Francisca, look at you. Thriving without me,' he said tenderly. 'I need not have cajoled Cardinal De Praed into travelling all through the night these last many days, in my eagerness to return to you, thinking you must have missed me as I did you.'

She smiled and looked into his hazel eyes. If she could look into his soul, she would find his true self. It had not been long since she had been excited to show him the fresco, but now, she was confused.

They entered the arch to the atrium, and he continued, 'You are just like your mother when she met your father. Radiant. All these months away, I had imagined you as a girl, still. I return to find you to have metamorphosed into a beautiful young woman.' His voice quivered with emotion.

It was impossible not to be moved by his affection, and soon it was impossible, too, to ignore the scaffolding and in-progress fresco standing before them.

'I see you have been busy. You did not mention in any of your letters that you had been tackling this. I look forward to seeing the finished product.'

'I found it the day you left. It was only by a trick of the light that the outline appeared. I wanted to surprise you. Father Alberto saw me working on it and reprimanded me. He told me to restore it to how I found it. Did you know it had been covered over with limewash?'

'That time is still a haze to me, Francisca. Perhaps I instructed it to be covered over. I cannot recall.'

She did not press the point, and instead, hesitantly asked, 'What do you think it represents?'

He stood back and studied the wall intently. 'It seems to be an imaginary landscape,' he said. 'Your mother did many canvases of a similar nature.' He smiled. 'It is quite impressive in terms of its size and scale alone. The colours you have chosen are striking. It will quite transform the atrium. I love it!' he declared.

Either he was a superior actor, or entirely sincere.

'I had wanted to finish it for your return, but alas...' Francisca needed time to gather her thoughts and so suggested, 'Let us see Mama.'

Soft orange rays of the burgeoning day filtered into the bedchamber. Marina, standing by the terrace doors, curtseyed and greeted Carlos formally. 'Your Grace.'

Carlos nodded, and greeted Marina formally too, but Francisca imagined their behaviour to be false, and that she was audience to a scene playing out before her. She wanted to pull the curtain down from the stage and unmask them.

'Raquel,' he said tenderly, bending down to kiss his sister's cheek.

He took his seat in the red velvet chair and folded her hand in his. When Francisca's mother opened her eyes and silently gasped, her unqualified delight was obvious, and Francisca could not help but smile at their reunion. It was a moment of joy, of recognition, and Francisca dared to hold on to the hope of her mother's recovery.

Buoyed, Carlos began to speak of his travels – of Valencia, Barcelona, Rome, and the Vatican. He mentioned some of his successes; in particular, that he had secured Seville's ongoing status as the principal trading port with the Americas. Francisca had been unaware that it had ever been in question. What would Seville be without its port? She had always taken it for granted, and she was again reminded of the responsibility of her uncle's position.

'I have extracted several months home. Then I may need to leave for England.'

'England?'

'To show the Pope's support for King Henry and Queen Katharine, our Katharine of Aragon. She is pregnant again. The

Pope thinks an ambassadorial visit might help instil confidence – to successfully deliver a child, and, God willing, a son.'

'You could visit Elizabeth and her father while you are there.'

'Yes, I would like that.' He said solemnly, 'I was going to tell you, Elizabeth's husband has passed away. She is bereft and has gone into God's service – a convent somewhere of strategic importance.'

Francisca smiled inwardly at her uncle's interpretation of the facts and said, 'I never thought married life would suit Elizabeth.'

'Francisca. What an astonishing thing to say. What other life could possibly be more noble for a woman?'

'Elizabeth was happy here,' she said, unable to conceal the bitterness in her voice. 'She was better suited to a life with more time for herself and others than as a slave to a man.'

'Is that what you think marriage is for a woman? Do you think your mother felt a slave to your father?'

'They were different. They had true love, they chose one another.'

'What about you, Francisca? Now you are a woman, we will have to find you a suitable match. I did mean what I said in my letter. Many would say I have been remiss to have waited so long, but I have one or two prospects in mind. You might too? Is there someone... special?'

Francisca froze.

He continued awkwardly, 'You and Fiel, returning just earlier... I thought, perhaps—'

A knock at the door saved Francisca for the moment.

'Your Grace. Welcome home,' the cook said as she curtseyed. She wheeled the breakfast trolley in, threw a cloth over the oval table by the terrace doors, and laid out the food.

Mama had drifted back to sleep, and Francisca and Uncle Carlos took their usual places at the table and sat down to breakfast. As Francisca poured the coffee, she changed the direction of the conversation. 'Bernardo has returned, Uncle,' she said. 'Did anyone tell you – he is staying here, with us.'

Carlos poured olive oil over the diced fruit and replied, 'I did not know that. We were not expecting him for some time yet. What happened?'

'He became ill. He is comfortable convalescing here and stays quietly. I had the guest bedchamber made up for him.'

'It was not on account of Bernardo that you have been out so late, then?' He took a deep breath and asked, 'Do you love Bernardo, Francisca? If you had the choice, would it be Bernardo you would marry?'

She finally had an opportunity to explain to Uncle Carlos. She must be clear. 'Bernardo and I are the dearest of friends. That is what we are and always will be to one another.'

He looked her in the eye and said, 'I accept your decision. I will look in on him later.'

'Thank you, Uncle.' With Bernardo's place and position in the house understood and secured, Francisca could not help but confront the subject of the Inquisition. She concealed her nerves by buttering her toast and said, 'Word is that the Inquisition is to resume here in Seville.'

The surprise on Uncle Carlos's face was evident but she did not know whether it was due to his own ignorance or the fact of her knowledge. 'Come, Uncle,' she said, feeling brave. 'You cannot keep me innocent of these things forever.'

He gripped the table. 'Who told you this?'

'Am I right to understand that we have nothing to fear?' she continued, evading his question. 'Only conversos will be brought before the Inquisitor Generale?' Her heart raced as she tried to catch his gaze, challenging him to lie to her.

He avoided her eyes and whispered, 'While I am archbishop, there will be no Seat of the Inquisition in Seville. Its time has passed.'

He spoke with sincerity. It could only mean one thing: that he indeed was ignorant of the King's plans. He could not protect her.

'Uncle, is it possible that you simply are not aware of what the King is planning?'

'All I can tell you, Francisca, is that while I am Archbishop of Seville, it simply cannot happen.'

The expression in his eyes told her he was willing to face the challenge of the dangers that might lie ahead. Now was the time to confront the issue that had been burning on her mind. 'Uncle, I support you in your resistance, but I cannot deny that I am afraid, for I know we are conversos.'

'Francisca!' His face turned crimson. 'One day I will tell you some things, if you wish to know.'

'You can tell me now. You might have told me before. Did you not think I might want to know who I am?'

'When you were a child, Spain underwent great tumult. We had to embrace a new life. I made choices for you, before you were able to choose for yourself.'

In his expression, she saw that he considered her his equal.

'Francisca, I wanted to talk to you but ultimately, I decided that it would not be helpful. Looking back is fruitless – it is like working at a festering wound. We must move forward.'

But she needed to ask another question, and it burst forth before she could measure it. 'Uncle, I need to know what happened to Mama and Papa. Were the perpetrators brought to justice?'

'I have told you all this before. The perpetrators were outlaws. Criminals. We never found them.'

'If you never found them, how do you know they were outlaws?' she asked quietly, barely controlling her rage. 'It could have been anyone.' She thought of all the characters in the wall picture and how she was no closer to solving it.

His colour still high, Carlos eased his collar. 'Francisca, we will talk later on this.'

If she pursued the questions, she would boil over, and she did not want that to happen now.

'Please, tell me about your work,' he said. 'Señor Ceretti is treating you well, I trust?'

'I shall show you what we have achieved.'

Carlos nodded. 'I look forward to it. Now, I shall return to my quarters for some rest.'

She followed him and, as they closed the door behind them, she felt the enormity of all they had endured together over the years.

'Francisca, I did not foresee us exchanging words on topics such as these.' His tone was conciliatory. 'I have been looking forward to seeing you.'

She was sorry for her part in raising these matters so soon after their reunion. He deserved a better homecoming. 'I am sorry, Uncle. I am glad you are home.'

He smiled. 'Well, I am glad of that. Now, I have arranged for a gentleman to visit tomorrow afternoon.'

She held onto the door handle. 'I have to be at the cathedral. Señor Ceretti is running to a tight schedule, as you know.' If she had dreaded the prospect of marriage before, there was now no world in which she could abide it.

'Do not concern yourself about the work. I will speak with Señor Ceretti.'

As he turned to go down the corridor to his bedchamber, he paused and asked, 'I almost forgot – I could not help noticing a broken window in the reception room. Do you know anything about it?'

She had forgotten about the glass, but she replied without faltering, 'It must be recent.' That, at least, was the truth.

'It is mystifying – no one seems to know about it, yet the glass splinters have been cleared away.'

As she sank her head into the pillow, her thoughts turned to Gabriela's final words – that there could be no mixed loyalties once she committed to joining the Insurgeants. She had already gone too far to turn back. She thought of Isabel, and she was determined to have her chance of happiness, regardless of the consequences.

CHAPTER TWENTY-NINE

Cardinal De Praed sat on the edge of his small chair, pinned between the table and the volumes of books in Father Alberto's vestry study.

'Might there be some wine, Father Alberto?' he asked, finding it difficult to contain his irritation. After the long and arduous journey, he'd expected nothing less than a formal reception with local dignitaries.

Father Alberto located a decanter on the window ledge behind a book, wiped his robe around the inside of a soiled goblet and poured a generous splash from the decanter.

Cardinal De Praed hesitantly brought it to his nose to test it and recoiled.

'Never mind.' He sighed, waving his hand. 'Let us turn to the schedule.'

The pupils of Father Alberto's eyes dilated. He leaned back, steepled his hands and looked into the mid-distance.

'We are gratified The Holy Father has ordained a new Seat of the Inquisition, for which, as you know, I have been agitating these many years past. The people's complacency has become all too apparent.' He sat forward and fixed his eyes on the cardinal. 'You will be shocked, I am sure, when you see it for yourself: citizens are more interested in commerce than leading a disciplined, God-fearing life.' There was a pained look in his eye as he added, 'Jewish practices are resurfacing and, unfortunately, the archbishop is not as interested as he should be – not in the way we naturally are.'

'Indeed, indeed.' He asked again, 'The schedule?'

Father Alberto patted his hands out reassuringly and said, 'The Auto-da-fé is Friday.'

'Do you mean, in just two days' time? With all the travel, I am losing track of the days...'

'That is correct. Today is Wednesday. Here is the list of those to be tried. You may take that copy with you and peruse the names at your leisure. All the evidence necessary is here.'

Father Alberto reverently tapped the rows of volumes stacked on his desk. He swallowed loudly and said, 'These will be delivered to the Inquisitor Generale tomorrow – he needs only a day to familiarise himself with the facts. The arrests will be made under cover of darkness. A new moon will ensure secrecy. The prisoners will be brought to the Castle of San Jorge in Triana, across the river.' He pointed out the window in its general direction. 'Everyone who needs to know has been fully briefed. I will not burden His Eminence with further details.'

'A tight schedule, but you have it all under control, Father. I am glad to have arrived in time for the drama.'

'As am I.' Father Alberto smiled smugly.

'And the imperative for it *now*?' Cardinal De Praed's brow furrowed as he adopted a concerned countenance. 'Is it simply the complacency you are concerned about – of course that is sufficient imperative. I just feel I should know all the material facts.'

'Thank you, Your Eminence. Detail is important. And you are correct.' Father Alberto shook his index finger at the ceiling. 'There is a rising support for the Insurgeants.' He looked to the volumes lining his vestry walls. He nodded and clipped, 'My instinct tells me we need to strike sooner than later. Take the offensive. Cut it off before it takes hold.'

'Absolutely right. The moment the masses get a sniff of freedom, danger looms.' Cardinal De Praed shook his head.

'I do have some information.' Father Alberto lowered his voice. 'There is to be a regional meeting of the Insurgeants, scheduled for tomorrow evening.' With an edge of agitation, he added, 'They will be shaken by what they will see at the Auto-da-fé, and, whatever it is they have planned, they will buckle – I guarantee it.'

'I agree with your strategy.' The cardinal nodded solemnly. 'Now, tell me more about the archbishop. He seems an affable man, but do I need to be concerned?'

'Oh no. Carlos is perfectly pliable.' Father Alberto inhaled twice before resuming thoughtfully, 'Sometimes, he needs to be reminded as to who put him here – and who keeps him here – but there is nothing to be concerned about. He simply gets distracted and confuses priorities.'

'Excellent. I admit, Father, I am curious. How did it all come about exactly? It is a situation that could never happen in Italy. Help me understand.'

Father Alberto sat back, peering at the moulding on the ceiling, and spoke like he was reading from a story book. 'He was a young man when he came to my church.' He squinted, thinking back. 'And desperate to do something with his life. He had missed out on love and, blaming his parents, refused to carry on the family business. He was lost. Adrift.' He shook his head. 'Even through his plight, I could see the clarity of his face – like an angel. His voice had a resonance, perfect for rousing a congregation. I knew they would believe every word this man would utter from the pulpit, and I thought to myself, *we* must have him. He was wasted as a Jew, and I told him.' He leaned forward, confidingly. 'And of course, the timing was perfect – he had little choice, really. He would be my frontman. All his problems would be solved.' He could not conceal his pride at his protégé's rise, and ended his tale simply with, 'So, I found him a home, a place where he I ensured felt he belonged. He worked hard and learned quickly.' He raised his hands as if to say, that is all there is to it. 'The people love him.'

'Fascinating. By all accounts, you make an excellent team.' The cardinal knew Father Alberto had started life as a mere orphan. 'You have done well with him, provided, of course, we can be sure he is on our side? There is no concern I should be aware of?'

Father Alberto harrumphed. 'Carlos does not want the Inquisition; I will not deny it. He is quite content with the way things are, and he prefers the quiet life. But ultimately, I have no doubt he will be with us. After all – as you rightly say – he still needs to prove whose side he is on, particularly now.'

The cardinal raised an eyebrow. 'You haven't briefed him about it? Why does he think I am here?'

Father Alberto gestured casually. 'Carlos thinks what he wants to think. He does not need to know until Friday.'

Cardinal De Praed chuckled. 'I shall make myself scarce Friday morning, then.' He hesitated, searching his memory. 'Another matter – I heard Carlos has a niece. Is she under control? She dabbles in painting, I hear. No childish notions of avenging her race, I trust?'

Father Alberto had prepared for this question. He looked Cardinal De Praed directly in the eyes and replied steadily, 'I have her under lock and key. You need not be concerned about her.'

Evidently, Cardinal De Praed was satisfied, for he moved on. 'Carlos told me about that painter – Ceretti – commissioned for the cathedral. What a muddle. I cannot set eyes on him; I am sure you understand.'

Father Alberto raised his hand in acknowledgement and grinned as he replied, 'Fear not, it has all been arranged.'

CHAPTER THIRTY

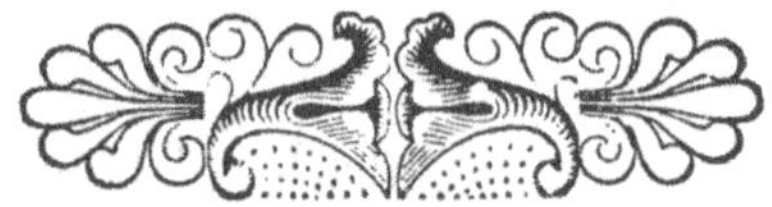

Sleep came only intermittently, and Francisca tossed and turned, battling disturbing dreams. Her bedchamber was stiflingly hot and, after a time, she rose and flung the windows open but there came only a semblance of a breeze. Finally, exhausted, her body relaxed into the mattress, her mind emptied of all thought, and she slept, but it seemed only moments before a knock at the door woke her.

'Señorita, a woman named Isabel is here,' Marina said. 'She says it cannot wait. I have asked her to take a seat in the atrium courtyard.'

Francisca's mind was woolly with sleep and she asked, 'What time is it?'

'Eight o'clock.'

'I will be down presently.'

She estimated she had slept for no more than half an hour, but she changed quickly. Her heart leapt at the sight of Isabel, seated on the fountain ledge. But by Isabel's posture, she sensed all was not well, and she rushed down the stairs to her.

'Isabel.' Francisca took her hands in her own.

'Francisca,' Isabel said. Despite her tender smile, Francisca sensed her agitation and saw that her eyelids were heavy.

'I am sorry to come so early. I have not slept all night,' Isabel said as she passed her a letter and gestured to her to read it:

My Dear Isabel,

Father Alberto has offered me a house in the countryside, where I can work without distraction:

La Capilla (by the church in the main square)

Olivares

Please join me. Father Alberto will assist with the travel arrangements for you.

Your loving,

A

Servants were rushing about nearby, and she quickly reread the letter, trying to absorb its implications.

'He must have left last night,' Isabel said quietly. 'Something about this troubles me. It is not explicable. The countryside reminds him of his childhood, and he would never choose to work anywhere other than the location where his paintings are to be displayed.'

'Of course – the cathedral's light. It cannot be replicated.' Francisca's mind was racing to keep up with Isabel's words. 'What do you think it means?'

As she whispered, Francisca recalled Elizabeth's letter and she surmised that Antonio's retreat to Olivares was likely to be connected to the arrival of Cardinal De Praed.

'I do not know. I do not wish to involve you in this, but I wanted to ask if you would speak to Father Alberto about the travel arrangements. In addition, I wanted you to know where I would be – in case, well, in case something happens.' Isabel looked meaningfully at Francisca as she added, 'I do not want to stay longer than necessary with him but I need to talk to him. I wanted to talk to him last night. I need to conclude matters properly.'

Francisca could see Isabel's mind whirring, and, whether rationally or not, she feared Antonio's temper. Impetuously she said, 'Isabel, we will go together. Olivares is half a day's journey by coach, and we can ride faster with Fiel. If we leave now, we have a chance of returning by nightfall. I will stay out of sight, but I want to come with you, to make sure you are safe.'

'I do not want to waste your time.'

'Only time away from you is wasted time, Isabel. Let us go; we must call in on Gabriela en route.'

'Isabel, Francisca – wait.'

Gabriela emerged from El Flamenco, striding towards them with a set of keys which she dropped into one of Fiel's panniers. She pressed Francisca's hands and said, 'The keys are to my cottage. If you need somewhere to stay, go to El Santuario, behind the taverna as you enter Salteras. It is the last village before Olivares. Bless you both and be safe.'

Thick, dark clouds rolled swiftly in their direction of travel. The light dimmed as they navigated the narrow lanes on the outskirts of Seville. Fiel set out at a slow, easy gait. Despite the weather setting in, Francisca relaxed into Isabel's back and drifted in and out of sleep.

It was already midday but the detour to El Flamenco had been necessary. It was important to inform both Isabel and Gabriela of Cardinal De Praed's early arrival in Seville. Their discussions, however, failed to yield agreement amongst themselves as to whether it signified that the arrests and the Auto-da-fé would be made correspondingly earlier. It was possible that his early arrival was as innocent as Carlos's eagerness to return home. But the answer to the question was important. To secure the best chance of

Valentina's escape and ensure the safety of those members of the Insurgeants charged with her liberation, the guards at the Castle of San Jorge needed to be occupied and distracted by bringing in the new prisoners for the Auto-da-fé.

In the end, they agreed that, until they knew for sure, there was little choice but to continue with their schedule as planned: the Insurgeants meeting would be held after Isabel's performance, and the prison break for Valentina's release would occur in the early hours.

As they left Seville behind, there was an icy edge to the air, and Isabel wrapped her shawl tightly around her shoulders. How long ago the wild abandon of last night seemed already, but Francisca did not wait to be invited and she curled her arms around Isabel's waist. Desire coursed through her.

They rode without conversation, and Francisca could not help wondering what Isabel was thinking. Could she be regretting last night? What did it mean to her? She feared it meant less to Isabel than it did to her. She knew she would never again in her life experience the enormity of the feelings. Perhaps, she fretted, it was a fleeting love affair, perhaps one of many for Isabel.

Whatever it signified to Isabel, it would not alter the fact that Isabel was set on leaving Seville to find her aunt. Isabel had made no promises to her. She fought the questions from her mind and tried simply to enjoy the moment, like Fiel seemed able to do.

As buildings, smallholdings and other signs of the city dwindled, and the meandering road to Salteras opened out ahead, Fiel picked up his gait to a steady trot and Isabel and Francisca sat up, observing the changing scenery and incoming weather front. Each was quiet and solemn in their respective contemplations. Fiel would need to maintain speed if they were to outpace the storm, which now, ominously, whipped up directly ahead of them, the clouds twirling in eerie shapes.

Francisca pondered on the multiple explanations of Señor Ceretti's letter and his sudden departure, and every thread of thought returned to the fact that Father Alberto had 'offered' Señor Ceretti a house. If this were true, it suggested Señor Ceretti had expressed a wish to work somewhere quiet, away from the cathedral. And yet, if that had indeed been the case, why had he not mentioned it to Isabel? Why would he not have chosen instead to work from their apartment? And why did he leave in the middle of the night rather than wait to travel together? What was the haste?

With the dark, brooding clouds looming, she pictured Señor Ceretti, alone in Olivares. He would be wondering if Isabel would come.

Francisca tried to still the other matters troubling her. Her confrontation with Uncle Carlos had unsettled her. She may have upset the one person in her life on whom she had always been able to rely. He had nurtured her as if she was his own child. She had loved him as the father she had lost. She had never questioned him. Implicitly, she had always trusted him. And she felt sick to think that the conversation – which had been uncomfortable for them both – had yielded very little in return.

The fact of Carlos's admission in 'making choices' for her did not establish anything, other than that, she surmised, her conversion occurred after the attack on her parents – for it would have been for her parents to have made such a choice for her, had they been able to. Even that fact seemed to lead nowhere, for what it signified she did not know. What concerned her most was her uncle's hopeless vagueness about the identity of the perpetrators of the attack. She could not deny he had been defensive in the face of that specific question. If it amounted to a lack of enquiry on his part, then, at a minimum, he was guilty of turning a blind eye – the sin of omission, as he would refer to it.

And as for the resurgent Inquisition, she felt frustrated in how little she had elicited. She had been too emotional in the way she approached the issue with him. She did not give Uncle Carlos the time and space he may have needed to reveal what might have been useful. The few comments he did make, she turned around in her mind. She believed his professed ignorance of any resurgence to be genuine; likewise, she believed his opposition to it to be sincere. Carlos had been proud to preside over Seville's rise as the Mediterranean's principal trading centre with the Americas. His ambition was a noble one: for Seville to become a city to which artists and intellectuals would be attracted, as well as a centre for business. He believed in progress, not a harking back to earlier times.

And yet, it seemed to her that if Carlos was indeed ignorant of, and opposed to, the Inquisition – and if it progressed nonetheless – then he could be no more than a figurehead. He was in office for others' bidding. Father Alberto's bidding, she presumed.

At the crossroads to Salteras, she recalled herself to the present. She and Isabel had barely spoken since they had set out from El Flamenco. 'We have both been lost in our own thoughts,' she said. 'Are you concerned for Antonio?'

'Hopefully it is a simple explanation,' she replied distractedly.

'You still care for him.' The words – a question or a statement, she was not sure herself – escaped her lips before she could measure them.

'There was a time when I thought we would be together forever.'

Francisca allowed the silence to linger, to give Isabel time to gather her thoughts.

'Antonio and I had a child but she died.'

The words fell from her with the sadness of late autumn leaves, and Francisca wished this had not been the answer to Isabel's melancholy. She could not imagine her sorrow.

'We grieved in different ways, and it changed us, individually and also in the way we were together.'

Francisca felt Isabel struggle for the words.

'It means that our souls can never truly be free from one another.' Isabel said it like a confession. 'Do you understand?'

Isabel was telling her she could not leave Antonio, but

Francisca understood this was not the time to dwell on her own feelings. 'What was her name?'

'Lucena.'

'What happened?'

'After her second birthday, it was a difficult winter. A simple cold developed into something serious, and she had not the strength to recover. She was delicate from birth.'

'Oh, Isabel.' Isabel's tears welled up. Tenderly, Francisca pressed herself into Isabel's back. 'She brought you light for the brief time with you.'

'Yes.'

'And now you must keep her light alive within you until you join her again. I cannot imagine your pain.'

There seemed a new kind of intimacy between them.

Salteras came into view. Ahead they could see a taverna and a small house behind. Francisca discerned the name by the door: El Santuario, and she made a mental note of it in case they could not return to Seville by nightfall.

They passed through Salteras and left it behind.

At the crossroads where a signpost pointed to Olivares, Fiel broke into a mighty gallop. Isabel held tightly to his reins and Francisca to Isabel's waist.

In the receding light, the sky shrank. Thunder rumbled. The way was marked by intermittent flashes of lightning. A church steeple, rising in the mid-distance, irradiated.

Even in the tumult of the weather, they located Olivares's modest square easily. It was but a small village and the streets were deserted. Under the church portico, they sought shelter from the storm and watched as the date palms bent and swayed in the deafening wind.

'I will wait here with Fiel,' Francisca said, raising her voice in an effort to be heard over the ferocity of the storm.

'At least go inside the church.'

'No – I want a clear view of the door.'

Isabel looked unsure but Francisca was insistent. 'Don't worry, Fiel and I are accustomed to storms.'

Isabel leaned into the wind as she ventured towards the cottage of La Capilla.

Francisca prepared herself for a long wait and was shocked to see Isabel emerge from the cottage after only a few short minutes.

Isabel shouted above the storm, 'Let us leave here.'

Francisca helped her into the saddle and was unable to read her feelings. As she hoisted herself up onto Fiel's back, they set off, through the storm, back to El Santuario in Salteras, for there could be no question of returning to Seville tonight.

CHAPTER THIRTY-ONE

By the time Francisca entered El Santuario after securing shelter for Fiel, she had a sense of the cottage having awaited their arrival. Isabel was dressed in nothing but a shawl – her wet clothes were hanging over the kitchen chairs – and she had prepared a fire. The cottage was small and sparsely furnished, but Gabriela's flair was unmistakably present. A large, tapestried rug decorated the broad bare floorboards, lanterns dotted the small tables, and dried flowers casually graced the kitchen table. They would be comfortable and safe from prying eyes here. At the sight of Isabel's exposed shoulders and bare legs, Francisca blushed and was unsure where to look. Isabel's eyes were fixed on the fire and her expression was still one that Francisca could not read.

'I found a place for Fiel in the taverna's stables,' Francisca said, attempting a cheerful tone. 'They were very kind. Look... provisions.'

Isabel smiled absently. 'Well, that's some good news.' She patted the place beside her by the fire. 'Why don't you change out of your wet clothes and join me? There is a dry towel and another shawl on the bed.'

Francisca did as Isabel suggested and arranged the provisions on a small table between them by the fire. Goblet of wine in hand, they stared into the fire. The flames crackled and danced, drawing up and tossing about in the wind whistling in a high pitch through the chimney. The rain beat down in angular sheets against the window shutters rattling in the wind against the wooden frames.

She wanted to reach out to Isabel and assure her that all would yet be well, but she held back, and decided to let Isabel speak if she wished to.

Eventually, Isabel broke the silence and, when she did so, her voice sounded unlike her own. 'Some of Antonio's things were there but he himself was not.'

'That's strange – I can't imagine there are many places to find entertainment in Olivares.'

'Who knows. Antonio finds diversions in the most unlikely places and circumstances.'

'I suppose we will find out more in the morning?'

'Yes, the morning usually brings some clarity,' Isabel replied vaguely.

'Try not to worry, though it must be difficult, I can imagine.'

'Oh, I could spend my life worrying about Antonio, running around in circles and achieving nothing.'

Francisca stoked the fire and tried to make her voice sound easy. 'Isabel, if you regret what happened between us, I have no expectations. Whatever you need to do—'

'What makes you think I am so changeable?' Isabel interrupted her. 'Not for one second do *I* regret it.' She looked up, her eyes filled with tears and a fiery grey-green hue, such that Francisca had never seen. 'But do you? With all my encumbrances and complications, I would not blame you.'

Francisca put down the fire iron. She was filled with apprehension and longing. 'Of course I don't. What you told me on the road – about Lucena – I thought you were trying to tell me you want to be true to Antonio; to be with him. Whatever there has been between us, I will cherish it, for always.'

'I had already decided, long before last night, that Antonio and I were over. It is for the best. How could you think I would return to Antonio after what passed between us?'

And with that, all the tension between the two lovers dissolved.

'I simply wanted you to know that there will always be a part of Antonio and me that will go on together.' She hesitated and pointed to the ceiling. 'Out there, in the cosmos, even when we part ways.' Her delicate collar bones quivered with emotion as she spoke. 'It is because of Lucena. I should have told you before, but it is so personal and difficult to talk about. You deserve better.' She placed her hand on her heart and said, 'I feel it here, your clarity of spirit and innocence. You have your whole life ahead of you, a chance to be unaffected by other people's choices... my choices, my losses and sorrows.'

Francisca took Isabel's hands in hers and looked into her eyes as she replied, 'I love you as you are, Isabel. I will hold dear your memory of Lucena and light a flame for her in my heart also. I want to know you, how you feel, what gives you joy, what gives you sorrow. I want to know all of you, not just the parts that you feel are untarnished. I don't want you to conceal your pain from me.'

Tears continued to spill in a great torrent down Isabel's face. 'Until yesterday, I had not uttered her name for such a long time. Lucena!' She howled and let out her years of silent pain. Francisca cradled her in her arms. 'After she died, friends recoiled if I talked about her. It was like, if I avoided mentioning her name, then she never existed, and it made everyone feel better – except for me. Lucena was a person, with her own character and feelings. We made each other laugh. My soul danced with hers. She was not a nameless child whose place in my heart died with her death. For such a long time I tried not to speak about her, hoping that – like everyone told me – if I just buried her inside, it would make things better.' She drew herself up and looked at her hands, drenched with her tears. 'But, apparently not.'

Francisca rubbed her back and said gently, 'Accept your pain.

Do not try to erase it. Time and effort cannot erase some things. Sometimes all we can hope for is to live with the pain and somehow find a place to keep it safe.'

Isabel cried herself to exhaustion in Francisca's arms until she fell deeply asleep.

The fire crackled against the grate. The rain rattled against the shutters. They were warm and dry and safe from the elements.

Francisca stroked Isabel's locks and observed the gentle rise and fall of her breath. She wanted to learn her heart and soul, to give the best of herself to her for the rest of her life. This was what love is, she thought – no concern for yesterday or tomorrow, simply being in the present, wanting only the present, to continue forever.

The fire reduced to a weak flame. She eased Isabel's head onto a cushion and stoked the fire back to life. From the bedchamber, she took a blanket and sheets and lay down beside Isabel, on the tapestried rug, and held her close. Soon, she fell asleep also.

Outside, the sheeting rain eased to a gentle patter against the shutters, and the wind subsided. The fire continued to burn slowly.

When it was still dark and the room warmed by the fire, Isabel awakened to find Francisca curled into her side and she thought of how, in her love of Francisca, there was no gap to bridge, no adoption of a role of submission on one part and of command on the other. There was an equality that she had never before experienced.

She could not help it and she kissed Francisca on the lips. Francisca stirred and they kissed tentatively and then fervently. They kissed to heal their pain. They kissed for some certainty, for sanctuary from the madness and cruelty of the world. They kissed to give and to take, for desire and the simple joy of being alive and in love. They kissed for both the impossibility and inevitability of their togetherness. Their limbs entwined and Isabel eased

Francisca onto her, so that she could feel all of Francisca's weight on her, and she explored her suppleness in her shoulders, down through her spine, and to her hips, and below, to where the flesh merged with her thighs, and, with her lover's hands, she enjoyed there.

They entered another realm and all the light that had been between them was extinguished and replaced with something new. With the rhythm of their bodies, they pressed and released, and pressed and released, over and over, and gave pleasure to one another, and they murmured, long into the night, climaxing over and over.

CHAPTER THIRTY-TWO

They awakened at the same time, enraptured and gazing into one another's eyes – the avenue to their inner world, the place of giving and receiving, as Leonardo put it.

Had they not looked into one another's eyes before? Is it possible to look into another's eyes and not truly see them? This kind of seeing felt so very different. There was no instinct to look away, no difficulty in holding the gaze, no embarrassment or self-consciousness. Francisca felt Isabel could read her very thoughts and she did not mind. They smiled, letting one another in, and lightly linked fingers. And each felt as a warrior in a battle against the world prepared to die in defence of their love. Their love itself, a covetous key to paradise.

Warm sunlight filtered through the shutters, casting faint undulating stripes of light across the sensual contours of their bodies. All was still. Yesterday's storm had returned from whence it came. The scent of last night's cherry wood fire mingled with their pheromones and hung in the air as a fragrant incense. Neither Francisca nor Isabel had any desire to move from the tapestry rug or think on the day ahead.

'You are a natural,' Isabel said, playfully.

'What are you implying?' Francisca feigned insult.

Isabel straddled across her, allowing her a fine view of her body, her intoxicating scent transporting Francisca.

She pinned Francisca's hands on the floor behind her head and teased, 'I'm just one of a long line of conquests, am I?'

Francisca squealed in protest and half-heartedly struggled to free her hands. 'I hardly dare ask about you.'

'Let me see.' Isabel pretended to be counting all her lovers, but then she laughed and released Francisca's hands. 'I did love a woman once. We even kissed but her father sent her away.'

Her hands freed, Francisca took the opportunity to use Isabel's hips as a point of reference from which to explore the soft texture of Isabel's skin and she gently massaged the muscles and tendons, so that she could know her sinews and forever recall the details.

'When I was growing up,' Isabel continued, 'it seemed the most natural idea – to love a woman – but in real life, it never seemed possible. I suppose it was the same with other things that I had imagined I might do or become. Now, I know anything other than this – *precisely this* – would be second best.' She traced the contours of Francisca's mouth and said, 'I am in love with you, Francisca Mendez.'

'And I am in love with you, Isabel de Flores.' Isabel leaned forward and lightly rested her hands on Francisca's shoulders.

It was as though they had scaled a great mountain peak. How different the world seemed from here, the air sweeter, life free from imperfections.

'Let us stay here, in El Santuario forever,' Isabel declared joyfully. 'Only Gabriela knows where we are, and she can bring us food and anything else we need.'

'Unfortunately, the whole of Saltares also knows. Last night, everyone in the taverna stopped and stared at me like I had landed from the moon.'

'I see. So, we need another plan.'

'Yes, and quickly. Carlos will have me married off by the end of the week if left to his own devices. He has found a "gentleman" to introduce me to this afternoon. *It's time a man takes control of you.*' She mimicked Uncle Carlos's baritone voice, trying to make light of the predicament.

'Oh, Francisca, how dreadful.'

'My life would be over, only as it has just begun.'

Isabel lay down beside her. They fixed their eyes on the ceiling, seeking inspiration.

In an altogether different voice, Isabel said, 'Have you really thought about it though? There might be a suitable man – you could lead a normal life, have children. Perhaps we could continue to see one another if we were careful.'

Was this what the day after was like, Francisca wondered? Undoing the night's words and deeds so truly expressed? But she tried to keep her voice light as she replied definitively, 'I should rather die fighting bare-handed alongside the Insurgeants.'

Isabel raised herself onto her elbow and asked, 'Have you always imagined yourself with a woman?'

'When Elizabeth was here, I felt like there was nothing else I needed or wanted; the emotional rapport, gentle sensibility, and understanding. Being with you is the same – only on an entirely different level of course.' She smiled. 'It is what I want. Why should I not have it? Should I change how I feel to accommodate Uncle Carlos or anyone else or to make life less difficult?'

'Well, your life *will* take a more difficult path, you know that.'

'I think I can manage difficulty. What I cannot manage is my soul withering like fruit on a vine rotting from its very roots. Having what we have had, how could I marry a man? Anyway, it is not like I will be a pioneer. Gabriela has lived as I want to. Plato wrote about it. And then there is Sappho herself.'

'Tell me one of her poems.'

Francisca closed her eyes and recited:

You may forget but
let me tell you
this: someone in
some future time
will think of us.

'How sad. But I have no intention of forgetting you, Francisca.'

Francisca rested on her elbow so she could see Isabel too. 'Then stop saying I could forget you and be with a man.' Stroking Isabel's cheek, tenderly she asked, 'Did you think about having another child? Might you like it yet?'

'Only with you, and that would be quite something.' She smiled sadly. 'But right now, I feel that love itself is creation enough. We have created something out of nothing – that is a kind of miracle.'

'Yes, I feel the same way. I have always wanted to live with animals. They need homes too, and they help us be our best selves.'

They talked it over and agreed that they liked the idea of their love sprinkling beyond themselves, for it seemed that in doing so, it would evolve and thrive, and they agreed to live on some land filled with animals.

They continued on joyfully and linked hands as they imagined what their future might be.

'So, it's settled,' Isabel said. 'We want to be together. The days ahead are going to be difficult and fraught with uncertainty. If we have a plan for our future, it will give us courage to face whatever might be thrown at us.'

'I thought we agreed to meet at Lyra?' Francisca grinned.

'Francisca, be serious,' Isabel insisted, tugging Francisca's locks.

'Do not ask me to solve this like it is some problem of perspective. It is not that simple. You need to find your aunt, and I cannot leave Seville at the moment. Being here is not a matter of choice for me.'

Francisca couldn't leave her mother. That unchangeable fact

entered the crevices of the room and their minds. She sat up and, knowing the answer would change her life one way or another, asked, 'I know it is asking you to make a sacrifice, but would you consider Seville being a base from which to find your aunt, and return here to Seville on the tri-lunar cycle? One day, when I am free, I will go with you, anywhere your heart desires.'

Isabel did not make Francisca wait for an answer, and she took her into her arms as she replied, 'If Seville is where you must be then Seville will be my point of reference. So the answer is, yes, my darling.'

They lay together, their hearts swelling with the joy and certainty of the decisions just made and imagining the time to come like some long-fulfilled promise of happiness.

'With Gabriela's help and the band growing in popularity, I can earn a living here.'

'I will have to fend off all your admirers.'

Isabel smiled and followed the contours of Francisca's face with her index finger. 'But we must be discreet. The tide is once again turning against the likes of us, remember.'

But Francisca grinned. 'I think I could make a fine gentleman. Papa's wardrobe is still filled with his suits – I have even tried some of them. It feels wonderful.'

Isabel straddled Francisca again and, adopting the voice of a surgeon, said, 'Let me examine you, Señor Francesco.'

Eyes closed, her hands firmly and slowly followed the line of Francisca's shape.

'Here – señor's fine, slender neck. Here – señor's soft, smooth skin and gently sloping shoulders. But what is this? Señor's generous breasts? And shapely hips?'

Francisca simultaneously laughed and groaned with pleasure at Isabel's touch.

Isabel opened her eyes. 'Señor makes a most singular man. But I am open to being convinced.'

They laughed, even as Francisca guided Isabel's hand down and said, 'I will show you later.'

And they made love over again.

Afterwards, their conversation turned to the day ahead. Isabel would take Fiel to Olivares while Francisca waited at El Santuario.

Outside, it was like yesterday's storm never happened. The air was fresh and still, and the birds sang a morning chorus. The sunlight dazzled, indulgently extending its autumn warmth upon them.

But the nearer Fiel trotted towards Olivares, the more Isabel's mind turned to the task before her, and she felt torn between the ecstasy of her new love and the pain of what she knew she must do. As she approached the church square, it occurred to her that Olivares, devoid of any obvious sign of inspiration, even in the morning sunlight, was a peculiar place for Father Alberto to send Antonio to work.

Isabel looped Fiel's reins over a hook nailed into a tree in the church square.

The front door of La Capilla was ajar and swinging on its hinges. With trepidation, she stood before the threshold and called out to Antonio. The house echoed out her voice, and hesitantly, she entered. Antonio's things were gone. On the kitchen table, was an envelope with her name scribbled across it and she broke the seal.

Dear Isabel,

Being here, alone for these brief, yet interminable hours, I realise I cannot stay. You and I need time apart. It was a mistake for me to have accompanied you to Spain, I can see that now. I have decided to go to a place from where I need not run. You know where it is.

I must tell you: I know of your childish infatuation with Francisca. Others are also aware. People are watching and my love for you requires me to advise you to be careful and to restore yourself to your true, God-given, nature. God forbid that people arrive at the wrong conclusion; that you are indulging in unnatural acts (or would such a conclusion be wrong?).

If you decide to join me, it must be on the basis that we make a new start; our failures to one another would be forgotten and freely forgiven.

I shall hope for that time.

Until then, be sure that I remain your loving,

Antonio.

Isabel slumped into a nearby chair, choked of air. She held a hand to her racing heart and looked blindly around the room.

His words about Francisca and herself shook her. Precisely what was commonly known? Precisely what had been said, and by whom? Was it pure conjecture, based on something intangible – such as Francisca's portrait of her as Mary with the Christ Child? If so, she hoped it would be a simple matter of explaining away. Or did someone know? Had someone been 'watching' her, as Antonio's letter expressly stated? Her mind turned to Father Alberto. Regardless of the answer, deep down, she knew from bitter experience that evidence was not required for those who have the power to condemn and a wish to do so.

Although Antonio's departure shocked her, her primary feeling was one of relief. She examined her conscience and concluded that her feelings for Francisca had not been the cause of the breakdown in their relationship. Rereading the letter, she considered that it did not seem to have played a factor in Antonio's decision. Their troubles had started long ago, even before Lucena's death; she tried to think back, but her memories of that time were muddled now. What she knew with certainty was that this past year, still fresh in her mind, had been almost intolerable. How much more should they endure before permitting themselves the freedom of letting go? Everything had been done that could have been done.

She read the letter again and turned her thoughts to Antonio's reference to not needing to 'run' and she thought of his recent restlessness – even during their daily travels on the road from Rome to Seville. She had tried to ask him if something had been on his mind, she had tried to understand him, but the more she asked, the more he withdrew.

She forced herself to breathe and collect herself and she ran from the house. Swiftly, she mounted Fiel. He felt her agitation and bolted away. En route to Saltares, her mind tied itself in knots. Should she share the information with Francisca? If she concealed it, she knew she could not continue with any semblance of normality towards her. But if she shared it, Francisca would be fearful, and she baulked at that prospect. Francisca had only just found happiness. How brief their time of joy had been, she thought bitterly.

She entered the front yard of El Santuario and saw the towels and bed linen hanging out to dry. She opened the front door to find Francisca sweeping the remnants of last night's fire. Despite the disquiet in her mind, she smiled at Francisca's productivity.

Francisca looked up. Aghast, she declared, 'Isabel, you look like you've seen a ghost. What's happened?'

'Come, let us sit together.'

'What has happened?' Francisca repeated.

'I think you should read this,' she said, handing over the letter.

The colour drained from Francisca's face. 'Do you have any thoughts as to who might know and how?' she asked.

Isabel shook her head. 'I do not know anything for sure, but I am guessing what I think you are guessing: Father Alberto. He makes it his business to know everyone else's business. And I am guessing he knows by the same means I suspect he knows of your own awareness of your Jewish parentage. There must be an informer in your household.'

Francisca tried to swallow but her throat seized up. With a cold thrill of insight, she finally saw it. 'My journal,' she said in a dry voice.

The words fell like an executioner's axe.

Guilt and fear took hold of her. 'What if Uncle Carlos knows too? Father Alberto would tell him, surely? We must return to Seville immediately. I need to destroy my journal.' She grasped for some reassurance. 'Without evidence they cannot do anything against us, can they?'

'They will do what they like.' Isabel stared into nothing.

Tears streamed down Francisca's face at the helplessness of the situation and her own naivety and carelessness in bringing danger upon them both.

Isabel wrapped her arms around her and soothed, 'Do not blame yourself and be not afraid. Fear is the worst danger we face.'

CHAPTER THIRTY-THREE

Their journey back to Seville loomed with trepidation. The only comfort was their resolution about their future together.

Approaching Calle Almansa, they agreed that if it were not possible to meet before, they would at least meet at El Flamenco that night for Isabel's performance and then the meeting of the Insurgeants. As they parted, they hardly dared look at one another, for fear their intimacy would be visible to any passers-by.

Francisca entered the palacio's courtyard hoping to go straight to her bedchamber unseen, but Uncle Carlos emerged from the reception room.

She feared her legs would not support her but, somehow, she walked towards him.

His face was red with anger as he demanded, 'Where have you been? I have been worried sick.'

Those words were enough to tell Francisca that he did not know about her relationship with Isabel, and she found the courage to answer him assertively, 'I have been trying to find Señor Ceretti. He has abandoned your commission.'

'I thought you knew – he has gone to Olivares to work without distraction.'

'I can update you, Uncle. He has already left Olivares and he is not coming back.'

Confusion clouded his expression, and he stuttered, 'You might have thought to tell me where you were going instead of leaving me to worry all night.'

'I am sorry you were worried, but you must understand – you have been away more than half a year, and I have had to manage on my own without you. So, please, do not treat me as if I am still a child.'

He had no answer to that. 'The gentleman will be here before the new hour. Get changed.'

'Who is he?'

'A respectable man, and a friend of the Church. You will see. There is nothing objectionable about him,'

Was that the standard to be applied? 'And you think I will agree to marry him?'

'Please, just get changed,' he said, fingering his rosary beads. 'You will soon see. All will be well.'

She rushed upstairs. Exposed on her writing desk was her journal, the letters from Elizabeth filed within it. She felt sick to see it so vulnerable to prying eyes. How could she have been so naïve? Her hands shook and heat rose to her temples as she tore out the offending pages and set them to the flame of a candle.

She dressed and sat on the chair by her desk and tried to calm down. All the household had access to her bedchamber, but, unfairly and irrationally perhaps, her mind kept returning to Marina. Such a betrayal was almost impossible to contemplate. Why would she commit such a breach of trust? Surely not for money? But, if not for money, then why?

At a knock on her door, a voice called out softly, 'Francisca, it's me.'

This was the one person she did want to see.

'Bernardo,' she said as she let him in and fell into his arms.

'Francisca, what is it? I couldn't help hearing...'

'I am in love,' she said, gasping for air.

'Is that so bad?'

In a matter of just a few sentences, she told him everything.

Bernardo nodded sagely. 'There is rot in the fabric of the Church. I do not blame Carlos – he is the one bright light – but he is only one man and cannot do everything on his own. Let me come with you tonight, to El Flamenco. I am stronger now. Please, let me help you. Let me help the cause.'

And so, it was agreed.

From downstairs, Francisca heard voices. It was time.

She took her place in the reception room. She had an awareness of her mind feeling displaced from her body, of being introduced to a man, of a conversation ensuing, and that she was incapable of engaging in it. When the ordeal was over, Uncle Carlos told her she had performed well, that the man was impressed and that her life could yet be excellent. Her betrothed lived near Seville. She would see Mama from time to time. The marriage date was set for the day before el Día de Todos los Santos. That was two weeks from now.

Francisca changed and, in the fading afternoon sun, ran through the gardens to the cathedral. As she entered the Prince's Doors, a wave of nausea overcame her. She lay down on the bench by the doors and covered her ears to muffle out Father Alberto's denunciation of sinners. In his Latin verse, few of the congregation comprehended, but it mattered little; the tone of his voice was unambiguous, and Francisca felt his sermon directed at her personally.

She rose from the bench, determined to finish what she had come here to do. If she was to be reviled for a painting, she wanted it to be the finest it could be. At the trestle table she looked at the canvases scattered about on easels and felt proud of what they had achieved.

She prepared the pigments and oils and took the palette to her unfinished Mary with Christ Child. When the light disappeared, she gathered some candles to illuminate the canvas, but it was more out of habit than necessity: she could do this blindfolded.

Ángel circled the minaret and let out a piercing cry. An icy draught whipped through the columns. The very foundations seemed to creak; the cathedral felt alive with supernatural forces.

Francisca continued, unafraid even while she imagined there to be other lives beneath the flagstones. As she applied cochineal glaze to Isabel's hands, she thought of the mosque that had graced this spot before the Catholics destroyed it. Years ago, she had found a painting of it in Uncle Carlos's library. In the background, a synagogue and a church were clearly visible. Suddenly, she was overcome with sadness, at a whole world destroyed. Not only the world of the Moors and the Jews, but the world of acceptance that had permitted a church and a synagogue to stand side by side with the grand mosque. Does one world need to destroy another in order that it may flourish? Might they not coexist? She thought, one day, a coexistence might again be possible. But she knew blood would first be shed. She thought on the Insurgeants meeting set for that night.

Did the Moors lose their mosque and their place in Seville to neglect, or had they died fighting? She thought of Isabel's words, out on the terrace all those nights ago – about the fragility of liberty and progress, and how they would be in jeopardy if not fought for and protected. Isabel had said that Sevillanos' liberties were built on the shifting sands of good fortune because they had taken them for granted. Francisca did not understand at the time. Now, she knew what was at risk, and there seemed no option other than to join the Insurgeants' cause. She hoped they would not be too late.

She placed the brush down and, with her fingers, delicately applied the paint to the canvas, wanting to feel the texture and to see the strokes, not disguise the fact that this was a mere painting, a mere representation, and an approximation of love. This was no veneer.

As she applied the glaze to Isabel's fingers, she wondered what was to become of the few Jews and the Muslims remaining in Seville and of the others, like her, that offended King Ferdinand and Father Alberto's ideals. What was life, she thought, other than all the love that we have within ourselves, for one another? Was that not what Moses and Christ taught – and Rumi too? Was that not what Abraham himself knew and spoke of? It was what her father taught her also: that it was by deeds, and not by creed, that a life of worth was led. Perhaps, she thought, this was what Carlos, in his own way, had endeavoured to do, but fear had led him to make too many compromises.

It was Isabel's eyes that she attended to last, and she mixed colloidal silver, and applied a drop of mercury, so that her eyes sparkled with her radiant clarity of thought and spirit. There was a restless unease to the finished work, an evident attempt at reconciling the irreconcilable aspects of her soul and intellect. She was at once spiritual and sensual, full of joy and anguish. Her expression suggested she was about to say something. The viewer would ask themselves what words she was imparting. Might they perish before her, in seeking the answer?

When it was finished, Francisca felt it could not have been other than it was, and yet each stroke and application of pigment had been fought for.

CHAPTER THIRTY-FOUR

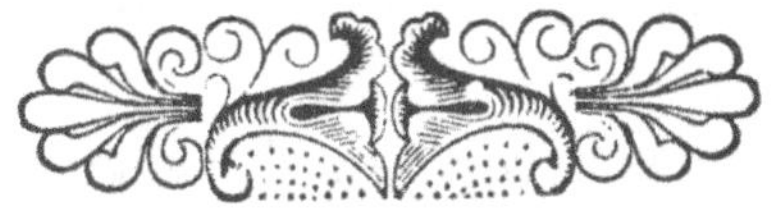

With a sense of unreality, Francisca and Bernardo pressed through the crowded hall of El Flamenco. A single candelabra suspended high above the stage illuminated the space. Even in the shadows, the crowd's excitement was palpable.

Francisca looked for Gabriela. She needed to pass on her suspicions about Marina. Marina's absence earlier that evening had fuelled Francisca's fears about her betrayal, that Marina might be connected to the Guardia Royale, absurd though the conjecture may have seemed. Francisca had searched the palacio for her. All her belongings were gone. None of the servants could tell her anything.

At a gasp from the crowd, she turned to the stage. The candelabra was lowered. The candlelight glowed over Isabel as she walked to the centre. She was like a visitation from the ancient past: dressed in a loose white robe, a crown of gold-dusted leaves adorning her head. Elaborate make-up had been applied around her sparkling eyes. Tonight (and, in Francisca's mind, forever more) she was Aphrodite.

With arms extended, Isabel surveyed her devotees. She spotted

Francisca, smiled and, just for a moment, their eyes locked. Francisca was in no doubt that this performance would be for her.

The audience erupted. The band members and three actors entered the stage, all dressed as ancient Greek slaves: Aphrodite's slaves. The band members took their positions, the actors surrounded Isabel and extended around her a silk cloth, sliced with star shapes.

For a spellbinding moment, there was complete silence. Expectation filled the hall.

The tambourine struck up a steady beat, the lute thrummed a harmony and a reedy shawm recorder wound melancholily above. Isabel's voice found its way through the line, dancing above and below in question and answer. Soon it found its own vanishing point where, for a time, it felt sure. Then, suddenly, her voice soared off, in an arc all of its own.

The song had a ritualistic and trance-like pulse. The actors danced around Isabel, revealing tantalising glimpses of her. Under Isabel's spell, the audience paced back and forth, in time with the music.

An uneasy feeling began coursing through Francisca: that this could be Isabel's last performance. She thought back, to how Isabel described performing as an imagining of death and then ahead, to what was planned for later in the evening. There would be no guarantees as to how it might end.

She tried to put her anxiety aside, and to be present and absorb the music. She caught Bernardo's eyes, and they smiled, sharing the moment.

Within the sounds and the silences, a space opened out within her. It was a space where she found her mother, Leonardo and Elizabeth, and she felt their aspiration to seek something higher than themselves. The feeling filled her up, and she yearned to follow them. This was what her life must be. She must follow that path.

Finally, the actors wrapped Isabel in the silk cloth and lifted her above their heads and spun her around. She continued singing, even as they carried her from the stage, and the song faded.

The audience erupted in applause before eventually dispersing. Bernardo took Francisca's hand and, gradually, the emotions that the performance had inspired dispersed too, as they turned their attention to what lay ahead. They pressed against the crowd and went up the stairs to Gabriela's apartment.

From Gabriela's entrance hall, there was already a small throng, talking excitedly. The parlour was dimly candlelit. Anticipation hung in the air. Something remarkable was about to happen.

When the parlour was full, Gabriela entered from the terrace. She stood formidably before them: tall, dressed in a long black velvet gown, her luxurious hair flowing freely.

As Gabriela held the gathering's attention, Francisca realised she had become part of a higher cause. There could be no going back. It was both frightening and thrilling.

With a gravity to her voice, Gabriela addressed the gathering.

'We know why we are here. The persecution of our friends and loved ones is no longer something we can passively observe.' There was a murmur of acknowledgement. She nodded and continued, 'Had fate dealt her hand differently, it could have been any one of us.'

A chill ran through Francisca at the truth of those words.

Gabriela paced the floor, her gaze fixed. 'In recent days, I have been asking myself whether providence will be on our side.' Dramatically, she looked into the eyes of those present and clarified her question, '*Can* providence be on our side? What we plan, after all, is treason.'

A murmur rushed through the room at the mention of the word, and Gabriela briefly acknowledged it. 'Yes, treason. Have no doubt as to the danger of what we are about to embark on. But, having reflected,' she continued with a lighter quality to her voice, 'I am unchanging in my resolve, because what this signifies goes beyond the law. It goes to the very core of who we are. Our friends have been incarcerated because of their courage to live unrepentantly, according to their creed, faith or nature. For them, to relinquish that part of themselves would be a nonsense – an insult to themselves and society – for the lie it would represent.'

Her voice rose with emotion as she declared, 'The King has not God's authority to demand the lie.'

The gathering roused in agreement, but Gabriela continued, her tone dropping. She spoke quickly. 'Our intelligence tells us that King Ferdinand, with full Papal authority, is on the cusp of launching another Inquisition. Seville is now under the watchful eye of the Vatican.'

Francisca froze at the mention of the word 'Inquisition', and at her uncle's denial of what was about to befall the city.

Gabriela continued, 'We are told, this time will be different. This time, Ferdinand will not sit in judgement of faith.' She tapped her right index finger to her temple and declared, 'This time, he will sit in judgement of the purity of our thought.'

The gathering gasped.

'Conversion will not be an option. That time has passed.'

A heavy silence filled the parlour, as the purport of Gabriela's words filtered into the hearts and minds of those gathered.

She continued, 'Yes, having reflected, I am unchanging in my resolve, although I am not ashamed to tell you I am afraid. But I draw strength from the fact that we are here together. We are each here freely, fighting for what we believe in, for a better life: for ourselves, for our friends and for all of Spain. Let there be no mistake: we will risk our lives for it if required.' She looked directly into the faces of her friends and colleagues. 'What is at stake tonight is friendship – that very delicate and cherished wonder – and of justice. Indeed, the very soul of Spain is at stake tonight. She is a glorious country, rich in history and diversity. But I hate what Ferdinand is doing to it, and to us. He is dividing us and making us afraid.

'I, like all of you, have aspired to a quiet life,' she continued. 'I have wanted to pursue the things *I* wanted to do, to enjoy the time God has granted to me. I have not sought out political vendettas, but the Insurgeants' cause has been thrust upon me, and, in the end, I have felt compelled to take it as my own. For, what choice is there? Do we cower in the face of injustice and let our friends suffer and die alone? Our souls perish each day that we stand by and permit this to continue. We cannot subjugate our reason to the King's perverse ideology.'

The gathering uttered murmurings of agreement.

'Each of us has been set a task tonight,' she said, adopting a practical tone. 'Great care has been taken to minimise the risks, both to those whom we are to liberate from the Castle of San Jorge, as well as to ourselves. And we are blessed that tonight is a new moon and there is a thick cloud covering. Darkness will be our ally.

'Once the prisoners are liberated from San Jorge, we will disperse and retreat to our assigned places, but our work will not be complete, for we must not discuss tonight ever again. Not with each other, not with another soul. Now, let us eat and drink and enjoy each other's company until the appointed hour. Leave here tonight knowing that providence *is* on our side. Let safety and courage be our companion.'

Gabriela raised her goblet, and all gathered shouted, 'To Freedom! To Spain!'

CHAPTER THIRTY-FIVE

By a small inlet of the river, Francisca and Isabel crouched into the base of a shallow cave formed by a craggy overhang of rocks. Like a distorted looking glass, the river reflected the mighty Castle of San Jorge, towering on the upper banks behind them.

It was a cramped space, and they tried to derive comfort from one another, the waters gently lapping at the shore, and Fiel, grazing quietly on tufts of grass at the mouth of the cave. But, as the moments passed, anxiety rose. They felt trapped inside the cave and had a keen sense that their security depended on events beyond their control.

Ángel skimmed the river's surface and glided towards the mouth of the cave, her wings outstretched like an angel sent to bid them courage.

'Do you remember the Rumi poem?' Isabel whispered.

Eyes closed, Francisca recited:

Who gave this soul to me?
The one who hooded my eyes
like a falcon's, who soon
will set me loose to hunt.

Isabel squeezed Francisca's hand. 'Ángel is a portent for good.'

Isabel had tried to dissuade Francisca from volunteering tonight, but she would not hear of it. Francisca's knowledge of the woods and Fiel's lightness of hoof would be invaluable, and, in any event, there was not a world in which she would abide Isabel risking danger without being by her side.

In turn, Bernardo had also insisted on taking a role. His allegiances had always been with the Insurgeants, and this was his chance to apply his skills for something he believed in.

The plan for Valentina's release had thus been finessed. Rather than Valentina being delivered to Gabriela's nearby waiting carriage – which would be slow-moving and difficult to conceal – she would, instead, be delivered to Francisca and Isabel, waiting in a secret cave by a small inlet below San Jorge.

En route to their position, Francisca and Isabel had taken care to not attract the suspicion of the guards on the Puente del Herra, and so had crossed separately. Isabel had walked on ahead, a shawl concealing her face. Francisca had held back and watched on from the shadows, aghast when the guards stopped Isabel and she was forced to reveal her face. It was a brief interrogation – but an interrogation, nevertheless. Isabel had her answers prepared. She was to visit an aunt, taken ill in Triana. They let her pass without pressing for more information.

With an appropriate elapsing of time, Francisca and Fiel emerged from the shadows and began their crossing. The guards, accustomed to seeing Francisca at this time of night, let her pass without interrogation, but she was under no illusions – they would have minuted the fact and time of her passing.

They had continued to their meeting point separately, each following the banks of the river close by the shadows of the cliff walls. The other Insurgeants had accomplished the river's crossing by boat. Bernardo had been tasked with navigating and lookout. His comrades had continued their journey to San Jorge on foot, under cover of darkness.

'Do you think Valentina knows what we have planned?' Francisca whispered.

'I do not know. Imagine, all those years, locked up, wondering if anyone remembers you or if your loved ones are still alive. I would have gone mad.'

'As would I,' Francisca said, glancing at the water.

'I worry for Gabriela,' Isabel muttered, almost to herself.

'Imagine her anxiety at this moment.'

'Yes of course. But will Valentina be the person Gabriela remembers her to be? Gabriela made El Flamenco into something of a shrine to their dreams. That is how she has survived.'

'Did they perform?'

'Yes. They had always wanted a place of their own. Gabriela made it happen, even though she stopped singing. The singer in her faded when Valentina was arrested, and Valentina's daughter taken from her.'

'All they have endured is beyond imagining.' Francisca asked, 'What happened to Valentina's daughter?'

'We are still not sure. We heard rumours that she was forced into servitude in some household of strategic importance. Perhaps worse. But, if the plan has gone as we hoped, she will be with Gabriela now, waiting for Valentina. Someone amongst the Insurgeants has known of her whereabouts all these years and kept it secret – for her own safety.'

A distant sound alerted them. They listened out and peered through a small crevice in the cave. A line of carriages slowly proceeded across the Puente del Herra. Francisca recognised the silhouette of the driver of the front carriage. Like the grim reaper, Father Alberto led the procession.

The carriages rolled stealthily on and, once lined up on the coach road, broke into a gallop and thundered towards San Jorge. Whips lashed the horses' backs. Soon, carriage doors flung open, and orders were barked out. There was a scuffle, followed by a dull thud.

Silence.

The new prisoners had arrived.

Inside the cave, anticipation rose within the two women. They had been told enough details about the escape plan to know that the Insurgeants would now make their attempt at breaking in, to take advantage of the inevitable chaos during the incarceration of the new prisoners. Neither Francisca nor Isabel knew precisely how the Insurgeants would execute the plan, but they presumed it required assistance from at least one of the Guardia Real.

The minutes that followed felt like days. Francisca had an urge to pace up and down, but she could not stand to her full height inside the cave, and it would have been reckless to step out from its shelter. She tried to still her shaking hands by clasping them together.

'Are you scared?' Francisca threw a glance at Isabel.

'I would be lying if I said I was not, but your presence, and focusing on the reasons we are here, helps.' Isabel also clasped her hands tightly between her knees, but Francisca saw they were shaking.

Soon, out from nowhere, they heard footsteps. Again, they peered through the crevice. Two men approached, one carrying a bundle wrapped in a blanket. They were nearer now, and Francisca and Isabel recognised the men from tonight's gathering at El Flamenco.

Francisca rose but Isabel caught her wrist.

'Francisca, I want you to know,' she whispered, 'that if, for whatever reason, we are separated tonight, I will wait for you.'

'Darling, be in no doubt that if the worst happens, I will wait for you too, but I do not plan on losing you. Not tonight or ever.'

They kissed briefly but fervently.

There was no time for more words.

They emerged from the cave and identified themselves to the men.

The man gently let the bundle down, and Francisca saw that it was a woman, dressed in rags, her head shaved. She gasped. It was the woman she had seen all those weeks ago, shackled to the back of the carriage. The woman was Valentina!

The other man passed Valentina a satchel and he whispered, 'Valentina, quickly, change into this.'

Francisca looked at him, querying the expenditure of time.

'We must do the small things we can, to enhance our chances. She must appear to be a civilian.'

Isabel sheltered Valentina with her shawl and helped her wash by the shore of the river and change into her clothes and tie her bonnet.

When she emerged, she stood tall, with a quiet dignity, and, in that moment, Francisca understood that Valentina's spirit had survived, and a wave of optimism washed over her.

Together, the three women mounted Fiel. Isabel took the reins and Francisca wrapped a shawl around Valentina's shoulders and held on to her fragile waist.

There was no time to lose. Every passing moment was a moment closer to Valentina's escape being discovered.

Isabel whispered down to the men, 'Is there any chance you were followed?'

'No. It went as planned.'

But, in their countenance, Francisca detected uncertainty.

'Now, go!' they commanded, prohibiting further discussion.

The men hurried away into the darkness and Fiel started on the path, keeping close to the cliff face, on the lower path by the river's edge. Soon, they had no choice but to take the path rising to the upper bank, beyond San Jorge. At the top of the rise, Isabel held Fiel back until she was sure the way was clear, and, on her signal, they crossed the exposed coach road, Fiel trotting at his silent clip.

They made it to the other side, seemingly unseen and breathed a little more easily. Never had they been more thankful for a dark, moonless night.

In forming the escape plan, the Insurgeants had reasoned that the Guardia Real would suppose the escapees would flee downriver, by boat or on land, to the coast – to Huelva or Cadiz. So, the Insurgeants planned their dispersion in opposite directions: Valentina into the woods by Triana, the others, south and southeast, to the villages beyond Seville.

Francisca glimpsed back at San Jorge, towering like an ogre over Seville. Horsemen circled menacingly, and the horses bucked and neighed in distress. Isabel signalled Fiel to quicken his gait. Francisca held Valentina close to her.

They navigated the crisscrossing narrow back streets of Triana's small ceramic workshops. Even with the stalls closed and streets deserted, the area felt purposefully industrial, in contrast to the decorative beauty of the city on the other side of the river. Fiel made barely a sound on the cobblestones and kept close to the side of the buildings' where the shadows were deepest. At a crossing, they turned and started down a seemingly endless lane, but the woods were at the end, and not far beyond they would find the path that would ultimately lead them to the clearing where they had agreed to rendezvous with Gabriela, and Valentina's daughter.

'May I ask where we are going?' Valentina asked, her voice raspy from lack of speech, but her diction perfectly clear.

Francisca and Isabel had been so focused on making haste that they had revealed nothing to Valentina of the plan.

'We are taking you to Gabriela and your daughter,' Francisca whispered. 'They are waiting in the woods. From there, they will take you in a carriage to a safe house, where you will rest until ready to continue.'

'Gabriela and my daughter are waiting?'

'Yes.'

Valentina's shoulders shook as the emotion took over her.

'We can only imagine what you have been through,' Francisca whispered. Her heart went out to her at what she had endured.

'I did not know if they were still alive. I had almost lost hope,' Valentina uttered.

'They are alive. They have been waiting for you, and you will be reunited,' Francisca assured her. The flame that had been kept alight in the woman's soul through all her suffering had been the hope of love itself enduring.

Finally, they reached the end of the lane, and Francisca surveyed the thick woods to locate the entrance. As her eyes adjusted to the endless trees before her, she recognised the two ancient horse chestnuts, signifying the path.

All three women sighed with relief as they entered the thick canopy. The most treacherous part of their mission was behind them. The woods were cool and teemed with nocturnal life. Owls hooted and insects buzzed. The cacophony itself was soothing and there was a kind of comfort in being amongst sentient beings that wished them no harm.

But as they pressed on, deeper into the woods, Francisca's senses became more acute. At every sound, she glanced back, imagining the Guardia Real in pursuit.

They carried on, eastward at each crossroad, and straight on at every fork, maintaining a constant but slow pace. With the darkness and narrowness of the path, speed was impossible.

At last, the atmosphere began to lift. The dense woods opened out into a clearing, marked by a circle of cypress trees, signifying they had reached their destination. Fiel stopped by the cover of an oak tree, surrounded by a copse. Silently, they watched, trying to find their bearings within the clearing. Francisca spotted a reflection, like light shining off metal, at the far side. She pointed so that Isabel could see what she saw. Isabel nodded and held Fiel back as Francisca dismounted to inspect on foot. Slowly, she stepped out from the shelter of the oak tree and furtively walked on. Suddenly, there was a snapping of twigs nearby. She froze and turned to see the source of the sound. Out from behind the shadows, a figure, like that of a slender deer, emerged.

Francisca gasped when she saw the deer was in fact a woman.

The woman extended her hands in a gesture of peace, and whispered, 'I am here, with Gabriela.' She revealed her face.

'Marina!'

'We have been waiting for you and Valentina – my mother. I am sorry, Francisca. I could never tell you.'

Francisca's mind was reeling.

Isabel, witnessing the exchange, dismounted and helped Valentina to do so also.

Marina and Valentina beheld one other, in disbelief. Valentina nodded and smiled, tears streaked her face, and they embraced. The pain of all the years of separation already began to heal. Francisca choked back tears at the sight.

Isabel cleared her throat and interjected, 'I am sorry, but we must make haste.'

Valentina turned to Francisca and said, 'I knew your mother.' She put her hand to her heart and said, 'Please, thank her for me.'

Some of Francisca's many questions were finally being answered.

Marina took Valentina's hand and led the way to the carriage.

Gabriela rushed out to greet them, arms extended. Her breath caught as she embraced Valentina. The years of suffering were over.

Francisca said, 'Quickly now.'

But Marina took Francisca aside and confessed, 'Francisca, you need to know – I had no choice but to inform on you and Archbishop Carlos to Father Alberto. I am sorry.'

'Whatever you may have done, there is nothing to forgive. You had no choice.' It was almost a relief to know the truth, however dreadful it was. 'But Marina – tell me what you know of my mother and father's fate. I need to know.'

Marina looked about nervously and said, 'The attack was meant against your father. Your mother wasn't meant to be there, but, as it happened, their plans changed at the last moment. I told

Father Alberto, but he said it was too late; the arrangements had been made.'

'Father Alberto? Why?' Francisca's heart raced with rage and revenge.

'Surely you knew. Your uncle was to be made archbishop, but your father refused to convert. It was the time of the Purge. Father Alberto had to fix it.'

Francisca felt she already knew this part of the story. What she needed to know was the part her uncle had played. 'Did Uncle Carlos know what Father Alberto was planning?'

'I do not know.'

'You must know!' she cried desperately.

Her hope of ever finding out Uncle Carlos's role in the crime faded as Marina shook her head. 'But I don't know.'

Marina climbed up the carriage steps to take her place as driver. 'I wish you well. We may never see one another again.'

Isabel turned to Gabriela. Her bottom lip was trembling.

'I will visit you,' Isabel promised.

Valentina and Gabriela stepped into the small carriage, and they waved farewell. Tears flowed.

But the night's task was far from over.

Quickly, Francisca and Isabel mounted Fiel, Francisca holding Isabel close to her. The path widened out, and Fiel trotted on at a steady pace.

Francisca relayed Marina's story to Isabel.

'You may never find out what Carlos knows,' Isabel said darkly.

'Oh, but I will.'

'Francisca, you must be careful.'

'I am beyond that now.'

Approaching the wood's edge where it merged into the olive groves, Fiel, unbidden, retreated and settled amongst a dense covering of bushes concealing them from the path. With deep foreboding, Francisca and Isabel sensed they must remain completely silent. They hardly dared breathe, even as their hearts raced.

Soon, there was a crescendo of a rumbling vibration. It grew louder and louder, like thunder, and then a roar unleashed, and it was all that Francisca and Isabel could do to stay still and silent behind the covering. Their hearts beat furiously with anticipation.

One by one, a dozen horsemen of the Guardia Real charged into the woods, galloping recklessly. Heat emanated from the horses' torsos. The horses bared their white teeth, their coats glistened with perspiration. The soldiers' fixed faces, like masks, were terrifying.

Francisca and Isabel's brief joy at reuniting Valentina with Gabriela and Marina vanished. They could only hope and pray that they had a sufficient lead and had made great haste.

Francisca said, 'There is nothing we can do. We cannot get ahead of them.'

'Francisca, I cannot bear it. After everything,' Isabel whispered, emotion choking her words.

There was nothing to be said.

They waited and looked back helplessly at the horsemen, knowing, even as they did so, that it was a futile expenditure of time and energy.

For Francisca and Isabel, it was now a question of their own survival, and they had no choice but to continue. Soon, they emerged from the woods and onto the coach road, which they crossed quickly and took the path down to the banks of the river. By the river's edge, they dismounted and looked for the spot where it had been agreed that Bernardo would wait. It would be risking too much for Isabel to re-cross the Puente del Herra. By now, the guards would be alert to the prison escape and would interrogate everyone, perhaps even immediately arrest them.

Finally, they saw a signal through some reeds, and they rushed over.

Bernardo's face was flushed with excitement. He was in complete command, and he beckoned them to him.

Francisca and Bernardo helped Isabel into the tiny boat, but

Francisca's hands felt like stone. A sudden terror that she may never see Isabel again took hold of her. She crouched down and looked into her eyes, willing herself to capture her image forever, to ensure all the details would be accessible, forever fresh in her mind. But a fevered panic rose within her, that this moment was somehow already a memory.

A forced frozen smile formed on Isabel's face, and she said uncertainly, 'Francisca, I will see you in the morning, remember?'

Francisca was unconvinced. She looked from Bernardo to Isabel, certain that something was being concealed from her, and she remembered Isabel's inexplicable words in the cave. She said, 'I want to come with you now.'

'But Fiel...'

'Then let's stay here tonight. It is not too cold,' Francisca implored, gesturing to the banks of the river. Even as she did so, she saw the impossibility of it.

Isabel touched Francisca's lips and said, 'We had reasons, good rational reasons, for planning it like this.' She repeated the plan, as if the repetition would assure its success. 'As soon as we get to the other side, Bernardo and I will re-enter the city walls at the unguarded section, and we will go straight home. And you, my darling, will re-cross the bridge – just like any other night. In the morning, I will see you at the cathedral – just like any other morning. Now, go. Let safety be your companion.'

Isabel took Francisca's hand and kissed it tenderly. She lifted her eyes to Francisca, and with emotion catching her voice, commanded, 'Now go!'

She released Isabel's hands and stood back, watching the tiny boat silently drift out and melt into the river's silvery mist until, finally, it disappeared from view.

Francisca remounted Fiel and they galloped down the coach road. When the port came into view, she did not give significance to a ship where sailors busily readied her for launch and one sailor looked anxiously upstream as if waiting for something – or someone.

Francisca steeled her nerves for the crossing on the Puente del Herra, trying to imagine it was just another night's ride.

She was calm when the guards questioned her. She had rehearsed her responses a dozen times.

No, I have seen nothing. No, I noticed nothing unusual. Yes, I was in the woods, but mainly on the coach road. Yes, I am going straight home now.

Either they believed her or not. They knew where to find her. They knew who she was.

CHAPTER THIRTY-SIX

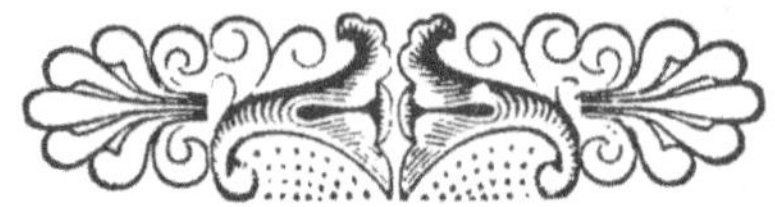

Francisca urged Fiel homewards. The interrogation had shone a light on the danger she and her colleagues – specifically Isabel – faced. The night's events played out over and over in distorted sequences, unsettling her equilibrium. Somewhere in the back of her mind, she acknowledged that, at the very moment she needed strength, she was afraid and filled with self-doubt.

She reached for Gabriela's words. *At risk is friendship and justice... the very soul of Spain...* But her words – that had rung so true and had so encouraged her – held no comfort now. She felt utterly alone.

No matter how fast she urged Fiel on, she could not escape her anxiety, and the source of her primary concern soon emerged. The Guardia Real would piece together her movements and they would know that it would have been impossible to be riding out tonight without witnessing any of the evening's dramas. They would conclude that she had lied to the guards on the Puente del Herra, and would draw the only logical conclusion – that she was one of the Insurgeants.

She grappled with the hope of weaving a coherent alibi that

would acquit her while implicating no one else. If only she could slow down her thoughts.

With each step closer to the palacio, something else became clear: something she had not foreseen. She had betrayed Uncle Carlos, and as a result, the palacio could no longer be her home, but she had nowhere else to go; not yet. She needed time to think and plan where and how she could take her loved ones – her mother, Bernardo, and Isabel – with her to make a new home elsewhere. They could form a life together as a family. Her mind expanded in hope.

Fiel cantered on through the darkness. Thick clouds smothered the stars. The city had a sense of abandonment. There were no revellers. No street flares lit the way. No light emerged from the town houses indicating life inside.

Madly, to quell her fear, she called out to the night, 'Tell me!!!'

Then, suddenly, the focus of her anxiety shifted from herself, and she thought of the reunion of Valentina with Gabriela and Marina, and how the joy had been crushed with the Guardia Real thundering in pursuit. Her thoughts turned to Isabel. Imprinted on her mind was Isabel's face, frozen in a forced smile, as the tiny boat drifted into the river's mist.

Like a missed stitch, she perceived another flaw in their execution of the plan. The Puente del Herra guards would have noted Isabel's passage out to Triana and, with what had transpired, would undoubtedly audit the book in the morning and find that she made no return passage. They would trace her movements. They would find her. She must warn Isabel. Isabel must leave Seville.

She passed through the palacio's courtyard as quietly as she could, walked up the atrium staircase, careful to make not a sound. At the top of the staircase, she listened out. All was quiet within the household.

Then, the silence was shattered. A crystal-clear sound chimed out. For a moment, she was disorientated by a sense of déjà vu – could her mind be revisiting the traumatic events of just a few nights ago? In her heightened state of stress, could her mind be playing it all out again?

But with a sickening feeling in the pit of her stomach, she knew this to be real, and she rushed across the hallway and flung open the door to her mother's bedchamber. There before her was the evidence: glistening splinters of glass littered the tiled floor. Amongst them was a stone, wrapped in parchment. Nausea rose in her throat as she took the stone and brushed pieces of glass off the parchment, bracing herself for the new message. On it was a crude rendering of two hyenas mating. She knew it was a derogatory reference to the homosexual act.

She ran to the terrace windows, pulled back the curtains and saw a man racing through the forecourt. Resisting the impulse to leap over the terrace, she turned to see her mother, bolt upright in bed, her eyes wide with terror.

Francisca hurried to her side. 'He is gone, Mama. No one can hurt you now. I'm here, we are all here.'

'What happened?' Bernardo appeared in the doorway, flush-faced, lantern in hand. He scanned the bedchamber, his eyes widening when he saw the broken glass.

'Thank God you are here, Bernardo.'

She had assumed she would arrive home before him, but she was too relieved to see him to give it further thought.

He discerned the question in her eyes and whispered, 'The tide was in our favour.'

'Do not leave Mama's side until I return.'

'Should I not come with you?'

'No. Stay with her, please. Comfort her.'

She raced down the atrium stairs and, within seconds, emerged onto the lane. This time, without hesitation, she ran towards the cathedral square. In the distance she saw the tall, hooded figure. Unmistakably, it was the same man whom she had chased without success on the previous such occasion.

Fear and determination drove her on, and her heart pounded.

The way was clear. Not another soul was in sight, but she soon heard someone in pursuit. Who could possibly be following her? She wished she had taken the rock with her. She was defenceless with no weapon. She looked back.

It was Uncle Carlos, his purple robes flying out behind him. Relief washed over her and she willed herself to run faster.

The tall, hooded figure disappeared into the cathedral's shadows. She guessed he had entered through the mighty Prince's Doors, and she followed.

Inside the cathedral, her eyes gradually adjusted to the soft light of the flares illuminating the crucifix in the Main Chapel. The hooded figure was nowhere to be seen but Uncle Carlos had now caught up to her. He pressed her hand.

A door clicked shut and its sound echoed out faintly.

The minaret, Francisca thought. Whoever the perpetrator was, he must have a key. Either he had been given it or he had stolen it. Uncle Carlos searched for his keys from the pocket in his robe, and he nodded to her. His eyes hardened as he gestured to her to remove one of the flares lighting the crucifix.

'Are you sure? The crucifix—?'

'Yes. The minaret is too dark, and we need speed.'

With flare in hand, they wound their way through the stone columns. At the Nave del Evangelio, the paintings stood about uncurated on easels, like stone heads in a graveyard. She gasped at the sight of Mary with Christ Child. Mary's mouth gaped open in a ghastly sneer. The painting had been slashed beyond repair. Francisca felt the injury inflicted on herself.

Uncle Carlos saw it too and he hissed, 'We will get him.'

Fresh rage coursed through her, and they ran at speed towards the minaret. She directed the light of the flare to the lock to help Uncle Carlos insert the key. Once inside, they listened out for footsteps. Gathering their breath for the long ascent, they started out on the ramp at a brisk jog.

'He cannot escape,' Uncle Carlos muttered.

Nevertheless, they kept up their pace. Francisca kept slightly ahead, lighting the way with the flare. At the halfway point, a sound from below dimly echoed out, and Uncle Carlos gestured to Francisca to wait and listen, and, at that moment, the metallic sound of the minaret door below slamming shut echoed out. Confused, they waited and listened, and soon, they heard the unmistakable clip-clop of a horse's hooves.

'Father Alberto with his pony,' Uncle Carlos whispered his surmise.

They continued, as fast as they could. At the top of the ramp, Francisca saw Uncle Carlos's fearlessness. On a nod and a sharp intake of breath, they entered through the arch of the viewing platform. Stealthily, Uncle Carlos took the lead. Francisca took the opposite direction. In only a matter of moments, they met at the halfway point, exchanging questioning glances.

They had encountered no one.

Francisca looked up to the sky of an impenetrable charcoal. The air was empty and lifeless. All was silent.

Then Francisca saw it: a glint of metal on the balustrade railing. With her free hand, she traced the metal's outline. It was a hook, secured to the balustrade. Attached to it, stretched taut, was a rope.

She hitched up her skirt and gestured to Uncle Carlos to take the flare but he held her back and shook his head and cautioned, 'You are not climbing over, Francisca.'

In that moment, the metal hook disengaged, flew, swivelled, and tumbled down. They leaned over and saw the tall, hooded figure, gathering his rope and hook and running with the grace of an acrobat across the metal-domed rooftops of the cathedral far below.

Almost simultaneously, the sound of horse's hooves was upon them and they turned to see Father Alberto. He was dressed in a black robe and his hair was tied back in a black bow. In the messianic way he smiled and raised his hand to an adoring congregation that did not exist, Francisca surmised that he had lost his mind.

As he dismounted his pony, he caught his foot in the stirrup and stumbled awkwardly to the ground. He reached up and took his sticks from the bridle, hoisted himself upright and shuffled to the balustrades. Together, spellbound, the three of them watched the cloaked figure disappear into the shadows.

Father Alberto chuckled and said, 'I wanted to know what all the fuss was about.'

Rage boiled over from within Francisca. She sliced the flare through the air, so that it illuminated Father Alberto's mad eyes and she said, 'Do not pretend you do not know what has been happening, Father Alberto. You have engineered it.'

'Our little friend has disappeared,' Father Alberto observed, unperturbed.

Francisca remembered the parchment in her pocket, and she thrust it in Father Alberto's face as proof, but Uncle Carlos intercepted it and he put it to the light of the flare. Lines wrinkled his forehead.

'You disgust me,' Francisca said, lunging at Father Alberto.

He stepped back, his face betraying shock but, almost instantly, he composed himself.

'Francisca, it is me that you have to *thank*. I did not know how else to warn you.' He squinted at her in the light. 'You need to be more careful. If it was not for me, you might have been taken to San Jorge tonight. You should know, the Guardia Real caught up with Marina and have dealt with her. They have not yet found her companions, but they will. Their methods are thorough.'

'Ohhhh!' Francisca cried in pain at the cruelty of Marina's freedom being taken from her just as she had reclaimed it. 'Just when she had found happiness.'

'What is this about?' Carlos demanded.

'Please tell us, Father Alberto.' She caught herself in time to withhold all that she knew, realising the less she said, the better.

'Someone had to take control.' Father Alberto said, regarding Carlos meaningfully.

Francisca directed the flare towards her uncle's face. He squinted into the naked light, and she saw his confusion.

Her emotions surged and she unleashed her questions, 'Did you know about the attack on Mama and Papa? What did you know? What did you do? Uncle Carlos, please, I must know. That imposter of a priest,' she said, gesturing to Father Alberto, 'organised it. He made it all happen, but I need to know what you knew and what part you played.'

Through his fingers shielding the glare of the flare from his eyes, Uncle Carlos asked again, 'What is this?'

He turned to Father Alberto for help.

Father Alberto shuffled towards him and the sky opened out from behind the clouds.

'Come on, Carlos.' Father Alberto said jocularly. As if teaching a new concept to a young child, he explained, 'You were to become archbishop. I had supported you in the face of everyone's counsel against it. We could not have Jews in your family. I told Joshua the tide had turned, that renouncing was nothing – not compared to everything else he had to lose.'

Father Alberto's focus shifted beyond Carlos, to all those years ago. A lifetime ago. Francisca tightened her grip on the flare. She was ready for anything.

Father Alberto's voice droned on, 'But Joshua would not *listen.* I told him he would lose Raquel and Francisca – that I would see to it that they would stay here, with you.' Father Alberto shook his head. 'He thought the Inquisition was not interested in people like him – he said he was just an ordinary man. I tried to tell him that he was *precisely* the kind of man the Inquisition was interested in, and that your rise within the Church made him especially vulnerable.' He clenched his jaw in disgust. 'He was arrogant.'

He shuffled towards Carlos, peered into his eyes and grinned wickedly as he elaborated, 'It required barely a whisper,' he said, and he drew his index finger across his neck.

At the suggestion of her father's decapitation, Francisca retched. Somehow, she had always known her father had met his death by an executioner's axe. Her mother had witnessed it and it had crushed her spirit.

Barely recovered, she shrieked at him, 'You stole my family! You robbed me of my childhood!'

Father Alberto ignored her outburst and continued explaining to Carlos, 'I did it for you, Carlos. For us. For our dreams. Do not tell me it was not worth it. Do not tell me you did not want it too.'

Francisca searched for the truth in Uncle Carlos's eyes. Like a coiled spring, Uncle Carlos leapt up, towering over Father Alberto. She had never seen him use his superior strength against anyone, and she was afraid.

'You... evil. It was you.'

Uncle Carlos looked to the sky for help and sank to his knees in agony. He cried out, 'But Raquel – why Raquel?'

Father Alberto shrugged as if it was inconsequential. 'Raquel was an unforeseen casualty.'

Something in Uncle Carlos unhinged and he sprang to his feet again. His jaw set and he lunged at Father Alberto. He clutched his neck, lifted him off his feet, and eyed him. Father Alberto lashed out with his stick and struck Carlos by his left eye. Carlos turned his head, wincing with the pain.

Francisca rushed to Uncle Carlos's aid and pushed Father Alberto away.

It happened so quickly.

Father Alberto overbalanced and tipped over the balustrades. Francisca reached out for his hand. Time seemed to lose a beat. It was too late.

Uncle Carlos and Francisca leaned over and helplessly watched as he tumbled and hit the ground with a thud.

'My God,' Francisca muttered. They ran down the ramp, the pony following.

As they emerged through the Door of Concepcion, all the horror of Father Alberto's shattered body lay before them. His body was splayed out by the fountain's ledge. His ribs protruded, his broken jaw gaped open, and his eyes bulged.

As gently as if Father Alberto were a bird fallen from its nest, Uncle Carlos stroked his head and closed his eyelids. His hands shook as he unclasped his own robe and covered Father Alberto's corpse.

A bird squawked. Ángel swooped by.

Uncle Carlos fell to his knees and, in a quavering voice, prayed:

Oh Lord, deliver Father Alberto's soul
from evil
Grant him eternal rest
In your loving mercy.

His voice faded and he looked to the sky in silent prayer.

'Uncle, look.' Francisca cried, as the ground shuddered and shifted.

From deep below the fountain's spring came a soft, long exhale. A short silence was followed by a soft rumbling which rose to a mighty roar. The slumbering dragon had finally awoken, and, as the fountain burst open and overflowed, it was as if she had finally purged herself of the damaged souls that had inhabited her.

Uncle Carlos lifted Father Alberto's body from the fountain and together they rushed into the cathedral. Tenderly, he lay him down on the altar before the crucifix. Francisca in turn replaced the flare to its hold, and she thought of the terror Father Alberto wreaked and felt no pity nor sorrow at his death. 'You loved him,' she said as she pressed Uncle Carlos's shoulder.

They linked arms and Francisca felt sure in the knowledge that Uncle Carlos was, and always had been, the one true and beloved uncle. She had been right to love him. Through all the pain and tragedy, he had returned to her. Yet she knew it was his weakness that allowed Father Alberto to commit his atrocities. Her family had needed someone strong to protect them. Uncle Carlos could have been that man, but he was soft. The power vacuum had to be filled, and Father Alberto filled it. Yet she could not find it in herself to blame him. He was a gentle man. His true weakness had been in seeking the best in people, and believing in their goodness, and she forgave him, for he could not help his nature.

In silence, they went home.

Francisca stiffened at the sight of guards filing in from the lanes and she kept close to Uncle Carlos, her gaze lowered.

CHAPTER THIRTY-SEVEN

The shadows cast by the flares on the atrium landing flickered on the walls like dancing demons, and a dark foreboding began to descend on Francisca as she and Uncle Carlos approached the door to her mother's bedchamber. Francisca's legs began to give way, and she held on to the wall.

Uncle Carlos turned and asked tenderly, 'What's troubling you, Francisca?'

'I'm afraid. What if Mama has been shaken by the intruder? She may not...' Francisca could not utter the dreadful words.

'I promise, you need not worry,' Uncle Carlos said with conviction. 'I'll join you shortly. In the meantime, go quickly and open the terrace doors to your mother's bedchamber. The room needs to be open to the elements.'

As Francisca entered her mother's bedchamber, she required all her concentration to put one foot in front of the other and she barely managed a glance at her mother, who was sleeping, or Bernardo, who was watching over her from the red velvet chair. She was grateful to have an instruction to comply with and went directly to the curtains and flung them wide open. She did the same with the terrace doors and fresh air rushed in, as though the room had been hungry for it.

Bernardo came to her and whispered, 'What happened?'

'The intruder escaped but Father Alberto is dead.'

'My God,' Bernardo said, automatically crossing himself.

'He fell from the minaret. It was horrible,' Francisca said, unable to convey any sorrow.

Bernardo's jaw slackened as he said slowly, as if piecing together a jigsaw, 'But that is uncanny. We felt the earth shudder. And, Francisca, your mother had a small seizure.'

Francisca put her hands to her mouth to silence her gasp.

'But as you can see,' Bernardo quickly added, 'she is resting peacefully now.'

No sooner did Francisca go to her mother's side than the energy in the bedchamber changed and became charged; her mother woke and became alert.

Francisca turned and saw the reason. It was Uncle Carlos. From the distant look in his eyes, it seemed he was in a trance. He wore plain white robes of uncertain priestly order, and Francisca noticed that he was barefoot. He proceeded throughout the room, quietly incanting, and swinging a chain attached to an ancient thurible that smoked with the raw scents of sage, basil, and sandalwood. The words of his incantation were foreign to Francisca, but they must have meant something to her mother, as she gripped Francisca's hand tightly, surprising Francisca, for she had never evinced such strength.

When every crevice became saturated with the scent of the herbs, and the room filled with Uncle Carlos's low chant, his voice suddenly rose to a booming crescendo.

'*Vade retro Santana!*' he commanded.

Her mother's entire body contorted in violent spasms and Bernardo and Francisca used all their might to restrain her.

When she became calmer, Uncle Carlos came to his sister and towered over her. He placed his hands on her forehead and instructed, 'Raquel, be released from Father Alberto's curse, for he is dead, and with him all powers he invoked!'

Sweat poured forth from her mother's face and she let out a scream.

Unperturbed, Uncle Carlos turned and extended his arms skyward and beat the air, and called out, 'Father Alberto, go from whence you came and do not return. You are not wanted here!'

Time extended and compressed. The silence that came after the rite was deafening but soon everything became still, and Francisca's mother fell back into a deep sleep.

When Uncle Carlos left, Francisca knew to follow him.

Downstairs in the atrium, Francisca and Bernardo gathered around Uncle Carlos and he explained, 'The curse has lifted and now your mother must rest. Tomorrow, her spirit will be restored. Then her physical recovery must begin in earnest. Her muscles will need training. She will need our help. Now, I suggest we all get some rest.' Uncle Carlos returned to his study, leaving Francisca no less than awed by him and at what she had witnessed. For the first time she understood Uncle Carlos truly to be the high priest that others had always presumed him to be.

The low chanting from the monks in the monastery wafted on the gentle air. It was already time for lauds and the morning's light shone through the atrium, marking the dawn of a glorious new day.

CHAPTER THIRTY-EIGHT

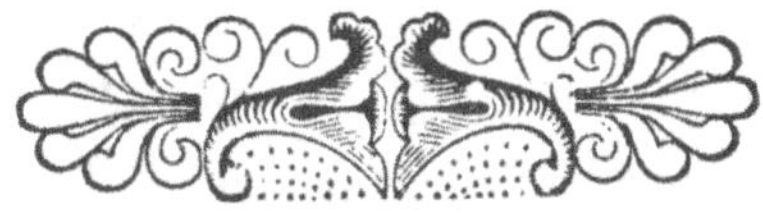

Francisca did not have the luxury of sleep. Quickly, she changed and set off through the cathedral grounds for her rendezvous with Isabel. In the soft morning light, the cathedral's limestone glittered like silver. Inside, the lead-light windows drew in all the light.

Francisca hurried to the Nave del Evangelio, careful to avoid the altar, where she presumed Father Alberto's shattered body still lay. She soon lost count of the number of turns of the nave she completed. Her anxiety grew by the minute as she waited for Isabel. Her brow sweated as she began thinking the worst and, by mid-morning, she knew in the pit of her stomach that Isabel was not coming.

Dark thoughts loomed at what might have befallen her. Perhaps the Guardia Real had broken into her apartment or interrogated her en route to the cathedral. Perhaps she was in custody, alone and frightened. Francisca needed air. Just as she began to plan her search, she heard a disturbance.

'Francisca,' Bernardo called in a whisper.

In the manner of his approach, Francisca sensed all was not well, and she ran to him.

'Let us sit together,' he said.

They huddled into a nearby pew and checked to ensure they were quite alone. In the bright light, Bernardo's eyes were as clear as indigo.

'Bernardo, what is it?' Francisca insisted. 'Reveal all.'

He nodded solemnly and she sensed his effort in ordering his thoughts.

'Francisca, you must be very brave. Please, listen to all that I have to say before drawing any conclusions.' He took a breath. 'Shortly after you left this morning, Cardinal De Praed met with Carlos,' he whispered. 'I listened to their conference. The city is under lockdown. By now, each exit point is likely to be under the Guardia Real's surveillance. No one can enter – or leave.'

Francisca's mind was awhirl as she tried to process the sinister implications of the information. 'We did not anticipate this,' she murmured.

'Your uncle told me to come and find you and take you home.'

'Is that why you are here? I will not return home until I find Isabel.'

'Francisca, please, listen to me.'

He had a look of more difficult news to convey, and she could hardly bear the anticipation.

'Francisca, Cardinal De Praed told Carlos he has evidence of your involvement in the Insurgeants' uprising.'

Her stomach turned. 'This cannot be happening!' she said, seizing on to the pew and swallowing the bile rising in her throat.

Bernardo continued, relentlessly. 'They seem ignorant of my involvement, so at least one of us is not under suspicion. Uncle Carlos pleaded with Cardinal De Praed for your clemency. He negotiated to keep you under house arrest in the palacio until your marriage.'

'Dios mío,' Francisca said, holding her head in her hands. 'Just when I thought things could not get any worse,' she muttered.

'Uncle Carlos committed to Cardinal De Praed that your marriage will take place the day before el Día de Todos los Santos.'

'My life will be over,' she said, her throat constricting and the blood draining from her body.

Bernardo lifted his index finger – he had more to tell her, and he lowered his voice upon seeing shadows shifting at the other end of the nave.

'Francisca, you need to be very brave. Believe me when I tell you, all will yet be well, but there is something else. Isabel asked me to give you this.' He handed Francisca *Occurrences with Light* and a sealed letter.

The seal was impressed with Isabel's initials, *IdF*. On the front of the envelope was Francisca's name, written in a flourish of turquoise ink. Francisca had never seen Isabel's handwriting. It was beautiful and intimate.

With trembling hands, she took the letter. It bore Isabel's musk perfume. She broke the seal and read:

My Darling,

Alas, everything has changed. Difficult times are upon us: as we foresaw, Spain is no longer safe, and I must leave. Put your trust in Bernardo alone.

Your love will give me the courage needed in the time ahead. Let my love do the same for you. Keep Rumi's book until we meet again.

Your loving,
Isabel

The words were clear but Francisca could not absorb their purport. Isabel had abandoned her. She felt numb with pain.

With barely a shift of her hand, she passed the letter to Bernardo.

His brow quivered as he read the letter.

'Isabel must have learned of the lockdown before we did,' he said, 'and so she did the only thing she could have done in the circumstances: she escaped. She would have been arrested had she stayed.'

Francisca thought back to Isabel's cryptic last words uttered in the cave and realised she knew even then that she would escape.

'What if she was arrested in her attempt?' she asked in a panic.

'I am certain she has succeeded.'

'Bernardo, what am I to do?'

'Francisca, listen to me,' he said again. 'We will find out where she is, but let me assure you, Isabel is safe. She would have planned it. I have never met anyone as resourceful and clever as she is.'

Francisca recognised the truth in Bernardo's words, and she reread the letter for insights. 'One thing, at least, seems clear. She has left Seville and is intent on leaving Spain.'

Bernardo took her hands. 'What you need to focus on now is that she is safe. The details will emerge in the fullness of time. We have sources.'

'I must find her, before it is too late,' she said, but even as she said it, she knew it was impossible. Even if she could escape, she could not leave her mother. She felt the bittersweetness of it.

With wide eyes, Bernardo replied calmly, 'It is too late for that. Seville is now a prison and Spain is no longer the land we once knew and loved. Who knows how long it will be before the tide changes?'

She clasped her hands to her head in frustrated desperation.

Bernardo gently took her hands and looked her in the eye. 'I have a plan. All will yet be well.'

CHAPTER THIRTY-NINE

The candle on Francisca's study desk flickered in the cool breeze. She sealed the letter she had written for her mother and Uncle Carlos and placed it on the stand of her bureau.

Not much time remained.

Her hands were steady, and she took the cook's knife, made a neat cut in one of her bed sheets, tore some thin strips, and bound them around her breasts as tightly as she could bear. Watching in the looking glass, she carefully applied the knife to her hair and cut it into the shoulder-length fashion that young men wore. She took her purse and the leather pouch containing the map, each strung with fine leather, and hung them around her neck. She buttoned up the high-necked shirt that had belonged to her father and put on his Guardia Real uniform, coat and boots. The costume hung heavily on her body.

She was almost ready.

The two weeks since Bernardo revealed his plan had felt like a dream. Uncle Carlos ensured she did not leave the palacio, but she felt strangely detached from the reality of her imprisonment.

The evenings she passed with Bernardo, dutifully completing the tasks he had set for her, and yet, in her mind, she was simply going through the motions, for she had no belief in his plan. It seemed an impossibility, and the consequences too grave for her to accept responsibility for. She would not be capable of acting upon any of it.

Every moment of every day she passed with her mother, and in no time at all, it was almost as she had always imagined. In the beginning, the family regarded each step of her mother's progress as pioneering and miraculous. Her mother's first utterance of Francisca's name brought floods of happy tears. Their first conversation, hug, meal at the table, engagement with nature in the garden. Each one brought its own delight and was celebrated over and over.

With almost every passing hour, her mother strengthened, and their joy not so much erased the pain of the lost years as diminished them into near insignificance. It was as though time had unwound, and the years of decay had been reversed. In her mother, Francisca saw the ideal of her childhood.

'I will never abandon you, ever again, Francisca. I promise. Please, forgive me.'

'Mama. There is nothing to forgive,' she cried, overcome.

Uncle Carlos too was at his happiest. On the first day, when his sister declared that she wanted to stride the hills and swim in the river, his eyes were moist with emotion. 'Raquel, we must be patient. It may take some time to regain your vigour.' But he laughed too, for nothing could contain his joy.

In Francisca's few quiet moments, she caught herself wondering what might become of her. As the days passed, and her marriage date approached, her resistance began to wear, and she began to think she might submit to fate. Her initial reluctance to show her mother the fresco, for fear of it triggering a trauma, proved misplaced. No mixed feelings were provoked in her mother, and in a burst of productivity, Francisca completed it as her mother watched on from the fountain ledge. Francisca no longer felt a need to know its inner meaning, and once it was finished and the scaffolding dismantled, she saw that it was as she had hoped: her father was in the midst of taking her mother's hand. That was all she needed to know.

Early on the morning that the scaffolding was to be dismantled, and the household was still asleep, Francisca's mother instructed her to closely examine the halo of the mysterious figure at the mountaintop and bring forth what it held.

For the last time, Francisca clambered up the ladders to the top level and walked along the plank to the mysterious figure. Her fingers worked at the plaster which had set well. It was hard and cool. She felt the finely cut edges. It was then that she remembered what she had noticed all those weeks ago when Father Alberto interrupted her work and warned her to discontinue. The area around the halo was different to the rest. She explored it carefully until she found a concealed wooden panel. She prised it open and, inside, found a hessian bag.

Francisca looked down at her mother, who nodded encouragement. Inside the bag was a mound of gold coins: more than she had seen in her life. The bag was heavy and it was with difficulty that she lifted it out. Cradling it in her hands, she slowly descended the ladders and brought it to her mother.

'Your father and I wanted somewhere safe to hide it.' She beamed a smile. 'It is for you,' she whispered, pressing the hessian bag back into Francisca's hands.

'Why, Mama?' Francisca said, feeling the weight of gold coins.

'You shall need it if you are to be free,' her mother said meaningfully, and in her expression, as she pressed the bag into her hands, Francisca sensed her mother's prescience, and that she was giving her blessing and instruction. 'Live the life you dare dream, Francisca. In time, I hope to join you, wherever you may be.'

She had never seen her mother's eyes so intense, and then Francisca knew. Not only was Bernardo's plan a possibility. It was a certainty.

From then on, she set herself in earnest to Bernardo's tasks, with a heavy heart but no misgivings.

She and Bernardo sewed the gold coins into the fabric of the coat she was to wear, stuffed some into the pockets and some into her purse. She could not imagine ever needing so much money, but Bernardo was practical and told her that she could not know how long she might be without means to provide for herself. As for the coins remaining, Francisca instructed Bernardo to share them with her mother.

Bernardo used some of the coins to buy Francisca's passage. Its disembarkation date was finely timed – the eve of Francisca's marriage. Bernardo's contact had told him the ship had a single passenger berth – small, but with the luxuries of privacy, a port hole, and a full-length hammock cot strung between two poles. Bernardo procured the berth for her, calling on favours he feared he no longer had. There was room for Fiel in the hull.

She regarded herself in the looking glass and, though her father's military uniform hung heavily, the fit was passable. Night had fallen. She looked outside. Bernardo was at his post, by the stables. He signalled to her.

The time had finally come.

Quickly, she gathered together a change of clothes and a pair of soft boots, some drawing paper, and charcoal, along with her tobacco case, and packed them in a small linen bag that she could carry over her shoulder. She slid *Occurrences with Light* and the letter *explaining some things* – that Bernardo had written and told her to open only upon reaching Elizabeth's – into a pocket of her coat.

With a strange sense of calm, she climbed onto the window ledge, dangled her legs over the edge, and reached for the drain-pipe. She had already checked its sturdiness and, weighing up the options, decided it was better this than risk interception on the atrium staircase. Escaping the palacio was, to her mind, the most dangerous aspect of the plan. Once she cleared the gates, Bernardo had assured her, she would blend in with the Guardia Real on patrol.

She clutched the drainpipe and began scaling down. It was more awkward than she had anticipated, and she used her hands and thighs to grip. Unexpectedly, the drainpipe finished short of the ground, and she had no choice but to let go. She landed hard. Her heart thumped furiously, and she feared it would burst out of her rib cage. Everything within her told her to run, but she forced herself to check her ankle before putting her weight on it.

She sought Bernardo for comfort and found him squatting at his post, calm as a Sphinx, across the forecourt. He smiled reassuringly and she smiled tentatively back. She tested her ankle, and carefully put her full weight on her feet and ran furtively amongst the shadows of the palacio's walls, and onward, across the forecourt, to the stables.

Fiel was already saddled, and she mounted him briskly. As he trotted out of the gates, she again found herself grateful for his lightness of hoof. Bernardo peered from the shadows. His eyes smarted with tears as he raised a hand in farewell. She nodded and fought back a sob at the possibility of never seeing him again.

Not in any of Francisca's fantasies of leaving home for foreign shores had she imagined it to be like this, and yet, somehow, as she cantered amongst the soldiers and horse guards and exchanged respectful nods with them, she felt that it could not have been otherwise.

CHAPTER FORTY

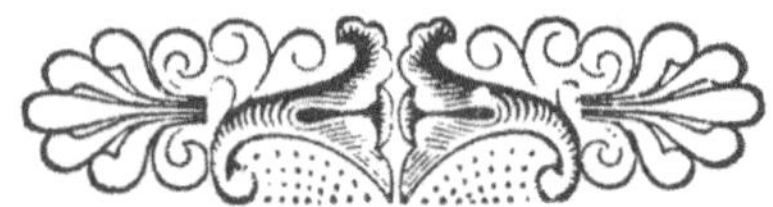

The sailors carefully manoeuvred the *Santa Fernanda* out of the port of Seville, and it began its long journey downriver. The waters lapped at the rudder, the oak beams groaned in sympathy with the oarsmen's efforts in the galleys below, and the oars clunked plaintively against the steel stirrups. The paddles struck and dragged at the waterline, over and over, like the slow beat of a dull drum.

Francisca leaned against the guard rail at the stern and raised her face to the night air. She fixed her sight on the minaret, softly glowing under a spray of silvery stars.

An icy mist rose from the river's surface in curious twists and curls like puffs from a giant creature beneath. The cold air cut into her skin, but she kept her face raised against it, willing it to blunt the pain in her heart. She had imagined her heartache would vanish once on board, that the sheer monumental act of leaving Seville would bring about the metamorphosis she craved. It proved not to be.

Despite her mother's permission, leaving her behind was something she could barely acknowledge she had done. And yet somehow the enormity of it made it unreal, like a stone statue instead of a living thing. Perhaps that is ultimately how she had managed to accomplish her escape.

She clung to Bernardo's words: *In time, we will be reunited.*

She needed to believe that.

Bernardo and Uncle Carlos had reconciled. He had truly found a home in the palacio. Uncle Carlos had begun to seek Bernardo's counsel. It would not be long before Bernardo would become the trusted adviser he had always truly needed.

Bernardo's enquiries had not turned up any reliable word as regards Isabel's whereabouts, and Francisca came to accept she would need to learn to live with the uncertainty for some time to come, but she rejected the idea that Isabel might be in her past. She continued to consume her every thought, and it seemed impossible that there would ever be a time when Isabel would cease to be her point of reference.

Bernardo's enquiries had, however, turned up word of Gabriela, Valentina, and Marina's fate. It was joyful news. They were safe and had arrived at their intended destination, the location of which was shrouded in secrecy. Father Alberto had evidently lied about Marina being 'dealt with' by the Guardia Real.

The *Santa Fernanda* glided slowly through the edge of Seville and made another turn of the river. The minaret faded into the last stars of the night sky. There was a moment of stillness.

She stole a brief glimpse into the future. She would be with Elizabeth, in the safety of the priory, and she would come to be a part of village life in Wilmington. The connections between Spain and England were well established, and, in Francisca's mind, there was the additional benefit that England was distancing itself from the clutches of the Vatican. England was taking its own path. There would be no Inquisitions in England.

She was not ready to confront more detail of the future awaiting her.

To stave off the tears, she bit her bottom lip. Soldiers did not cry, and she hardened herself. She conjured her mother, felt her presence, and told herself Bernardo's mantra: *All would yet be well.*

The glow of the city's flares faded. Nothing muted the light of the stars.

Francisca's thoughts were disconnected. She needed to rest, and she went down to the belly of the ship. Bernardo had warned her about Fiel's quarters, in the central chamber. There would be little natural light and the air could be stifling, he had said, but he had also said the journey should not be more than a week, assuming fair conditions.

No other animals were on board to keep Fiel company, and he kept quietly. She could not bear him passing the night alone, nor she without him. She spread out her coat beside him and steadied the candle to study the map, but it was more from a need to do something than necessity. She knew the latitude and longitude lines like the lines on her hand. She folded the map neatly and returned it to its leather pouch on the string around her neck.

She took Isabel's letter from her inner left breast pocket – the one by her heart – and held it close to the dwindling candle. It still contained the faintest hint of her musk perfume. She read it again, simply to feel close to her.

She marked off in her journal her first evening aboard. Bernardo had told her to do this each day to keep track of time. It was not long before the steady pulse of the paddles lulled her, and she slept a dreamless sleep, swaddled in amongst the hay by the warmth of Fiel's side.

At first light, she climbed the steep ladders to the deck. She hoped to avert company by adopting a forbidding countenance in her military costume. Bernardo had helped her practise a man's persona and gait. Their early sessions had mostly ended in fits of laughter but eventually she discovered the secret lay in taking longer strides, squaring her shoulders, and adopting a slightly arrogant expression by hovering her gaze above her usual line of sight.

The sky was clear, the mist had lifted. The air was filled with salt, pinching at her throat. Neat rows of vineyards lined the softly undulating terrain. She stood at the bow, took deep breaths, and looked out. Soon, the vineyards gave way to the meandering broad estuary waters.

The sailors gathered on deck and attended to their assigned tasks. Their organisation and athleticism were, in themselves, things of beauty. Some climbed the masts. Some tied ropes in elaborate knots. Others rearranged and secured items on deck. Their concentration, skill, and perfectionism were evident and reassuring. Nothing was left to chance.

The sailors gathered, eyes fixed to the horizon, and they saluted the open sea. A ritual of respect, invoking God's benevolence for the perils that lay ahead.

A whoosh whoosh came from overhead, and she looked up. The sails threw open, swelled, and became taut with air. She held on to the guard rail and felt the thrill of the ship lunging forward and launching onto the open sea.

The glare of the winter sun reflected the shimmering waters like a bejewelled floating tapestry of aquas, emeralds, and indigos. She dared to look down. It was unfathomably deep. She looked ahead and from right to left. Everything everywhere was sea and sky, stretched out, without beginning or end, melting into one another. There was no vanishing line. It was like nothing she had ever seen.

She looked back and her stomach lurched – already, land was out of sight. The *Santa Fernanda* was flying away from everything she had known and loved, and as she swallowed a sob, she heard a familiar squawk and looked up.

Ángel! She had followed her. Francisca smiled and waved and at last let out a sob, and her tears flowed.

Soon, not only the colours, but time, space, and distance merged into one another and lost their discrete meanings. She could not yet see the beauty and she knew that, if she was truly to make sense of this alien landscape, she would need to *learn* to see it, so she searched her mind for something familiar, and soon realised it was much like being immersed in the execution of a painting. Something, too, like when love had made her lose and forget herself, and a strange feeling rushed through her: that Isabel was close by, that, somehow, in undertaking this journey, it would lead her to her lover.

It was too soon to set herself to the task. Finally, she was physically and emotionally exhausted and she needed to rest. There would yet be time to learn the ways of the sea.

For almost three days, she slept. It was like she was in a fever, shedding herself of layers of her life. By night, she slept by Fiel, by day, in the comfort of her cot. Her dreams were like kaleidoscopes, as if purging herself of trauma.

On the fourth day she woke restored. She set off for the deck at the cusp of sunrise. The sun bled on the horizon. She breathed in the fresh salt air and, for the first time on board, felt sheer joy. She would not be marrying a man she did not love. She was free. And, for the first time too, she wanted to look forward.

Her instinct was to gather her painting materials, but first she knew she must study the landscape. The first step was to find something to hang some perspective on. Bernardo's advice came to her – to find the point of the sun in its arc in the sky and observe the light and shade. This must be done at multiple points of a day. By afternoon, her eye became keener. She was ready, and she sketched out the arc of the sun's passage.

That night, she drew the sky. It was a waning moon, and she realised two weeks had passed since she had last seen Isabel. She swallowed the feeling. In her mind's eye, she drew a line down across the moon's temporarily concealed horns. South. Spain. Bernardo. And she smiled.

Bernardo had taught her how to read the maps they had found in Uncle Carlos's study. In themselves, they were works of art – remarkable two-dimensional representations of the world and beautifully decorated. They had kept at their studies even after

Francisca had felt sure she could find her destination, which she marked with a large *E* that she circled.

Bernardo had taught her the rudiments of finding the points of the Earth – by night from the moon and the stars, and by day from the sun.

'The moon will rise by the northeast and set in the northwest.' He pointed to the corresponding points on the map. 'On a crescent moon, extend an imaginary line from the top horn down through the lower horn and down to the horizon. That is where you will find due south and that is how you will know where Spain is and where I will be – here, waiting for you.'

He had helped her relate the astronomical points back to the maps so that she might always keep her bearings during the journey, and he had told her, 'Wherever you are, whatever happens, the sun and the stars will be there for you,' he had said. 'Your training as a painter has helped you keenly discern light and shade – the essential skill to navigate by the sky. You will never be alone, Francisca. And,' he had added quietly, his hand to his heart, 'you know I will be thinking of you always.'

On the fifth day, she felt in the flow of the rhythm of life at sea, and she was able to begin to envisage the future. She clung to the one element of her plan that gave her certainty, solace, and hope.

Elizabeth.

Elizabeth would be waiting for her. Francisca imagined arriving at the priory in Wilmington, in the county of Sussex. The green there was greener than any other green, Elizabeth had told her. By Elizabeth's descriptions, it would not be difficult to find – opposite a 'giant', etched in chalk in the green hillside by the banks of a tributary of a gently flowing river, the sea just some distance beyond.

She would paint and learn the local techniques. Elizabeth had said the English canvases were as smooth as duck eggs and the English light as subtle as Mona Lisa's smile. These two things alone would yield a different style from her hand. No doubt the walls of the priory themselves could do with some decoration, and she imagined pleasing Elizabeth by applying a fresco to the entrance hall.

She imagined becoming known to the locals as *The Painter from Seville.*

As the sun sank below the horizon, thoughts of Isabel again rose to the very surface. Loving Isabel had occupied her every waking moment. In just those few weeks, Francisca's love for her had transformed her life. She had done things she had never imagined. Dangerous things. Things that had set her life on a radically altered trajectory – for here she was, disguised as a soldier, on a ship set for England, leaving behind everything she had ever known and loved.

And yet, on another level, she thought bitterly, for all the intensity, loving Isabel had amounted to nothing. She had nothing but the battle scars in her heart to show for it all. No trumpets had blasted to herald the end. No angel had looked over her to assuage the trouble and pain.

Would Isabel simply forget her? Might a stranger, in the not-too-distant future, approach Isabel and point to a painting of Francisca's, and ask her opinion of it? Might Isabel recognise her own resemblance, and might she think 'Oh, yes, I loved her once.' Might she even regret it or feel embarrassed about having loved a woman?

Francisca could now admit that, at the time, she had been aware of a flicker of warning light in a far corner of her mind, whispering to her that, if left unchecked, loving Isabel might swallow her up. It might reduce her to a mere shadow of herself and snuff out her own creative urge or reduce it to insignificance.

At the time, her love for Isabel had been so intense and Isabel's creative force so alluring, that Francisca stamped out the warning. She had told herself that Isabel would be her inspiration but what if Isabel became all that she would need?

Looking out to the fine line of the horizon, she comforted herself by telling herself that she needed to find the fire from within. She needed a kind of quiet around her. What she needed, she told herself, was to feel a yearning for something. Before meeting Isabel, that yearning had always been her mother's return to health. The agony she had felt for her mother had been the springboard for her urge to somehow try to make life better, for her mother, and for herself. Somehow, as a complement to that urge, was the yearning too – to find her way through life on her own terms, to see the way things really were for herself, and not second-hand, through the lens of Uncle Carlos or anyone else. Somehow, every painting represented this yearning. It had been the thing she had turned to, to try to make something from the pain.

On the sixth day, there was a sudden shift in the weather. Bernardo had told her about the seas teeming with fish, large and small. Francisca could not imagine any creature surviving these temperatures. Yet, gulls appeared from nowhere, swooped down and emerged with full beaks.

The air was decidedly colder, and a fog hovered visibly above the waters. The sea itself was still as oil. Her hands were too cold to draw, and she hunched inside her father's coat. In the afternoon, a charcoal smudge appeared on the edge of the horizon. Darkness pulled in heavily without the ritual of dusk.

Fiel neighed. Storm clouds rolled in like an advancing army.

She brought to mind Bernardo's words of warning.

'The Atlantic winds at this time of year, Francisca, can steer a ship off course, many miles,' Bernardo had explained with uncharacteristic reverence; the tone of voice she had learned he reserved for the sea.

Bernardo had told her too, 'You must not become complacent, Francisca. Anything can happen at any time. Do not let the sea hypnotise you. You must be prepared.'

His blue eyes had never been so intense. 'A charcoal smudge on the horizon heralds a storm. Do not wait for it to come. Get down to your berth and stay there. Put your trust in the captain, the ship, and God, in that order, and try to just let everything inside of you surrender.'

The sailors climbed the masts and furled the sails. The *Santa Fernanda* rolled, pitched, and plunged with the elements. Mighty waves turned about in a seething force, filling and occupying everything, even the sky and the horizon. Over and over, the ship rolled, pitched, and plunged violently, seemingly on the same spot.

Francisca was mesmerised but noticed, out of the corner of her eye, a sailor gesturing and calling wildly to her. He threw her a rope, and she caught it. He pulled her in, and she staggered from one fixture to the next. They linked hands and, with the gait of a drunkard, she retreated down into the ship. For a moment she feared he would discover her disguise, but she need not have feared. He was set on his tasks.

'Do not return to deck until the storm passes,' he called to her. He caught her eye and said, 'Do not worry. We will get through this one.'

Until that point, she had not felt afraid.

She almost tumbled down the ladders. Fiel had been tied in securely. His eyes were white with fear.

Without warning, she was thrown up and tossed about the chamber. She tried to cling to the floor, but it was helpless to hold her. The *Santa Fernanda* pitched as high as a mountain and plunged as deep as the very ocean bed. The walls, ceiling, and floor became indistinguishable. She sought the door, but it was like traversing the ocean itself. Nothing had prepared her for this.

A series of elegiac images filled her mind. They were extraordinarily clear and filled with a pathos utterly at odds with the chaos of the moment. She saw herself as a small child, when she trusted in the eternal love and protection of her mother and father and Uncle Carlos. She saw herself, watching on, as Marina, Gabriela, and Valentina mounted their carriage in joyful reunion and hope. She saw herself on the banks of the Rio Guadalquivir, bidding farewell that one last time to Isabel.

This was to be the sum of her life, she thought, and she remembered Bernardo's words and she surrendered to what would be.

She let go. As she was tossed about, she felt no more grasping or yearning. Her mind was filled with brilliant images, such as she had never seen. For all the preoccupations with texture, form, space, shape, colour, value, and line, it all amounted to nothing more than expressing something of what it was to be alive, with all its joy and pain. It was what she had done to make sense of it, to put her life into context and give it meaning. It was not a contrivance. It was not a papering over anything. It was deeply within her. She did it to commemorate life, to pay respect for the time God had granted her and to give something of herself for those she loved.

There was a break in the chaos. For a moment, the ship remained still.

She hardened herself for the next round of terror and tried again to find something to cling to. For all the willingness to surrender to what would be, she did not want to die. She saw a pole, and she crawled to it and hung on. She looked about for Fiel and found him across the chamber and saw the whites of his eyes as he looked over to her.

All was still.

That was when she realised there would be no more pitch and plunge. She crawled across to him and held his muzzle in her hands.

It was over. They had survived the apocalypse.

At dawn there was nothing left in her body to hold her upright but she needed air and slowly returned to the deck. There was a strong breeze at the stern and the ship sped across the sea. The sailors pointed ahead, muttering excitedly. The horizon was closer. There was a faint shadow. Land. England.

She resisted the temptation to study the maps one last time. It was courage and confidence in herself that would ensure she would find her way.

A shadow passed overhead, and she heard a pulsing in the air. She looked up. It was Ángel. She had flown the entire journey.

Francisca cried with emotion and wonder at the bird's empathy, beauty, and strength.

In a flash of honesty and self-knowledge, she knew that what she had been telling herself about love was not her truth. She must share her life with another who shared her nature. She had found that with Isabel. She had made herself vulnerable to it. To truly share her life would not mean any diminishing of her own creative urge, no swallowing up of her own self. On the contrary. It would raise her up. It would be the making of her. Every day would be a call to give the best of herself. It would be the thing that would help her face anything with courage and strength, to help her paint the best she could paint. It would forge the path for her to find her voice, both as an artist and as a woman. She knew she would spend the rest of her life searching for that kind of love again, for there could be no other way to bridge her solitude.

The faint shadow on the horizon took form. There were white cliffs and rich green undulations beyond. The contrasting light in the folds and creases was like the subtle chiaroscuro of a Leonardo da Vinci painting.

At the time, the voyage had seemed endless, and yet, now that it was all but over, it had passed too quickly. All that luxury – of time suspended, of having no responsibility other than the essentials of living – was almost at an end. She turned her thoughts to the reality of disembarkation and the next stage of her journey, and she began to feel a tingling excitement. Fiel would need to find his land legs. Once they set off, the onward journey time should be no more than a matter of a day. Elizabeth would be there for her.

She pressed her hands into her father's coat pockets, to bring forth his spirit for the journey ahead. Behind the fabric of the pocket was the outline of a book. It was Isabel's orange vellum book. She had forgotten all about it.

It fell open at a page marked in turquoise ink with the initials *I* and *F*. Curious, Francisca read:

Either this deep desire of mine
Will be found on this journey,
Or when I get back home!
If I had known the real way it was,
I would have stopped all the looking
around.
But that knowing depends
On the time spent looking.

It made sense to her. After all the searching within, she had found what she had been looking for and she knew that everything she ever needed had always been there.

Suddenly, the sails fluttered down. She looked ahead to the green undulating land with soft light. Her eyes adjusted to the land and the nearness of things. A small, whitewashed chapel set within its own clearing of green became discernible. A few simple houses with thatched roofs huddled around it. Closer by was a small inn made of timber.

The ship pulled into harbour. Francisca's stomach twisted in anticipation. By the pier was a simple port office. A small welcoming party gathered on the landing.

Light shimmered from a spot in the crowd. It seemed a mirage.

She looked again and checked herself. Perhaps she was dreaming?

It was a woman on a white mare. Francisca swallowed the lump forming in her throat. The woman's auburn hair flew in the breeze. She smiled and raised her hand.

Francisca's heart expanded. She was helpless to stop it, and she smiled back, raising her hand high above her head.

And she knew, whatever else the future might hold, the light would follow her, and she would follow the light.

ACKNOWLEDGMENTS

With thanks to my wife, parents, brother and sister, my fellow writing group members, and many dear friends who saw *The Painter from Seville* through its various stages, and provided invaluable feedback and encouragement. Thanks also to my sister and artist friends for generously sharing their experience of the artist's condition and painting technique.

Thanks to my publisher who believed in *The Painter from Seville* and ensured it was brought to life.

ABOUT THE AUTHOR

Sonya Van de Graaff was born in Australia where she studied music and law, and developed a love for the Renaissance. She now divides her time between London and the South Downs where she lives with her wife and two dogs.

instagram.com/sonyavandegraaff

linkedin.com/in/sonya-van-de-graaff

ALAYA BOOKS

Alaya Books is a vibrant and growing publisher committed to offering a diverse selection of titles spanning memoirs, biographies, self-help books, and children's literature. We are excited to introduce this exceptional debut novel by Sonya Van de Graaff and look forward to bringing you more captivating titles in the future. Stay tuned for what's to come!

www.alayabooks.com

Alaya books

The world needs your story.

www.ingramcontent.com/pod-product-compliance
Lightning Source LLC
Chambersburg PA
CBHW072006210726
48294CB00013B/1646
* 9 7 8 1 7 6 3 6 9 9 8 0 9 *